"All these folks are victims of the Prowlers. You got vengeance for me and some others in Boston. They're hoping you'll do the same here," Artie explained.

Jack glanced quickly over his shoulder. The ghosts had moved out into the street now, standing in the rain as a few errant rays of sun broke through and speared the pavement around them. Most of them hung their heads as though ashamed.

"I don't get it, though," Jack whispered. "One of them tried to get me to turn around. Now this bunch won't even look at me."

Artie did not respond at first. Jack had to look in the rearview mirror to make sure he was still there. Then those black, bottomless-pit eyes met his gaze, and he shuddered and returned his attention to the road.

"Artie?" Jack prodded.

"They're feeling a little guilty," Artie finally revealed.

Jack furrowed his brow. "Why?"

"They think you're gonna die."

Prowlers Series
by Christopher Golden

Prowlers
Laws of Nature
Predator and Prey (*coming soon*)

Available from Pocket Books

Laws of Nature
PROWLERS

Christopher Golden

POCKET PULSE
New York   London   Toronto   Sydney   Singapore

An *Original* Publication of POCKET BOOKS

 POCKET PULSE published by
Pocket Books, a division of Simon & Schuster, Inc.
1230 Avenue of the Americas, New York, NY 10020

ISBN: 0-7434-0365-7

First Pocket Pulse printing August 2001

10 9 8 7 6 5 4 3 2 1

POCKET PULSE and colophon are trademarks of
Simon & Schuster, Inc.

Cover art by Anna Dorfman; photo credits: Digital Vision/Picture
Quest; Corbis Images/Picture Quest

Printed in the U.S.A.

For my amigo,
Steve Bissette

ACKNOWLEDGMENTS

First and foremost, my love and gratitude to Connie and my boys, Nicholas and Daniel. Thanks, as always, to my agent, Lori Perkins, and to Lisa Clancy and Micol Ostow at Pocket Books. Extra special thanks to Tom Sniegoski and Rick Hautala.

PROLOGUE

Alarmed by the rumble of an approaching engine, a murder of crows took flight from the heavy trees that hung on either side of the Post Road. Against the early morning sky, the flurry of black wings that momentarily blotted out the sunlight seemed particularly ominous. Then they were gone, resettling in the sprawl of maples and elms on the far side of Henry Lemoine's property, and the sky was bright and blue again.

Phil Garraty shivered as the shadow of the birds passed above him, but barely noticed his own reaction. Truth be told, he liked seeing the birds. Crows, the odd hawk or three, even sparrows and such, were a welcome sight. Though Buckton, Vermont was about as rural as a town could get and still have cable television, they didn't have much by way of wildlife. He saw the occasional deer or rabbit, even a fox now and then, but no more than that, and with nowhere the frequency he'd been told was normal for towns in the area.

Some of the families in Buckton still hunted, and most of the tourists they got were hunters who'd found their way into town by mistake. Phil figured that was the explanation. Somehow, the animals must have developed a kind of sixth sense about areas where there was a lot of hunting.

In the ancient postal van he'd been driving for seventeen years as Buckton's only mail carrier, he bumped along Route 31 with early U2 blaring out of the speakers from the CD player he'd rigged under the dash. The narrow two-lane road led south out of town toward Rutland. Nobody in town called it anything but the Post Road, and Phil Garraty liked that; made it feel like it was *his* road.

It was just after nine in the morning and he was beginning the last leg of his rounds. He had started north of town at six A.M., made a circuit of the farm and dairy roads up that way, then delivered the bulk of each day's mail in the square mile that made up the downtown area of Buckton before heading south. Only a hundred-and-twenty-seven homes to deliver to, all told, with a dozen on the southern end of the Post Road and the last few on Route 219, which intersected with it a mile south of town and ran east to west. Lot of traffic passed on 219, but all of it headed somewhere else.

That was the way people in Buckton liked it.

Dave Lanphear and his boys at Public Works hadn't

been out to trim the trees on the sides of the road, and as Phil drove the van toward the junction with 219, the foliage grew thicker on both sides, spread out in a canopy above the pavement. From full sunlight, the road ahead plunged into profound shadow, branches swaying with the breeze. He took off his sunglasses and tossed them on the seat beside him. Suddenly, out of the warmth, he found the wind that blew through the van to be surprisingly chilly.

The plaintive wail of "Sunday, Bloody Sunday" surged from the speakers and Phil sang along. The van trundled along at about thirty-five miles per hour as he approached the junction. Though locals used the Post Road more frequently than 219, the east-west road had more traffic and a higher speed limit, so Phil was forced to brake for the stop sign. Just two stops on the other side of the junction, then he would double back for the four homes he delivered to on 219.

Sunlight flickered through the branches above, and Phil squinted against the brightness as the van rattled to a full stop. A car flew by on Route 219, doing at least sixty, and he sighed as it disappeared around a curve. He accelerated, and the van's engine grumbled as it picked up speed again, crossing 219 and continuing along down the Post Road.

He'd barely gotten it up to twenty-five before something dropped out of the trees above him. The windshield splintered and sagged inward, a mass of spiderweb cracks. Phil shouted in shock and momentary fear, then jammed his foot on the brake. The van shuddered to a stop and the engine quit with an exhausted whimper.

There wasn't much by way of a hood on the van, but the thing on the windshield held on just the same. He spied it through the many facets of the ruined windshield, and found that he could not breathe. Movement in the woods off to his left drew his attention, and Phil glanced over to see several huge, bestial figures slipping through the shadows beneath the trees. As one, they trotted into the road toward the van.

"Oh, sweet Jesus," Phil Garraty whispered to himself. "It's true."

Something landed on the roof of the van—a heavy thing with claws that clacked against the metal.

"I don't have it!" he cried out, the scream searing his throat.

Silence, as they all paused and gazed at him. And then the quiet was broken by snarls, breaking glass, and rending metal.

CHAPTER 1

The swinging door that separated the dining room from the kitchen of Bridget's Irisk Rose Pub was a portal between two worlds. In the restaurant proper, fans whirled lazily above brass and wood, and the Celtic-rooted melodies of the Chieftains were pumped into the room along with the air-conditioning. Only the steady chatter of the clientele and the bustle of the wait-staff disturbed the tranquility of the scene.

When Molly Hatcher, empty tray in hand, pushed through the door into the kitchen, it was like diving into chaos. The cooks in the back shouted pleasant obscenities at one another, dishes were clattered, and orders were shouted out. Somehow, the chaos managed to find a kind of focus whenever Tim Dunphy was on duty.

Tim was twenty-three, a powerfully built guy from South Boston who had little patience for fooling around. Molly had a feeling it was more the respect for Tim's ability to kick the hell out of any one of them rather than his prowess as a chef that made the other cooks obey him. Either way, he ran a tight ship. Loud, yes, and wild, but somehow the orders in his kitchen were filled and rarely wrong.

Molly stood with her back to the wall to let another waitress slide by her. A computer screen to the left showed that order number 0417 was up, and it was one of hers. She slipped her tray onto the counter and scanned the various dishes that were arrayed on the warming racks before her. Swiftly, she gathered the four dishes that comprised her order and turned to go.

"What, you don't even say 'hi' anymore?"

Tray balanced precariously on one hand and hip, Molly turned to grin at Tim on the other side of the counter.

"Hi, Tim," she replied, a tiny smile playing at the corners of her mouth. "I didn't want to interrupt. You guys are so busy."

"Never too busy for you, Miss Hatcher," he flirted.

Molly rolled her eyes, but she knew he would not take it harshly. Though she did not really know how to handle his advances, that didn't mean she didn't like them. Not at all.

Tim was a mess—greasy face, bandanna tied over his head to keep his hair from falling into the food; never mind the odd bump on the bridge of his nose, where it had been broken at least once. A fighter, no doubt. Growing up in Southie, he'd probably not had a chance to be anything else. And with her wild red hair and green eyes, Molly knew she was Tim's type. He'd made no secret of that fact. Truth be told, despite his rough edges, she thought he was sort of sweet.

But it was too soon. Way too soon. After what she'd been through . . . after Artie . . .

"So, y'know," Tim began, "I was thinkin' maybe we could—"

"Leave the girl alone, Timothy Dunphy."

Molly turned, startled—though not enough to unbalance her tray—and saw Tim's sister Kiera shaking a finger at him. Kiera was also a waitress at the pub, and she and Molly had struck up a friendship.

"Mind your own damn business, Kiera," Tim snapped, eyes narrowing.

"I make it my business. Why don't you just do your job?"

Her brother bristled. "You oughta learn to keep your mouth shut."

"I kicked your ass when you were twelve, boy, and I'd be happy to do it again."

Tim shot her the finger, then grinned broadly at Molly and disappeared back into the kitchen. A second later one of the other cooks slipped several plates of food onto the warming racks.

"Don't let him bother you," Kiera said, a smirk on her face.

"He's not," Molly insisted. "But I'm happy to provide you guys with something else to fight about."

"And we appreciate it," Kiera confirmed, eyes lighting up with mischief. "We truly do."

Molly shook her head in amusement, then carried her tray out of the shouting and clattering that was the kitchen and into the much more serene environment of the restaurant. The other difference, of course, was temperature. The kitchen was insufferably hot, with so many stoves and ovens going at once. The restaurant and bar area whistled along at a cool seventy-three degrees, according to the thermostat.

As she slipped around a recently hired waiter named Paul and waved at Wendy, the hostess up by the front door, Molly found her thoughts again drifting back to Artie. For most of high school, the two of them had been inseparable. Then, in April, her sweet, funny guy had been murdered. Surreal as it had seemed then, it was even more so now. For Artie had not been killed by a drive-by gangbanger or convenience-store robber. He had been butchered by a race of monsters that had been around before the first man walked the earth.

Monsters. After all she had seen, she still had a hard time wrapping her mind around that word. But there was no other way to describe them. They weren't were-wolves, though there were similarities. Unlike the were-wolves of mythology, the Prowlers had no human core whose basic moral structure might restrict their actions, though some of them lived peacefully, even benevolently, among humanity.

The rest were just savages, beasts who stalked the human race like lions on the veldt or hunted in packs along the fringes of civilization. Except sometimes they didn't stay on the fringes. A bold pack of Prowlers hunting in the city had killed Artie and Kate Nordling, one of Molly's best friends, as well as a bunch of other people. The authorities had finally caught up with them, and Molly and her friend Jack Dwyer had taken down their leader while the police dealt with the others.

But there were more out there. No one knew how many, but it was clear that they existed, scattershot, all over the world, in ones and twos and packs of various sizes. Molly shuddered at the thought of what might happen someday if they were all brought together. Their knowledge of the Prowlers had put both her and Jack on edge, made them suspicious of everything and everyone.

Jack. He was the other reason she did not know how to react to Tim Dunphy's flirting. All through the horrors back in April, Jack had been at Molly's side. He had been Artie's best friend since the two of them were very young, and he was the one who had first discovered the truth about the Prowlers. For her safety, Jack and his older sister Courtney, who owned the pub with him, had invited Molly to live with them and work there.

For safety, she had agreed. Once she was there, even after the crisis was over, Molly was not about to go home to her drunken, abusive mother and their filthy apartment in Dorchester. She only had six weeks left to go now before she started classes at Yale in the fall. Not a lot of time, and she wanted to spend it with Jack and Courtney.

She had to wonder if she didn't really just want to

spend that time with Jack. Even wondering filled her with horrible guilt. Just a few months earlier her boyfriend had been murdered, and now she felt . . . *something,* at least, for his best friend. But she could not help it. Jack was her best friend, now. No one had ever known her so well. Not even Artie.

Which didn't help alleviate her guilt at all.

"Miss?"

Molly blinked, stopped too quickly and only just managed to keep from letting the dinner tray topple from its perch atop her fingers. She frowned as she glanced at the woman in the booth who had called out to her. Then realization dawned, and Molly offered an apologetic, self-deprecating grin. The order she was carrying belonged to the three women at that table.

"I'm sorry," she said earnestly as she slipped the plates one by one onto the table. "Just a little preoccupied, I guess."

"No harm done," a diminutive blond piped up from across the booth. "As long as we all get what we ordered. I'm starved."

The other women chuckled, and Molly joined in.

As she slid the last of the dishes onto the table, she happened to glance over at the bar area. A small cluster of locals sat at one end, eyes glued to whatever sporting event was on the TV bolted to the wall behind the bar. A few empty stools down from them, however, there sat a man, alone.

Staring at her.

With a quick intake of breath that whistled through

her teeth, Molly turned her attention back to her customers. She forced a smile, all the while feeling the stranger's eyes boring into her from behind.

"Can I get you ladies anything else?" she asked.

One of them asked for an iced tea, but the others practically ignored Molly as they dug into their dinners. When she turned around, her gaze ticked involuntarily back to the bar again. The man wore blue jeans and black boots, and a stylishly tight powder-blue T-shirt stretched over a broad, muscular chest. One of his biceps bore a tattoo she could not make out at this distance. His hair was too long and his chin bore several days stubble.

He would have been strikingly handsome if he didn't look so mean, if his eyes didn't burn as he stared at her with a hunger that was almost . . . predatory.

Oh my God, Molly thought, heart skipping a beat. A horrible thought occurred to her.

Panicked, she glanced anxiously around the pub until she spotted Jack talking to the hostess up front. She dangled the large, round tray at her side as she made a beeline across the restaurant for him. When Courtney was not around, Jack was in charge. But even if his older sister had been there, Molly would have gone to Jack instead.

When he saw her striding toward him, Jack's conversation faltered.

"Molly, what is it?" he asked.

Her gaze flicked toward Wendy, who instantly got the message and returned to the tall desk the hostess used to take reservations and assign seating.

Molly purposely positioned herself in the line of sight between Jack and the man—the predator—at the bar. "Don't look right away," she warned him. "There's a man sitting by himself up at the bar who looks a little like a TV star or something. He's staring at me."

A small smile twitched at the corners of Jack's mouth. "Can you blame him?"

She grimaced. "Not in a good way, Jack. I get a vibe off him. I can't help wondering if he's . . . hunting."

Her friend's face blanched and his eyes narrowed. He was five foot ten and, though muscular, not physically intimidating. But Jack was stronger than he looked, and when his body tensed, she could feel the coiled power of a much larger man. Jack was not someone to underestimate. Not at all.

As Molly watched, Jack glanced past her shoulder. She saw no reaction in his features before he gazed at her again.

"Wish Bill was back from his break," Jack said, voice low and grave. "He'd be able to tell."

Molly hesitated a moment, then gave a tiny shrug. "What do we do?"

Jack nodded slowly. Then, without a word, he set off across the restaurant on a direct course for the bar.

The world around him shuddered and seemed to disappear as Jack strode the wood floor of Bridget's Irisk Rose Pub. The voices were gone and the other patrons ceased to exist, until all that remained were the guy at the bar and the music that lingered in the air.

Adrenaline rushed through him, and Jack nearly

quivered with it. His alarms were going off, and he did his best to tone them down. Molly was right. The guy looked out of place in here, like a model or an actor. Too perfect. And cruel, too. That was what disturbed Jack most of all. A powerful-looking guy, out of place, all by himself, and staring at Molly as though he were the hunter and she the prey.

Prowler, Jack thought, and the idea only solidified as he moved closer to the man, defiantly challenging him with his steady gaze. The man did not look away.

Jack took the two steps up to the bar area and stood directly in front of the man, staring down at him.

"You're pissing her off," Jack told him.

The man's eyebrows shot up, a glint of amusement in his eyes. It was an arrogant look, and Jack wanted very much to slap it off his face. "I'm sorry? I don't know what you're talkin' about."

Arms crossed, Jack glared at him. "The redheaded waitress, the one you keep staring at. You're pissing her off."

The guy laughed. "I'm watchin' her. She's pretty tasty-lookin'. No law against watchin'. And I'm wonderin' if maybe it ain't her I'm pissin' off. Otherwise maybe she'd be over here tellin' me herself. Doesn't look like the kind of girl who'd let a guy do her dirty work. Unless maybe she's scared a' me."

Tasty-looking. The phrase stuck in Jack's mind. It might just be the guy being obnoxious, or it might mean something else entirely.

"Maybe she is," Jack admitted. "So maybe you should go."

The guy shook his head in disbelief and stood up. He was a good four inches taller than Jack, a lot broader, and—Jack had to hand it to him—he was better dressed. He knew how the man must see him: punk nineteen-year-old in a cotton shirt with the name of the pub sewn on the breast, telling him what to do?

"I'm not done with my beer," the guy drawled in his slight southern accent.

With a frown, Jack tilted his head and regarded the man. "You've never heard of Tanzer, have you?"

From the flicker of confusion in the guy's eyes, he knew the answer. This man was not a Prowler. Just an arrogant, sexist moron with a chip on his shoulder.

Jack sighed. Prowlers were one thing. Jerks like this he had to handle just about every day, which got monotonous.

"You're gonna leave now," Jack told him.

"Who the hell are *you?*" the guy scoffed.

"The owner," Jack said coolly, gazing up at the man. He sniffed with a boredom that was only partially feigned. "Look, I know you think you're a badass. But you're gonna have to trust me when I say I've dealt with meaner. If you want trouble here, you shouldn't come alone."

For a few seconds the guy laughed at that. But even as he did, he watched Jack's eyes. Whatever he saw there, something in them convinced him that Jack was speaking true.

He reached behind the bar and grabbed his mug, sucked back several gulps of beer, then slammed it down hard and stalked off, not looking back.

When the guy was gone, Danny—who was subbing for the bartender Bill Cantwell—leaned over the bar. "Damn, Jack, I thought for sure we were gonna have to take the big bastard down."

Jack smiled softly. Danny was all of five eight and maybe one hundred and forty pounds, but he was a scrapper. Like a lot of the pub's staff, he was a Southie boy.

"He didn't pay," Danny added.

"Forget it," Jack told him.

Molly met him at the steps that separated the bar from the restaurant, a look of consternation on her face.

"No?" she asked, glancing toward the front door.

"No," Jack reassured her, placing a comforting hand on her shoulder and squeezing gently.

Molly cursed under her breath. "After two and a half months I'm still totally paranoid."

Jack reached out and tilted her chin up so that their eyes met. "Stay paranoid," he warned. "We have reason to be."

Though it was well past eight o'clock, it had only just begun to get dark as Tucker Marshall strode angrily into the street from Bridget's Irisk Rose Pub. He was glad he didn't know anyone in Boston yet. The kid in the pub had embarrassed him. He knew he could have snapped the boy in half if he'd wanted to, but Tucker had come to town to audition for the touring company of the new Lloyd Webber musical and had a callback in the morning. The last thing he needed was to spend a few days in jail, or worse yet, damage his face.

The buffalo wings he'd had at the bar sat heavily in his belly, sloshing around with a couple of mugs of beer. What unsettled him, though, was the anger that still roiled in him. Tucker wasn't the kind of guy to walk away from a fight. That sweet little redhead at the restaurant had been something, that was for sure. He'd made eye contact, thinking maybe he would start up a conversation. Not a crime, as far as he knew. Women liked guys who were intense, at least in his experience.

Grumbling, Tucker strode across the street, barely looking where he was going. A car ground to an abrupt halt to avoid hitting him and the driver laid on the horn. Tucker shot him the finger without even looking up. He turned toward Quincy Market, figuring he could work off some of his anger just walking around, maybe get an ice cream or something. There were a lot of beautiful women, both tourists and locals, down around that part of Boston that second week of July. If he could strike up a conversation, get a chance to run his line, talk about being an actor . . . well, Tucker usually had good luck reeling in the ladies.

The sky was dimming quickly now, the sun disappearing behind the cityscape to the west. Tucker gazed a moment in appreciation as the last rays of light shot scythes of gold between the buildings.

As he was starting to turn his attention back to the sidewalk in front of him, he slammed right into a bald man who was speaking with a friend. The man bumped into his friend and both of them almost fell before regaining their footing.

"Sorry," Tucker mumbled.

He started to go around them.

The guy he'd run into grabbed him by the hair, spun him around and shoved him up against the side of a building hard enough that his head bounced off the bricks with a painful thump. Tucker grunted as all the fury that had been building up in him in the previous few minutes combined with a new wave of rage. He forgot all about his audition. Fists balled, he cocked his right arm back and threw the first punch.

"You sorry son-of-a—"

The powerful hand that gripped his throat choked off his words. The bald guy batted Tucker's fist away with his free hand and leaned in close. His breath was rank with the odor of rotting meat, and his teeth were too sharp.

That wasn't the only thing Tucker noticed about the bald man in that instant. His teeth, yeah. But his eyes were wrong, too. Not like a person's, but rimmed with red like a wild animal's. And his face . . . his face seemed to change, to pulse. He sneered, and for an eyeblink it was almost as though he had the face of an animal, a snout like that of a dog. Or a wolf.

Hair shot through the man's scalp and his face, but only a quarter inch, just a bristle.

Impossible.

"Do you want to die?" the guy, who wasn't bald anymore, snarled.

Tucker shook his head vigorously.

"Apologize."

He was not about to argue that he had already done so. "I'm . . . I wasn't paying attention. I'm sorry." Tucker stared at his shoes a second; his body felt electrified with fear and astonishment. People did not grow hair in front of you. And the teeth . . . and the eyes.

"Hey."

The voice was soft and dangerous. Tucker glanced up nervously to see the bald man smiling at him. Normal teeth. Smooth scalp.

"Watch your goddamn step," the guy warned him. "You just never know who you're going to run into."

Then he spun Tucker away from the wall and shoved him on his way. Tucker stumbled a few steps and then hurried on without so much as a single glance back.

As quickly as he could, Tucker made his way toward the North End, where a friend was letting him crash on a futon in the living room. He had forgotten all about cruising Quincy Market, trying to meet women. He had also decided that he did not like Boston.

Not at all.

"What the hell are you doing?"

Braun frowned, glared at Dubrowski, and ran a hand over his hairless scalp. "Guy ran into me, Doobie. Pissed me off. What do you expect, I should let him knock me on my ass and not say sumthin'?"

Anxious, Dubrowski glanced along the street toward Quincy Market, watching to make sure the pretty boy had gone on his way. Then he shot a glance in the other direction, toward Bridget's. Nobody had come outside or seemed to have noticed anything. Finally, he turned his withering gaze upon Braun.

"Go after him. Kill him. Either make it appear to be a simple murder, or, if you must eat, do *not* leave a body, even if you have to gnaw the bones and toss them in the harbor. After what happened with Tanzer, we cannot afford to have anyone suspect there are those of us who have not fled this city."

"Fine," Braun said, sniffing petulantly. "Gotta tell ya, though, Doobie, I got no idea why we're still screwing around here. We oughta take off, find someplace safe to hunt."

"And so we shall," Dubrowski promised. His gaze moved back toward Bridget's across the street. "Just as soon as we have tasted blood, in vengeance for the slaughter of Tanzer and the others of the pack."

With lightning speed, Dubrowski's right hand lashed out, and he scratched deep furrows in Braun's left cheek. Braun hissed with pain and snarled loudly, but resisted making the change that such a break of concentration sometimes brought.

"What have I told you about calling me 'Doobie'?"

CHAPTER 2

Once upon a time, the department store on one of the few blocks known locally—and surprisingly with little irony—as "downtown" Buckton had been a Woolworth's. The old brownstone building had even had a soda fountain inside, where a root beer float or a thick milk shake could be had for pocket change. The Woolworth's had long since been replaced by Mackeson's. It was also a department store, little different from the old Woolworth's except it was now owned by a local family. And the soda fountain was gone.

Alan Vance was only twenty-nine years old, but he remembered the soda fountain, and he thought it was a damn shame old Bernard Mackeson had done away with it when he bought the store. He missed it.

Other than that, however, downtown Buckton looked as it had when Alan was a boy. Some of the storefronts had been freshened up, of course, and new signs added, but Alan never felt very far away from his youth when he walked along Pine Hill Road. Pine Hill—which did not become a hill until a half mile or so west of downtown—was the main street, but he'd always appreciated the fact that it was not *called* Main Street. It added character.

Most days, Alan walked through downtown with his chin up. Little Alan Nelson Vance had grown up to be Deputy Vance, and he was proud of it. The uniform felt right on him, the heavy leather belt and holster sat just so on his hip. As a kid, he had never been the best hitter in the ballpark, or the last one standing at the Vermont State Spelling Bee, but while a lot of his peers had been in a rush to leave Buckton, Alan had never wanted to live anywhere else. Even the time he had spent in college was too long away from his hometown.

His town.

Sheriff John Tackett was a good man, but he was also an old curmudgeon. Not that his being old was an excuse for his being cranky. Tackett had been sheriff for going on thirty years, and Alan had the idea he had been just as crotchety when he first got the job.

Someday Alan would have that job. Then it really would be *his* town. For the most part, he had always been satisfied to wait until that day came. It had been enough to wear the uniform and to patrol the streets of Buckton with the good will of the townspeople on his side.

Now, though, as he strolled past the Jukebox Restaurant, where he'd taken Carrie Dietrich on their first date back in the sixth grade, and Travis Drug, where he had bought comic books every week right up until he left for college, Alan no longer felt as if he had the townspeople on his side. Nancy McCabe caught his eye from just inside the Jukebox. She looked sweet in her waitress uniform, and normally she would have smiled and waved to him.

Today, she frowned and glanced away.

A few cars were on the road, but no one honked and slowed down to shoot the breeze with him. On the front step of Travis Drug Aaron Travis and Kenny Oberst sat in beach chairs, just old men soaking up the warm July sun, enjoying the breeze and the heat. Any other day Kenny would have glanced up and grunted the word *deputy* by way of greeting.

Not today.

Alan hitched his heavy belt up a little higher, set his back a little straighter, but his chin was not quite so high and his gaze was not quite so curious now, nor so friendly. He passed by the gorgeous façade of the Empire Theatre, and the smell of fresh popcorn wafted out the open front doors. For a moment he was tempted to go inside. Sitting in the dark with a bucket of popcorn would be running away, Alan knew that. But he thought in that moment that if the movie were good, if it distracted him enough, maybe he could forget how cowardly an act that would be.

"Damn it," he muttered under his breath, and his pace quickened as he kept going right past the Empire.

With a quick glance in either direction, Alan strode

across the street. On the far corner of the intersection of Pine Hill and the Post Road sat the Paperback Diner. These days it would have been more accurate to call it a café, but the owner, Trish Scharnhorst, had always loved the place when she was growing up, and had kept it, name and all, just the way it was when she bought it.

The front door was open—flies or not—and Alan walked in with his hands in his pockets. He was far more subdued than usual, but so was the Paperback. Trish was nowhere to be seen. Old Burt Johnston was behind the counter, and the new girl, whose name he could never remember 'cause she wasn't local, was taking orders from the tables. There were maybe a dozen people in the place, all told. Burt was the only one who greeted him, and it wasn't with hello.

The old man raised a hand, more of a salute than a wave. "Alan. Anything?"

"Working on it, Burt," the deputy replied, hating the helpless, useless taste of the words on his lips.

The Paperback Diner was unique in Alan's experience. It had breakfast, lunch, and dinner, and brunch on Sundays, and it had the best coffee in town, but it also had books. On shelves built around the wide windows and along the back wall, there were hundreds of paperback books, all of which were available to customers. If all one wanted was a cup of coffee and a good book, that was more than acceptable, it was encouraged. The books could be taken home, as long as they were brought back eventually.

When Alan surveyed the diner, he spotted Tina

Lemoine almost immediately. She sat in a booth against the far wall by an open window, only a glass of water on the table. He could not make out what book she was reading until he moved closer. It was Hemingway. *For Whom the Bell Tolls.*

Alan smiled. That was one of the things he loved most about Tina—her intelligence. He had tried reading Hemingway a couple of times but just could not wrap his head around it. But Tina would probably burn through the book in a couple of hours, while other customers at the Paperback engrossed themselves in Danielle Steel and Louis L'Amour. Not that there was anything wrong with L'Amour. He was a personal favorite of Alan's.

Tina was just special. She was something else, not like any other girl he had ever known. Ever since junior high school she had been a tiny flame burning in his heart. When she came back to Buckton after college, they found that they had their love of their hometown in common. It was the first of many shared passions they had discovered.

Tina always made Alan feel like the luckiest man on earth. Even after a week like the one he'd been having.

"Good book?" he asked as he slid into the booth across from her.

The smile on his face was genuine, an involuntary reaction to being in her presence, but there must have been something of his melancholy lingering, for when she glanced up at him her eyes narrowed, the skin around them crinkling with concern.

"Oh, Alan," Tina said and sighed. She marked the page in her book and laid it on the table. Then her voice dropped to just above a whisper. "You have just got to stop letting this thing get to you so much."

"I know." He nodded slowly, letting some of the stress seep out of his joints. "It's just . . . this kinda thing doesn't happen in Buckton. Now, in a week, we've had two . . . murders. God, I can barely say the word. Nobody liked Foster, true enough, but Phil Garraty was a saint, Tina. Do you realize we hadn't had an honest-to-God murder in this town since 1957? It's like the natural order is suddenly breaking down. People expect me and the sheriff to keep that from happening, and they're taking it out on us."

Tina sighed. She reached across the table and took his hands in hers. "Alan, nobody blames you for what's happened. People are just upset, that's all. Crimes have been committed, horrible ones, and they look to you and Sheriff Tackett to get to the bottom of them. To find the man responsible."

"If it *was* a man," Alan replied with a derisive grunt.

Immediately he regretted the words. The papers had reported that the murders were savage, but the details were more gruesome than anyone knew. He had been careful not to discuss them even with Tina. Now he saw the stunned, baffled expression on her face and knew he had made a mistake.

"What do you mean?"

Alan glanced around anxiously, then leaned toward her. Her hands clasped his a bit tighter, as if in acknowledgement of the secret he was about to share.

"Mr. Garraty and Foster? Both of them were . . . they were mangled, Tina. Ripped apart. Not the way you see in serial-killer movies and the like. Just . . . I wish I had better words to describe it," Alan revealed. He shuddered at the memory of the sight of Phil Garraty's body. "Then again, maybe I don't. Never seen anything like it in my life. We're wondering if it wasn't a bear or something. If it was a man, well, he wasn't alone, and he sure wasn't in his right mind."

"My lord," Tina rasped, her voice thick with revulsion. Her mouth hung open just enough to make her lower lip bow fetchingly, and her face had gone ghostly pale.

"Don't worry, honey. The sheriff and I'll get to the bottom of it," Alan vowed, though he did not feel half so confident as he sounded. But when Tina looked at him like that, so sweetly unaware of how amazing she was, he would have told her the Earth was flat if that was what she needed to hear.

Tina slid back in the booth. "Maybe that would be better," she said. "If it was a bear. People would realize that was simply its nature; tragic, of course, but just nature."

"I think you're right," Alan admitted. "That'd be better. If it was just animals. I surely hope that's the way it turns out. You can't blame animals for doing what they were born to do."

When the last of the customers had shuffled out on to the Boston street, Jack locked the door of Bridget's Irisk Rose Pub behind them, and only then did he allow himself to relax. Any time he was around a group of strangers these days—which was every time he worked or, truthfully, went anywhere in the city of Boston—he felt on edge. A seemingly innocent face in the crowd could take on sinister import if that face turned his way for slightly longer than was normal.

Jack didn't flirt anymore. Not that he had given up on it completely, but he always felt a certain reserve in himself, knowing that even the sweetest, cutest girl in the place might be less attractive on the inside. That any face in the crowd could suddenly change.

The pub was already abuzz with closing time activities. Jack flicked the house lights up all the way and the place became almost garish. Waitstaff moved about quickly, wiping down the few tables that had not been taken care of earlier and mopping the floor. Jack slipped down into the restaurant area and began to upend chairs, placing them on top of the tables, so that the waiter with the mop, Gary, wouldn't miss anything.

Behind the bar, Bill Cantwell wiped down the oak counter and stacked clean glasses. Even as Jack glanced at him, Bill flicked the cloth out, draped it over something under the bar, then glanced around one last time to make sure everything was in its place. Bill was fast. It never ceased to amaze Jack how quickly he could prepare the bar for the following day.

Bill took the drawer out of his register and tapped the computer keyboard a few times. Then he sat down to count out the cash in the drawer, to make sure it matched the computer's assessment. He would count his tips last, Jack knew.

"Hey."

Startled, Jack nearly dropped the chair in his hands. He glanced up to see Molly smirking at him, obviously amused that she had made him jump. Despite the harsh lighting and the long hours they had worked that day—and all week—she looked great. While most of the eighteen-year-old girls he knew always seemed to have put themselves together with great care, almost to have sculpted their appearance from makeup to fashion, Molly was always just Molly.

"A little on edge?" she teased.

He allowed a small smile. "Always, unfortunately. You never know when some wild woman is going to attack."

She cocked a hip and placed a hand on it. "You wish."

And there it was, unspoken between them. Only implied. The attraction Jack felt was undeniable, and he knew that she felt it, too. But neither of them was willing to do anything about it. Not with Artie's death so fresh.

"Penny for your thoughts?" she inquired.

"You couldn't afford them, Hatcher," he replied. "You done for the night?"

"Yeah. Kiera and I did the rollups for tomorrow. Only Tim and a couple of the other guys are left in the kitchen. Can I buy you a drink?" she asked.

Jack glanced over at the bar, where Bill slipped his drawer back into the register and began to count his tips.

"Bill will not be happy if we mess up his counter," Jack told her.

"He'll live," she said. "Besides, Bill loves me."

Molly set off toward the bar. The sounds of shouts and something banging came from the kitchen in the back. Tim Dunphy and the rest of the kitchen staff were blowing off steam, meaning they were finished for the night. They'd go out the back, and Dunphy would lock the rear door. He was the only one on staff who had a key to the place other than Jack, Bill, Molly, and Courtney.

Kiera and another waitress waved as they disappeared back into the kitchen. And that was that. The only people left in the front of the restaurant were Jack, Molly, and Bill. The place seemed surreal, lit up like that when it was empty. Jack moved to the hostess's station by the front doors and turned the lights down again, leaving only a few still lit at all.

"Hey, romantic," Bill said, looking up.

Jack gave him a halfhearted smile but did not respond. He didn't think the lighting romantic at all. In truth, he was happy to have his friends' company. When he was alone down here, in the shell of the restaurant, after all the life had fled from it and the lights were down, he could not help but think of the night of Artie's wake.

It had been the first time he had ever talked to a ghost.

Of course, it had happened a great many times since then, but that first night, he had been terrified. Artie had been murdered by the Prowlers and had returned from the dead to ask Jack to take vengeance for him. He had opened Jack's mind so that he could see the Ghostlands, the world side by side with that of the living, where lost souls wandered.

Artie had never really gone away.

Jack did not see him all the time, but it was rare for a whole week to go by without a visit. Artie wanted him to take care of Molly, had even suggested that there might be more between them than friendship. The ghost would rather see her with Jack, whom he knew would treat Molly right, than some other guy. Which totally freaked Jack out. Not that he didn't have feelings for Molly, but the last thing he felt he could do was talk to Artie about them.

And Molly . . . Jack had a feeling that she suspected. He had told her about his ability to speak to the wanderers of the Ghostlands, and she had never asked if Artie was among them, a fact that told Jack she did not want to know the answer. Which was fine, considering that Artie did not want Molly to know he was still around. The ghost was afraid she would not be able to move on with her life.

Much to Jack's chagrin, what had been a simple life for him had turned out to be very complicated. And, it seemed, death was complicated as well.

With a shudder, he glanced at the spot behind the bar where Artie's ghost had first appeared to him, and then went over to take a seat next to Molly. Though Bill was still counting out his tips, he had taken the time to pour her an iced tea.

"Oh, sure," Jack said, "you'll dirty up your nice clean workspace for her, but if I asked you, all I'd get is the evil eye."

"Sorry, partner," Bill replied. He paused as he silently counted the last few dollars. Then he glanced up with a devilish grin. "She's just a hell of a lot cuter than you."

"I happen to be very cute," Jack retorted.

Molly sipped her iced tea, but raised an eyebrow to look at him. "Eh, you're not bad."

They all shared a laugh, but it was followed by a long moment of uncomfortable silence. Jack took a deep breath and looked at Molly, who glanced away. He shook his head and turned to Bill instead.

"Do you think this will ever go away?"

"This?" Bill frowned.

Jack shrugged self-consciously. "This. The aftershock from what happened with . . . with the Prowlers." His gaze was locked on Bill's. "It's like an echo that won't fade."

"It'll fade," Bill replied instantly. His eyes ticked toward Molly. "Our girl here will head off to Yale in the fall, and life will go back to normal. The nighttime will go back to just being what happens when it gets dark."

Molly cleared her throat. They both turned to her. She stirred the ice in her glass with a straw.

"Maybe it shouldn't," she said.

Jack frowned. "What do you mean?"

"Maybe it shouldn't go back to normal. Okay, we could forget about it. I mean, at least partially. Forget in a sense that whole days might go by where we wouldn't think about it."

Her gaze, hard and sad, went to Bill. "Except you. I guess you couldn't forget, could you?"

"Not likely."

Molly reached a hand out to grasp Jack's wrist. "But if we *do* forget, what about next time?"

"I don't get you," Jack told her. Though he was afraid that he did.

"What about the next time it happens somewhere? And we could have done something because we knew?"

Bill placed both hands on the bar and leaned forward, a grave expression on his face. "No one will believe you. Even the people who know about Prowlers pretend it isn't true. Look at the Boston Police Department. Had to be twenty officers and detectives, maybe more, involved in the case in April. All of them saw, with their own eyes. None of them talked about it. Who'd believe them?"

"So we don't talk," Molly relented. "But I know how I'm going to feel if it happens again."

It was just after seven the following morning when Molly stumbled into the kitchen, wiping sleep from her eyes. The sun streamed in through the high windows and gleamed off the slanted floor. Jack sat behind the round table in a T-shirt and jean shorts, looking bright-eyed and ready to face the day.

Molly wanted to kill him.

His chin was covered with stubble, but that was the

only sign that he had not woken up much earlier than she had. With her hair more unruly than ever, slippers on her feet, and her ratty terry robe badly tied around her, she felt like roadkill.

"Good morning," he said pleasantly, a bowl of Wheaties on the table in front of him.

"Who says?" Molly griped as she trudged to the fridge to pull out the orange juice.

"You're really not a morning person, are you?" Jack teased.

It had been almost three months since she had moved in. He knew full well she was not a morning person, no matter how perfect and sunny it was outside.

"You're a sadist," she told him as she retrieved a glass from the cabinet. She sat down at the table and began to pour as Courtney walked into the kitchen.

"Jack?" his sister said.

Her voice was filled with a cold dread that sent shivers through Molly. Courtney walked with a cane and had done so for a decade, and though her features were still young and attractive, her handicap often made her look older than her twenty-nine years. But never as old as she looked in that moment. Her face was ashen and drawn.

"What is it?" Jack asked, voice tinged with concern for his sister as he went to her.

Molly had known them half her life, and she knew there was no one more important to Jack than Courtney. Courtney held pages from her computer printer in her hand, and she offered them to him.

Her eyes went to Molly's. "I've been sort of . . . keeping an eye out. On the Net. Like we talked about? I ran across this today."

Courtney let Jack take the pages and sat down at the kitchen table, resting the cane against her leg. Molly's gaze ticked from her to Jack and back again, wondering what she had found, but knowing exactly what it was all about. When Jack finally handed her the pages, Molly hesitated only a moment. It was a news piece about the mutilation murder of a mailman in central Vermont.

"It could be anything," she said, her voice sounding hollow even to herself.

Molly glanced up at Courtney, but Jack was the one who replied.

"It could be," he agreed.

With a sigh, Molly closed her eyes and dropped the pages on the table. When she opened them again, Jack was staring at her expectantly.

"But it's probably them," she allowed, resigned to the truth of it.

Jack reached out for her hand, gently lacing his fingers with hers. "There's only one way to know for sure."

CHAPTER 3

It took almost an entire day for Jack and Molly to arrange everything for their trip north. The schedule at the pub had to be considerably altered to cover for their indefinite absence. It was a sort of reconnaissance trip—at least they tried to think of it as such. Bill and Courtney were eager to reassure them that it was unlikely they would actually find anything, that the acquisition of a cell phone for each of them was merely a precaution.

Jack and Molly had spoken about the murders privately only once. The details sounded too familiar. While there were other explanations, now that they knew that Prowlers existed, it was natural to lay the blame for this new round of savagery on the ancient, monstrous race.

Bill had explained to them that contemporary Prowlers had no real unity, no cohesive society, and yet there did exist a kind of loose network, a matrix of connections and information. There were Prowlers who were cruel and a few that were benevolent, but most, he explained, were simply animals, their lives dictated by instinct and necessity, not morality. Though he had been less than forthcoming with tales of his own past, it was obvious he still had connections to that dark, underground semi-society.

The weapons were a testament to that. Bill did not tell them where he had acquired the guns he wanted them to take along—another precaution—and no one wanted to ask him. It was another part of his life, a link to his heritage that made them all uncomfortable. Ever since they had discovered that he was a Prowler, they were reluctant to ask him about his past. It was difficult enough to reconcile their love for the man with the knowledge of what he was.

Once upon a time, Bill Cantwell had played football for the New England Patriots. Whenever Jack thought about that, he marveled at the man's control of his physical appearance. Prowlers had to concentrate in order to look human, and it was nothing short of miraculous that Bill had been able to play a game as brutal as professional football and never reveal his true form.

They knew him as a former professional football player, a bartender, a friend. Yet it was clear that he was very old, perhaps centuries old. Before he had played for the Patriots, he must have been many other things. Logic indicated that Bill Cantwell was not even his real name, though that was something else no one wanted to ask him.

It rained all of Thursday morning. It was nearly noon when Jack pulled his battered old Jeep into the narrow alley behind Bridget's. Molly was upstairs, double-checking what she had packed and putting a call in to her mother. Mrs. Hatcher was an alcoholic and worse, and lived in a shabby apartment in a run-down section of Dorchester. Molly called her rarely and went to see her even less. It was not that she didn't love her mother, Jack knew, but that the woman did not care if Molly called or not, could barely seem to remember she had a daughter. Contact became too painful for Molly.

The only other vehicle parked behind the pub that day was Bill's enormous Oldsmobile. Bill bent over the open trunk of the Olds, hair matted to his head by the rain, which dripped in a steady flow from his beard.

Courtney stood just outside the open kitchen door of the pub with a huge black umbrella over her head. The umbrella and the grim expression on her face caused her to resemble a woman standing vigil at a graveside. Jack dumped his bags into the Jeep and walked back to her, ducking his head under the umbrella so that they were only inches from each other.

"Hey," he said, voice low, his words meant just for her. "It isn't a funeral."

Courtney blinked, her mouth dropping open in shock. "That was in really bad taste," she chided him. "I know it isn't a funeral, little brother. I'm just worried about you. About both of you."

The wind swept the heavy rain down at an angle; the buildings provided none of the protection they might have if it had been just a light shower. It was not. It was a storm, the sky low and dark, roiling like an ocean, pregnant with the promise of more rain. With her umbrella cocked at an angle to keep her as dry as possible and leaning on her cane, Courtney looked small and frail to her brother. For a long moment, he hesitated.

"I don't wanna go," he said at last.

She looked stricken. "Then don't go. Let somebody else fight them." Courtney's eyes, usually filled with such life, had none of their familiar sparkle. "We've done our share against these animals, Jack. Nobody's gonna think less of you if you and Molly just stay home. And I . . . if I lose you, little brother . . . you're all I have."

Her voice was so plaintive that Jack almost could not respond. Finally he smiled softly and stepped forward to hold his sister.

"Court, you've got it wrong," he said. "I don't want to go 'cause I don't want to leave you here. Me and Molly, we'll be all right. We find something, or even suspect something, you and Bill will get a call. We'll figure out what to do from there. I'm just . . . I don't want to leave you with the pub to run, and the possibility that . . . there might be more where Tanzer came from."

Mouth set in a firm line, Courtney nodded once. "I'll be fine. Not that you're not a full partner these days, Jack, but you weren't much help back when you were nine. I can handle it. As for the . . . as for *them*, I'll be careful. And I've got Bill."

Jack narrowed his eyes. Courtney noticed, and seemed pained by his expression.

"You don't trust him?" she whispered.

He barely heard her above the rain. "It isn't that. I mean, he's still Bill. We'd probably be dead without him. I guess I just . . . I don't know if I can ever put aside knowing that he's one of them."

Courtney bristled. "He *isn't* one of them. Same species, that's all. But so are you and Hitler and Jeffrey Dahmer. Doesn't make *you* one of *them.*"

Jack took a long breath. He glanced at Bill, who was down the alley, still fussing with something in his trunk, and wondered how good his hearing was. Then he turned back to Courtney and nodded.

"We've been through this. I know you're right. He's the closest thing to an uncle or whatever I've ever had. The closest thing to family we've had since Mom died. But it's hard not to hold something back, y'know? I mean, they're a whole *race* of Hitlers and Dahmers, and the decent ones are the exception. But I know you'll be safe with him. He cares about you."

There was a bit of extra weight to Jack's last words, an emphasis that Courtney caught immediately. She smiled and rolled her eyes.

"Bill is staying here while you're gone, but he's sleeping in *your* room, Jack."

"You're a big girl," Jack replied nonchalantly. "You run your life the way you want to. None of my business. All I ask is that you stay alive."

Courtney grew suddenly serious again. Her gaze caught his, and they locked eyes. "Same here," she said.

A moment later Molly appeared inside the open

door with a canvas suitcase that had once belonged to Jack and Courtney's mother. There was a melancholy air about her that would have been impossible for Jack to miss. Courtney apparently noticed it as well, for neither of the Dwyer siblings asked Molly how her conversation with her mother had gone.

"All set?" Jack asked.

"Yeah. Let's go. The weather shows no sign of letting up, so we should just get on the road and take our time."

As the three of them turned toward the vehicles again, they saw Bill slide a large black chest—like an old sea trunk—into the back of Jack's Jeep. It had a thick padlock on the front. Though it was heavy enough to make the back of the Jeep sag a bit after he lowered it, Bill moved the trunk effortlessly. His strength was incredible, and it reminded Jack just how badly outmatched he and Molly would be if they ran up against any Prowlers unprepared.

Bill strode toward them, seemingly unaware of the rain sluicing off his head. "When you're parked, I want you to throw some blankets over that trunk so it will draw a little less attention," he told Jack. "But the things in that trunk are only a precaution. If you see any Prowlers up there, I want you to call me and we'll figure out the next move then. Check in with us regularly."

Jack's eyes widened. "Yeah, of course. But if you're playing cavalry, why do we need weapons now?"

All traces of a smile disappeared from Bill's features. "Just in case, Jack. I'm not taking any chances. There's a goddamn arsenal in that trunk, and that should tell you how seriously I'm taking this. You know how I feel about weapons. I know you feel the same." He glanced at each of them in turn, lingering a moment on Courtney's face before looking at Jack and Molly again. "None of these are traceable, unless you leave prints on them. Don't get caught with them. Don't shoot at anyone human unless it's to save your own life. Hell, don't ever shoot at *anything* you don't intend to kill."

"Bill," Courtney said hesitantly, "I don't know if—"

"We have to have them," Molly interrupted. Her face was pale, but her voice was clear and strong. "We've got to be prepared."

Bill nodded and handed Jack a small key that would open the padlock on the trunk. When Jack took it, Bill clasped his hand tightly and pulled him close.

"Be careful. Don't take any chances. Call for me and I'll come," Bill said, his voice a low rasp.

In the huge man's powerful embrace, Jack found reserves of strength he would sorely need if he and Molly found what they were looking for.

"You'll protect her, if anything happens?" Jack asked.

"With my life," Bill promised.

A sudden rush of guilt filled Jack for the doubts he'd had. Bill might be a different species, but he was part of their life and family. These people were just about all that mattered to Jack.

"Let's get on the road," he said as he turned away from Bill.

Molly carried her suitcase to the back of the Jeep.

Jack took it from her, put it on top of the trunk, and closed up the back.

"Wait, I'll get a couple of blankets," Courtney said quickly.

Jack and Molly climbed into the Jeep, he slipped the key into the ignition, and the engine roared to life. Anxious, Jack stared at the rain pelting the windshield. Molly reached over suddenly to take his hand and his fingers twined with hers as he turned to face her.

"It'll be all right," she said, an uncommon tenderness in her voice. "If nothing else, it'll be an adventure."

With a laugh, Jack shook his head. "Let's *hope* it's nothing else."

Pine Hill provided an idyllic backdrop for the town of Buckton. Almost anywhere else in New England, it would have been striped with ski slopes and chairlifts, but this part of Vermont had far less tourism than some other areas. The name of the "hill" was misleading, however. It was not quite a mountain, but certainly far more than a hill, and there were far more than pines along its span.

Though there were numerous small streets off it, Pine Hill Road, in addition to being the main street of Buckton, was mainly a throughway to other areas of the state. Very few Buckton residents chose to make their homes in the deep forest of the hill. Given the realities of snow removal, garbage collection, and postal service, what little new home construction there was in Buckton tended to be in the areas already populated.

As such, only hikers, hunters, and amorous or adventursome teens made their way into the densest parts of Pine Hill. Among those, only a small percentage stumbled upon Bartleby Road, a densely overgrown dirt path that had once accommodated wagons and carts laden with building materials. For, once upon a time, there had been an enormous estate built atop Pine Hill, more than a mile from the nearest road.

Before there was a Buckton, there had been the old Bartleby place. And yet only the eldest members of the community were certain it had existed. Others knew of it only as a legend, a whispered story to frighten young children, a house full of bogeymen, perhaps. The ghost of a house, most thought, if it had ever existed at all.

But it had.

Now only the ruins of the Bartleby place remained, tumbled fireplaces and fire-blasted brick, charred lumber under nearly a century's worth of detritus. The estate had burned to the ground in 1904. The only human beings who had seen it in the past few decades had literally stumbled across it. Almost all had continued on, thinking nothing at all of it.

Almost all.

A few had poked around, even tried to camp there. Hikers, mostly, and mostly from out of town. Some of those had never made it home.

It was a sacred place to the Pack, for it was where Bartleby himself had been slain those many years ago. The Prowlers who had lived upon that land had been driven off, not to return for decades. Once they had returned, however, and created of Buckton a sanctuary where all Prowlers were welcome so long as they followed the rules, the ruins became their meeting place, the chapel within which they worshipped all that was wild.

If the Prowlers could be said to have a religion, that was it. The wild and the wilderness. And the blood of prey.

It was late afternoon that Thursday, nearly one hundred years after Bartleby's murder, that the Alpha bounded along paths human eyes would have missed, up the Pine Hill toward the ruins. Rain pelted from the sky and slicked back his fur. He barely noticed the storm, however. His blood raged with a fury that had been all too common in recent days, and yet this latest development had upset him more than anything else.

A steady, ululating snarl emerged from his throat as his claws tore at the ground, and he burst from the last stand of trees beside the remains of Bartleby's sanctum.

The others were already there. At times—particularly when, as now, they met during the day—some of them would choose to appear in their human forms. In the rain, especially, they might have opted to wear coats or hold umbrellas to protect them from the elements. Such things disgusted the Alpha. The elements were part of the Wild. The Prowlers were part of it as well.

Among the ruins, nine members of the Pack awaited his arrival, mostly elders. The rest were in the town, going about the business of their human lives in a community filled with people who had no idea that monsters lived amongst them. Other pack members were still far from home, wandering across the world, though they would return someday.

When the Alpha reached the ruins, he paused, then advanced slowly, head high, establishing his primacy within the Pack. The others approached cautiously, lowered their snouts in greeting. Even those in human form cast their gazes at the ground. He waited until all such proprieties had been dispensed with before he spoke a single word.

It rumbled from his chest like rolling thunder.

"Desmond."

The young Prowler, who had challenged him three years earlier for Alpha and lost, raised his head with a start and a barely audible whimper. Then Desmond slunk back a step from the circle they had made among the ruins of their history.

"You have much to answer for," the Alpha went on.

Defiantly, the other Prowler bared his teeth. "I did what I thought was right. If you had not written the book—"

With a roar, the Alpha rose up to his full height and slashed Desmond across the snout, tearing bloody gashes in his fur. The cur cried out in pain and clasped long talons to his face.

"What you did!" the Alpha growled. "Oh, what you did, you little bastard. That book is our legacy, our history, to be passed down to those who come after us, so that no one shall ever forget Bartleby and the principles upon which this sanctuary was founded."

Desmond sneered, blood dripping from his wounds. "That book is an abomination. You claim to despise human things, but you write this . . . this *bible* for the Pack, just like a human. Oral history has—"

"Silence!" the Alpha growled, and Desmond obeyed instantly. "Oral history is little better than mythology, particularly with the packs scattered and so many nomads drifting in the world. When they come to find sanctuary here, they need to understand what they have found."

The Alpha paced a moment, then leaped at Desmond, the sheer force of his presence forcing the younger beast to back down.

"Enough of this. I do not have to explain myself to you," he snarled in the guttural voice of the beast. You have put this sanctuary and everything it stands for at risk. The first law of our Pack—the law that has allowed us to survive so long when so many of the Great Packs upon this continent have died out or been hunted to extinction—says that we must never hunt at home."

"It was not hunting," Desmond replied, though tentatively, eyes downcast. "It was self-preservation."

The Alpha sat upon his hind legs and addressed the upper hierarchy of the Pack arrayed about him. "What he did, this foolish beast, was slaughter Foster Marlin and Phil Garraty, right here in Buckton."

"Marlin found the book. You didn't hide it well enough. He found it, and he read it," Desmond went on, voice tinged with pleading now. "Worst of all, he *believed* it. He had to die."

The Alpha growled low in contemplation. "There were other ways. You know the laws of this sanctuary. We have lived among the humans long enough to know there were other ways. Marlin may have read the book, but with him dead, we have no way to know what has become of it. And what of the postman?"

"Garraty brought the letters, the demands," Desmond reasoned, almost whining now.

At the young one's words, the Alpha reared back and slashed him again, this time long gashes upon his shoulder. "Garraty was the postman, you idiot!" he screamed. "It was his job to bring the letters."

"We could not know if he had read them! We could not know what he knew. And he was Foster Marlin's friend. Perhaps the man's only friend. And he knew of the book. He confessed as much before we killed him."

"And what have you accomplished?" the Alpha asked him. "Two men killed and left where they could be found. The postman's murder was in the newspapers, Desmond. I've had phone calls from Hartford, Boston, and New York. You have compromised us, and we are no closer to discovering who now holds the book. Until it is safely back in my hands, the secrecy, and thus the safety of the pack of our sanctuary, is in jeopardy. Now that you have set us upon this path, we may have to kill again before it is through. We may once again be forced to abandon this place, our pack's original home upon this continent. The sanctuary we provide to others. And you are to blame."

There was a weight to his words that was unmistakable. Worse, though, was the low growl that began to emit from his throat when the last of his words had been drowned in the rain, stolen by the wind.

Desmond's eyes were wide. "No."

"You have shamed me. You have endangered the Pack," the Alpha declared. The single word that followed, a low and guttural sound, was spoken in a language more ancient than humanity.

Desmond tried to flee, his cowardice another example of his shameful behavior. He did not get far before the others dragged him down and tore him apart.

Unnerved by what lay hidden in the chest in the back of his Jeep, Jack never drove more than five miles per hour above the speed limit on the trip to Buckton. Though normally the drive would not have taken more than four hours at the outside, the heavy rain that had enveloped all of northern New England slowed them down even more.

All along the way, as they went north on Route 93 into New Hampshire and then continued northwest on Route 89 right up into the mountainous heart of Vermont, Jack did his best to keep Molly's mind off their destination. Though there was no way she would have let him go up to Buckton without her, that did not mean Molly was not nervous. Quite the contrary. It was clear in the way they both talked around the subject of Prowlers that neither of them was free of anxiety, even fear, as the site of the murder of Phil Garraty drew ever closer.

Molly also seemed reluctant to talk about her mother, and the conversation she had had with the woman right before they left Boston. Not that Jack minded, however. He preferred not to speak about Molly's mother at all. The woman's behavior toward her daughter, and the way she seemed to have flushed her own life down the toilet, were inexcusable. And yet, for all the pain her mother caused her, if anyone else spoke against her, Molly was just as likely to defend her as she was to join in. That was something Jack had learned the hard way.

So they talked about the few friends Molly still kept in touch with from high school, and who was going to what college, and what Yale might be like for her in the fall. Jack was surprised at the reticence in her voice, as though Yale were yet another subject she would rather not discuss. They did talk about it, though, and he found himself, despite the errand they were currently occupied with, hoping that the six weeks left of summer would crawl by.

When fall came, and Molly left for college, nothing would be the same for him. It was unsettling how vital a part of his life she had become. Whatever mystery or trouble they were traveling into now, there was a thrill for him in just being with Molly. Though their conversation dissipated to almost nothing by the time they were halfway across New Hampshire, and though the rain continued to darken the sky ominously, he knew that there was something about this trip that was precious and newly formed, and might never come again.

As they passed through White River Junction, just over the border in Vermont, Jack glanced over to see that Molly had fallen asleep, her leggy form curled up tight where she leaned against the door. His eyes ticked toward the passenger side door, and he was reassured when he saw that it was locked. It wouldn't do to have her tumbling out onto the highway.

He smiled to himself and punched the buttons on the radio until he found a soft rock station, something soothing. With the forbidding nature of their destination and the contact she had had earlier with her mother, Molly's dreams were likely to be of dark and perilous things. Jack hoped the music would soothe her. Keep the predators of the mind at bay.

The bruise-dark sky made the long July afternoon seem more like one in midwinter. Even though it was only beginning to edge toward dinner time, it was as though night had come already. Traffic had thinned as they continued northwest, until there were only a handful of cars on his side of the road. The rain began to let up when they were twenty miles or so from the tiny dot on the map where Buckton was supposed to be.

That was when Jack saw the first ghost.

He frowned and narrowed his gaze at the figure standing alone on the side of the highway. *A man,* he thought. Hands up, he waved his arms at Jack, who began to slow the Jeep. *Someone in trouble.* Scenarios flashed through his head of accidents and cars off the road in the storm. A Volvo station wagon behind him honked loudly and sped past in the next lane.

Jack squinted as he peered through the rain-spattered windshield, the wipers squeaking back and forth as they dragged across the glass. The Jeep rolled almost to a stop as he cut in toward the breakdown lane just slightly. Just enough so that his headlights washed over the man waving emphatically from the side of the road. The lights cut right through him . . . as did the rain.

The man had kind, sad eyes behind thick glasses and wild hair. But his hair was not wet. He was not, after all, really there. He was a ghost.

Jack shivered, but it was not the chill of the rain that brought it on. He had seen ghosts before, had spoken to them. They had saved his life more than once. Artie, after all, still appeared to him. But these lost souls of the mournful dead were still tethered to this Earth by grief or confusion or some unfinished business. He would never get used to seeing them or to the twinge of sadness he felt when he did.

The spirit appeared to be waving at him, but had not noticed when he began to pull over. Jack wondered if the man had died in an accident on the side of the road, and stood there for eternity trying to flag down some help, unaware that it would never come. He suspected that if he looked into it, he might find reports of other sightings of the ghost, a lost soul.

Ever since Artie had first appeared to him as a ghost, Jack had been able to see into the Ghostlands if he wanted to. Sometimes, though, it just happened, whether he wanted it to or not. Artie had explained to him that the phantoms who wandered the Ghostlands were spirits who were still tied to the earthly plane by grief or some sort of unfinished business. Many of them had died horribly, suddenly, such as the victims of Prowlers. Among those were ghosts who were not even aware that they were dead.

This man was probably one of them, killed so quickly in a car accident that his soul could not accept that he was dead.

Some of the ghosts Jack saw *chose* to be seen, to draw his attention to them. Others he simply noticed, sometimes out of the corner of his eye, like a spectral little boy he had seen a few weeks earlier, standing on a street corner as though waiting for a school bus that would never come. It had unnerved him, seeing that boy.

It seemed that whatever door Artie had opened in Jack's mind could never again be closed all the way.

Chilled, Jack did his best to push the thoughts away. He accelerated again, left the ghost behind. A short way up, he found the exit for the local, two-lane highway that would eventually lead him to Buckton. It took a moment for him to figure out which direction he ought to drive, but then they were moving again.

Three miles farther on, he saw another ghost. A woman, this time, standing in the center of the highway, arms raised above her head in what might have been prayer or a supplication to heaven. The rain passed through her, spattered the pavement around her. His headlights caught on the wraith-like mist of her phantom form, like the glitter off morning fog.

Unlike the first ghost, this one noticed him. As the Jeep bore down upon her, Jack moved into the oncoming lane to avoid her, though the vehicle would have passed right through. She dropped her arms and turned to stare right at him.

As he passed, their eyes met.

She mouthed the words "Go home, Jack."

"Holy shit," he muttered under his breath, heart rate speeding up, adrenaline pumping through him. His eyes were wide and he glanced in the rearview mirror, but she was already gone.

Molly stirred but did not wake. An old seventies love song came on the radio. Soothing, yes, but his heartbeat did not slow. He blew out a few breaths, trying to tell himself it was nothing, not to be so freaked out.

The road ahead was dark and slick with rain, the sun only a glimmer between black clouds. There were no other cars on the road. Now that he had gotten off Route 89, he was alone, with only Molly's sleeping form and the spirits of the dead for company. He wanted to scream.

Jack would never get used to it. They were dead, and it always felt to him as though they wanted something from him that he could not provide.

Life.

Go home, Jack.

Though the road was slipperier than ever beneath his tires, he risked a quick glance at Molly. She was cute as hell, her lips parted just a bit, a tiny bit of drool at the edge of her mouth that he would tease her for later. He mentally willed her to wake up, but resisted the urge to reach out and shake her. After all, what would he say? She knew about the ghosts, but just as she did not like to discuss her mother, he was reluctant to talk to her about the Ghostlands, because that might lead to questions about Artie.

A few miles farther on, he rounded a corner and the road began to climb up. All around there were hills and small mountains. A green sign at the side of the road announced that Barlow was three miles away, and Buckton eight. Jack never saw a trace of Barlow, and imagined it must be off the main road.

A short time later the Jeep rolled to a stop at an intersection where more than a dozen ghosts stood along the side of the road, like spectators at a parade. As one, they turned to stare at the Jeep, and at Jack behind the wheel. With the rain sluicing through them, they then lowered their heads and would no longer meet his eyes.

He froze. The engine idled as he sat there staring at the ghosts, hoping they would look up at him. If they did, and they told him to go as the other specter had, Jack knew he would turn the Jeep around and keep driving until he saw the lights of Boston.

But they did not glance up again. *Would* not.

"What the hell is this?" he whispered, his voice too loud in the Jeep with Molly sleeping beside him, even though the soft music on the radio drowned out his words.

There came an answer.

"Call it the welcome wagon, bro."

With a start, Jack glanced in the rearview mirror. In the backseat, the rear of the Jeep visible through him, sat Artie Carroll. Artie was a ghost now and a part of the spirit world that Jack could never understand. But Artie was still Artie.

"What do you think of it up here, Jack?" he asked. "Weird country, I think. I mean, on the one hand you've got plenty of liberals, all that PC Ben & Jerry's stuff and the push for gay marriages. On the other hand, you've got enough hunting to make Charlton Heston wet himself. An NRA festival. Damn peculiar, wouldn'tja say?"

Jack felt a chill run through him, and he did his best not to let Artie see how it all affected him.

"Good . . . good to see you, Artie," he said, voice barely above a whisper. Molly would hear him if she woke up. If he was lucky, she'd think he was talking to himself.

"You're freaked out, Jack. Don't lie to me. I don't come around for a few weeks, maybe you stop believing I'm still here," Artie said, sadness creeping into his voice.

Jack could clearly see the upholstery through Artie's body. Every inch of him was transparent, and sometimes his legs seemed to be disappearing. He drifted more than moved.

Every inch . . . but not his eyes. Artie's eyes were black and gleaming with sparkles that might have been stars. Something swirled inside them, something solid. His eyes were not transparent, they were windows into somewhere else. Jack thought it was the Ghostlands, but if it was not, he did not want to know what else it could be.

Molly began to stir, so Jack accelerated again, even

more slowly. They crossed the intersection and rolled past the ghosts, but not one of them looked up.

"What do you mean, 'welcome wagon'?" he asked quietly.

"They've heard about you. Word travels in the Ghostlands. All these folks are victims of the Prowlers. You got vengeance for me and some others in Boston. They're hoping you'll do the same here," Artie explained.

Jack glanced quickly over his shoulder. The ghosts had moved out into the street now, standing in the rain as a few errant rays of sun broke through and speared the pavement around them. Most of them still hung their heads as though ashamed, though one or two had looked up.

"I don't get it, though," Jack whispered. "One of them tried to get me to turn around. Now this bunch won't even look at me."

Artie did not respond at first. Jack had to look in the rearview mirror to make sure he was still there. Then those black, bottomless-pit eyes met his, and he shuddered and returned his attention to the road.

"Artie?" Jack prodded.

"They're feeling a little guilty," Artie finally revealed.

Jack furrowed his brow. "Why?"

"They think you're gonna die."

CHAPTER 4

Artie.

The moment Molly awoke, the dream began to slip
away. As her eyes flickered open, the only thing she
could recall was that he had been there. For a moment
it was as though she could still see him; the image of his
sweet grin lingered. Then it was gone.

Molly frowned. It was very dark outside, but with
the rain pouring down upon the windshield and drum-
ming against the roof, she could not tell if it was truly
night, or if the storm had brought evening prematurely.

The engine still idled, but the Jeep had stopped.

She moaned a little, stretched—the last thoughts of
the Artie-dream skittering back into the recesses of her
unconscious, like night creatures fleeing the sunrise—
and glanced over at Jack.

His hair was a mess, and his chin had a shadow he
could never seem to be rid of for long. Yet, though rum-

pled, he looked strong and confident. It gave her hope, seeing him like that, before he had noticed she was awake. Jack had always been the one out in front, the leader, and Artie always the loyal, devil-may-care side-kick.

But Artie was dead now. And Molly doubted she would ever allow herself to be anybody's sidekick.

She stretched again, and this time Jack noticed. His eyes sparkled as he glanced at her, and a smile blossomed on his lips. Molly might have seen something in his gaze just then, when he looked at her like that, just waking up, that sent a pleasurable shiver through her. But she pushed the thought away. It was hard for her to think of Jack in that way, but even more so with the last echoes of her dream still haunting her, as though Artie hid somewhere out there in the dark, amidst the rain.

"Well, hey there, sleepyhead," Jack said in a whisper, barely audible over the radio and the rain.

"Mmm," Molly replied, stretching one final time before sitting up in her seat and glancing around. "Are we here?"

She squinted and tried to get a good look at the storefronts on the street around them.

"Well, if 'here' is Buckton, then, yeah," Jack replied. Then he shrugged. "But I've gotta tell you, there isn't much 'here' here."

"What was it you expected, Metropolis?" Molly asked. "It looks quaint."

Despite the rain she could clearly make out the glowing marquee and façade of an old-style movie house, the Empire Theatre. There were a few small stores, mostly dark now, and what looked like a tiny Chinese take-out restaurant, given that its name was written in both English and the spiderwebbed characters that must have been a rough translation.

"Quaint, yeah," Jack agreed, his smile fading, his voice growing far more serious. "But it doesn't seem like the kind of place a pack would go unnoticed."

A cold fist of ice formed in Molly's gut. "No. I suppose not. On the other hand, they didn't really go unnoticed in Boston, did they? Maybe this is *exactly* the kind of place they could blend in."

For a moment neither of them spoke.

At length Jack shifted in the driver's seat and shut off the engine, casting them into darkness and killing the radio.

"I guess we should get something to eat and see about finding a place to stay. You've gotta wonder if they even have a hotel here. It isn't like it's a hot vacation spot."

"We'll find something," she assured him.

Jack hopped out of the Jeep and ran around to the back to get an umbrella for her, then went to the door. With the doors locked, the two of them crowded under the now-inadequate shield from the rain and looked for somewhere to eat. They spotted a place called the Jukebox Restaurant.

"It looks harmless enough," Molly observed. "And it's dry in there."

"Sold," Jack replied.

Together they ran to the door and slipped inside. The Jukebox was much nicer than Molly expected. Not that it was anything special, but the tablecloths were clean and each table had a small candle on it. It was relatively crowded as well, which Molly thought boded well.

A minute or so after they had come in, a waitress walked over, wiping her hands on her apron. She smiled oddly at them, as if she thought they had inadvertently stumbled into the wrong place.

"Can I help you folks?"

"I hope so," Jack replied. "Two for dinner."

The waitress blinked. "Oh. Oh, sure. Smoking or non?"

"Non," Molly said quickly.

As the waitress grabbed a couple of menus and turned, Molly frowned. *Nothing like being wanted,* she thought. Maybe it was the girl's first night, or maybe it was that they just did not get too many travelers passing through, but she thought the waitress's hesitancy was extremely rude.

With a curious smile, the waitress laid the menus on a table against the back wall. As Molly sat down, she glanced around and saw that a lot of the other diners had turned to observe them. A shudder passed through her.

Enough to make a girl paranoid, she thought.

"Can I get you folks a drink while you're deciding on dinner?" the waitress asked.

Jack ordered a Coke and Molly asked for lemonade.

The second the waitress was gone, Molly tried to tear her attention away from the surreptitious glances she was getting from others in the restaurant.

"Boy, I guess they really don't get a lot of tourists through here," she whispered to Jack. "I feel like I'm in a fishbowl."

"Could be they're just entranced by your ravishing beauty," he suggested.

Molly swore at him under her breath, and he laughed. A few minutes later the waitress returned with their drinks and they ordered. Jack had steak teriyaki. Though Molly would have liked the pasta primavera, she ordered the chicken parmesan; she reasoned that was the one thing on the menu it would be really difficult to screw up.

"Okay, anything else at the moment?" the waitress asked, eyes on Jack.

"Actually," Molly put in, almost forcing the girl to turn to her, "we were hoping you might be able to tell us if there's anywhere in town for us to stay. A hotel or a bed-and-breakfast?"

"Hunh," the waitress replied, face twisted up in an expression that implied the question might be too difficult for her. She was clearly stumped. "Do you have relatives in town?"

"No," Jack said good-naturedly, "just passing through. Seeing the sights."

"Yeah," the girl replied cynically, "it's just too bad there aren't any sights to see. There isn't much to do in Buckton."

Molly and Jack just waited, watching her. After a moment the waitress shrugged.

"Well, the only place to stay in town is the Buckton Inn. It's just up the Post Road a ways, about a mile and a half on the left. You can't miss it, considering it's the only thing there," she said, her expression, like her tone, filled with disdain for her hometown.

"Thanks," Jack said.

"Not at all," the waitress replied. "Just do me a favor? If you're going anywhere that's even remotely like a city after this, give some thought to the idea of taking me with you."

Molly actually chuckled at that, feeling far less impatient with the girl than she had been. "We'll take it into consideration," she promised.

Deputy Alan Vance stood in the lobby of the Buckton Inn and tapped impatiently on the counter. The fingers of his right hand drummed out the theme from the ancient *Lone Ranger* television show.

Behind the counter, Tina was on the phone with Mick Bradley, who had been unwilling to come down from his third-floor room to complain about the small leak in his roof. It had been raining like hell all day long, and the old three-story inn was likely to have a leak or two in at least one of its twelve rooms. It was just a tragedy that it had to be Mick's. Like four of the other guests, he used the Inn as his primary residence. Ever since Marianne had thrown him out on his behind three years earlier, Mick had been living at the inn and making a general nuisance of himself.

Before Tina had bought the place—or, more accurately, had her father buy it for her in order to lure her back to Buckton after college—the Buckton Inn had been a moldy, run-down shambles of a place, with broken windows, stained carpets, and sagging ceilings. But the Lemoines had never been short of cash. Tina had infused enough money into the inn to make it look wonderful. It would never be a five-star hotel, but there was a simple elegance to the decorating, plenty of brass and glass and timelessly impressive carpets, and Tina always kept fresh-cut flowers around.

During the spring and fall, when hunters and hikers would often take up the other rooms in the place, Tina offered a continental breakfast, and even had entertainment in the lobby on Friday nights. Just Joe Kenneally with his fat-bellied guitar, but Joe was a heck of a singer.

The inn was the nicest place in Buckton, even if most of the people in town had never been through the front door.

"Mick," Tina snapped into the phone. She turned to look at Alan and rolled her eyes. "No, Mick, listen! I've called over to Byron to come and repair the roof, but there's nothing he can do until it stops raining, and that's going to be tomorrow morning. Just keep dumping the bucket into the toilet . . . or out the window, if you want. It's only supposed to rain for another few hours. Then tomorrow morning, I'll take care of it."

Jaw set in a firm, angry line, Tina closed her eyes and sighed. The phone was clutched tightly in her fist.

"Then find another place to live!" she shouted into the phone before slamming it back down into its cradle.

"Wow," Alan said, unable to hide the amusement he felt. "You sound just like my mother. Is that a good idea, chasing your customers off?"

"Where would he go?" Tina replied, shaking her head slowly.

Alan heard someone clear his throat and turned quickly to see a young couple standing in the lobby with a dripping umbrella. The guy was average height and muscular, with dark hair and intense eyes. His girl-friend, if that's what she was, had an alluring mess of rich, red hair and a way of standing—hip jutted out to one side—that told him she wasn't the type to put up with foolishness from anyone.

"Oh," Tina squeaked. "That's not exactly good pub-lic relations, is it?"

With a frown, Alan glanced at her. There was a light-ness in her voice that was unusual for her. She even seemed to have flushed a bit. He understood that she was embarrassed that the guy and girl, neither of whom looked like they could possibly be over twenty—probably college kids, he reasoned—had overheard her tirade against Mick. But Alan did not think she should be concerned.

"Don't worry. Tina only snaps at the regulars. She's real nice to out-of-towners," Alan said.

"So," Tina asked, "you two want a room?"

The two young people glanced shyly and a bit awkwardly at each other. Alan thought it was fairly precious. He had been to college out in the real world, but even in a little town like Buckton you didn't often find kids who were nineteen or twenty years old who still had it in them to display that sort of hesitation. They weren't that much younger than Alan himself, but he knew that most kids their age were all bluster and swagger. That was how they dealt with each other.

He liked these two.

"So you two are hikers, I take it?" Alan ventured.

The guy glanced at him, and suddenly everything changed. His eyes, so innocent a moment before, became veiled and suspicious.

"Well, amateur hikers, I guess. Just exploring New England, Officer."

"Deputy," Alan corrected. "Deputy Sheriff Alan Vance, at your service."

He held out a hand. After a slight hesitation, the kid shook. The girl did the same, and now she, too, seemed to have retreated within herself. Alan had liked them on sight, that much was true. But all of a sudden he wasn't sure if he could trust them.

"I'm Molly Hatcher," the girl said. "This is my friend, Jack Dwyer. We've heard you have some beautiful terrain. Excuse us if we seem surprised, but we're from Boston. We're not used to the police being so hospitable."

She smiled so charmingly that Alan laughed. "All right, Miss Hatcher. No pushy law enforcement around here. Just being friendly, is all."

"He does look rather imposing in the uniform, though, doesn't he?" Tina said, teasing him.

Molly and Jack smiled, and Alan shot Tina a withering glance. Though he supposed it was better for her to hassle him in front of tourists than in front of locals.

"Actually, I'm glad you're here, Deputy Vance," Jack put in casually. "I was wondering if there were any special precautions we ought to take, hiking around here?"

Alan frowned. There was something in the kid's tone again. It was weird how he kept shifting from friendly to guarded.

"You mean to avoid getting lost?" Tina asked. "Because people always find their way back to the inn. It's my animal magnetism."

Jack narrowed his gaze. Tina had been flirting a little, but Alan was glad to see that for once it had not had the effect she had wanted. Not by the look the kid gave her.

"Actually, we were concerned because of the murders," Molly explained, pushing her hair away from her face.

Alan froze. "Murders?"

"That mailman and the other guy," Jack explained. "We read it in the papers down in Boston, but we didn't want to change our plans so late. That's what I meant about precautions. Should we be concerned?"

"I . . . I don't think so," Alan said hurriedly. "Isolated incidents, you know?"

"Any theories?" Molly prodded.

For a moment Alan felt as though he were being

interrogated. Something gleamed in Molly's green eyes, a fire that added weight to her questions.

"A few," he said evenly, more confident now. He was the law in Buckton. Part of that job meant keeping the peace, and part of keeping the peace was keeping the people calm. "If you're experienced hikers, you should have no problem. Just keep to the trails and watch for wild animals."

"What kind of wild animals?" Jack asked.

"Coyotes. Bobcats, though they don't really bother people as long as you don't try to pet them."

"Lions and tigers and bears," Molly said with a small laugh.

Yet the laugh sounded hollow to Alan.

"No lions or tigers, but possibly bears," Tina put in. "There may have been a sighting or two in the last couple of weeks. They're not uncommon up this way."

A sudden and unwelcome silence fell over the lobby. It was slow this time of year, and Alan found himself wishing for an interruption, even another phone call from Mick. After a moment, though, Tina smiled again.

"Well, you two will be all right, I'm sure. So, would you like to check in?"

"That'd be great, thanks," Jack said.

Molly shuffled closer to the counter and blushed fiercely. "Do you have a room with two beds?"

Tina raised an eyebrow toward Jack, then smiled at Molly. "I think we can take care of you, hon."

Before she went on, she glanced over at Alan. "So, eight o'clock at the Empire? What are we seeing again?"

"To Catch a Thief," he replied, distracted now by thoughts of their date later. "It's finally been restored."

"I'll meet you there," she told him, and in her tone was an obvious dismissal.

Alan lingered for just another moment, as Tina checked in the Buckton Inn's unexpected guests. Then he smiled at her and went out the front door and down to his patrol car.

He had an hour before they were supposed to meet for the movie. More than likely, Tina would be late. Alan took one cruise through downtown Buckton before heading home to change. Though he was really looking forward to spending more time with Tina, and going to the movie, he had a hard time getting Jack and Molly out of his head. Some of the people in Buckton—most of them, he mentally conceded—had a disdain or at least a dislike for out-of-towners. Alan did not feel that way at all. But he was a sheriff's deputy, an officer of the law, and he had been trained to trust his instincts.

His instincts told him that there was something off about those two. Alan decided it would be a good idea to keep an eye on them.

He had a feeling that they were either going to get into trouble, or they'd brought it with them.

Though he was only three weeks shy of seventy-three, nothing gave Kenny Oberst more pleasure than watching cartoons. When cable television came through town a few years earlier, the only reason he had gotten it was in order to watch the Cartoon

Network and others. He didn't just like the shows from his youth, either—though they were his favorites. He also liked the new stuff on Nickelodeon.

Kenny Oberst thought of himself as a cartoon connoisseur.

In his little two-bedroom house on Elm Street, just a few blocks away from the town library—where he had worked as librarian for more than fifty years—was a veritable second library, though this one was more eccentric. He had hundreds of videotapes of various cartoons, some of them quite rare.

Tonight, Kenny was treating himself. He had managed to get his hands on a tape of Max Fleischer's Superman cartoons that had been made from the originals. It was pristine, better-looking than anything he had ever seen broadcast on television. He had seen the first of those cartoons way back in 1941 at the Empire Theatre downtown, and seeing them so sharp and clear now made him feel, just for the time he was watching them, that the little boy he had been was perhaps not so far from him now.

Fleischer's *Superman* was extraordinary, a feat of animation that Kenny firmly believed modern cartoonists, particularly those with computers, ought to pay more attention to.

In an old leather recliner whose seat cushion hid years of stale popcorn—his other great weakness— Kenny sat with a cold Michelob in one hand and the remote control in the other and slipped back into another time. The room was filled with videos, leafy plants on high pedestals, and books he had not gotten around to returning to the library. Not that he was concerned—in fifty-two years, he had never fined himself, despite his chronic tardiness.

When the first knock came at the door, Kenny did not even notice. He was an old man now, and his hearing was not what it had once been. The volume on the television was up too loud as it was, though he had no neighbors close enough to complain.

Only when the rapping came a third time, and hard enough to shake the door on its hinges, did Kenny glance over and realize he had company.

His mouth twisted into a grimace as he pressed the pause button on the remote control. With a sigh, he put down the recliner and stood up. Beer still in hand, he walked to the door and opened it.

Kenny blinked in surprise. "Well, I'll be," he said pleasantly, but also a bit mystified. "How long has it been since you showed up on my front step?"

"A long time," the man at the door replied. "A very long time. May I come in?"

" 'Course you can!" Kenny told him amiably. "Why, what a surprise. Hey, come here a second." He led the way into the living room and gestured toward the frozen picture on the television set. "Remember those?"

The man studied the television for a moment, then shrugged. "Superman. But I can't say I remember that particular cartoon. That's always been your passion."

"Sure has," Kenny replied proudly. He sat back down in his recliner, though he didn't lean back. He thought that might be rude. With a sweep of his hand, he indicated that his guest should take the sofa, and the man did so, first stacking some books to clear himself a seat.

Kenny glanced suddenly at his beer, and felt a bit guilty. "Say, can I get you a beer or something?"

"No, thank you," his visitor replied. "I'm not going to stay long. I only came to ask one question."

The cartoon started up again unannounced, music blaring, narrator moaning dramatically about Superman. Kenny shot his guest a sheepish glance and clicked the stop button on the remote.

"Sorry," he said. "It just does that if you leave it too long. So, what was your question?"

The man smiled. His teeth gleamed in the light from the white snow static on the television.

"Where's the book?" he asked.

Kenny frowned. He did not recall having borrowed a book from this man. In truth, he had not had any conversation of real substance with his visitor for many years.

"Come again?"

Again with that smile. "Foster Marlin stole a book from me. Word has it that he may have come to see you before he died. I want to know if he gave you anything, or told you anything about the whereabouts of my book."

"Foster?" Kenny asked stupidly. "What the hell's he got to do with some book?"

The guest glared at him, eyebrows raised, looking sinister. Kenny shifted uncomfortably in his chair and put the beer down on the tray table, hoping to look more sincere about things himself.

"He stole it from me. He came to see you before he . . . died."

For one seemingly eternal moment, Kenny was stumped. He stared at his guest, shaking his head. Then a flicker of memory raced through his mind like a ghost in a darkened hallway. His eyes went wide.

"Wait," he said, backing up into his chair.

"Yes?" the man asked, a grin on his face. He leaned forward, almost coming off the couch. "We've known each other a long time, Kenny. If you have something to say, by all means, spit it out."

Kenny shook his head. "Look, I don't know about him stealing anything. Don't you think I would have said something? But he said he'd found this book, he wanted to show me. Said he was going to make a lot of money with what was written inside it. Secrets, he said. Secrets about this town. The people here. I didn't want anything to do with it."

"That was wise," his visitor told him.

"Yeah," Kenny replied, nervous but uncertain as to the cause of his anxiety. It was not as though he had done anything wrong.

"You knew Foster. Where would he have hidden such a thing if he wanted to hide it?"

Kenny shrugged. "I don't know. Could have hidden it anywhere, I guess. Thing about Foster, though, he wasn't all that inventive. Not dumb, mind you, but he usually figured his first idea was his best one. If he wanted to hide something, it shouldn't be difficult to find. Hide in plain sight, that's what he would have done."

His guest glanced slowly around the room, eyes narrowed. "You have an awful lot of books here, Kenny. Are you certain that while he was here with you, he did not hide anything in your house, getting you in trouble?"

"Trouble?" Kenny frowned angrily. "Look, like you said, we've known each other a long time. You know if I had this thing I'd give it to you."

"Maybe you don't know you have it."

"It's not here. Trust me. I know my house, and I especially know my books and my videos. Wherever Foster hid the thing, it wasn't here."

"But you don't mind if I have a look around, do you, old friend?"

Kenny bristled. He picked up his beer and took a long pull from the bottle. He wiped his hand across his mouth and glared at the visitor, who suddenly seemed more like an intruder.

"You know, I *do* mind," Kenny told him bluntly. "I don't have the damn thing, and I think you should go now."

The visitor shook his head. "I'm sorry to hear that."

He stood up. Even as he did so, he began to change. Thick hair or fur sprouted right up through his skin, tearing it away as though it were made of tissue paper. His face bulged as though he were holding his breath, and then it stretched with a sound like ice cracking, and pushed out to become a snout. The horrifying, slavering beast began to snarl and snap its jaws as it dropped to all fours.

Kenny stared at the impossible. The man had changed, bones and flesh altering. Now only a beast remained, an ancient thing with wisdom in its eyes. Wisdom, and hunger.

The beer bottle dropped from his hand and smashed to the floor. Kenny screamed. As his voice cracked, the front door slammed open hard and three more of the snarling, drooling monsters bounded in. Slowly, they advanced on him.

"Find it," the first one barked at the others.

He shuddered at the sound of that inhuman-yet-familiar voice. With all the energy left in the old man's muscles, he scuttled away from the monsters who had invaded his life. They began to tear through his books and tapes, and Kenny whimpered in real pain as they destroyed his things.

One of them, a sleek female, moved closer, eyes locked on his. A thick, purple tongue snaked out and slithered along her sharp teeth, and she sniffed the air as though savoring the scent of him.

"No," barked the one who had been his friend. "Leave him to me."

The other creatures moved off, still searching, trashing what little life he had made for himself. The leader studied him closely. Though the female beast lingered nearby, she did not dare approach.

The monster's jaws snapped as he leaped at Kenny.

He scrambled backward, felt something hard-edged under his butt, and realized it was the remote control. The VCR hummed and the static snow on the television became Superman once again. The music blared. The narrator pronounced Superman's heroic deeds with a deep and sonorous voice.

The beast pounced on Kenny's chest. His yellow eyes glared down upon him and drool dripped onto Kenny's cheek. Kenny began to cry, and he felt warmth beneath him now as his bladder gave way.

"I'm going to eat you myself," the monster snarled. "For old times' sake."

...

...

C H A P T E R 5

The rain stopped overnight and Friday began
bright and hot. Though the faded cotton nightshirt she
wore was cool against her skin, the heat and humidity
made Courtney uncomfortable. She lay in bed, only
half-awake, and struggled briefly to return to sleep.
Soon enough she surrendered and allowed her eyes to
flicker open; she gazed balefully at the alarm clock
beside her bed. Only minutes left before seven A.M.,
when it would have begun to jangle angrily to rouse her
from dreamland.

But there were no dreams for Courtney this
morning.

Already preoccupied, she reached out and clicked off
the alarm, then swung her legs over the edge of the
bed. Her hair hung across her face and she brushed it
away, feeling just as rumpled as the sheets that were
bunched at the foot of the bed. She had not slept well at

all, waking frequently, mind awhirl with thoughts of Jack and Molly, and of Prowlers.

Courtney had responsibilities—the pub, the bills—but she had somehow convinced herself to set aside her primary responsibility, the safety and welfare of her little brother. Of course, Jack was not exactly little anymore; he could take care of himself. Still, she worried, and she cursed her bad leg for making her a liability. If not for that, she might have gone with him, all other responsibilities be damned.

Jack would call to check in with her, tell her where they were staying, all of that. But it was barely seven, and it wasn't likely he'd call before eight. It was going to be a long morning.

With a low sigh, Courtney reached for the lion's head cane she had inherited from her grandfather and stood up. In the mirror across the room she could see herself—just as rumpled as she had imagined—with the faded nightshirt hugging her body. She thought she looked pretty good, all things considered, even though the old shirt was decorated with cavorting teddy bears.

Her mind flashed to Bill Cantwell, asleep in the next room while Jack was away, and she blushed at her image in the mirror. With the support of her cane, she walked to the closet and pulled out an old striped robe that had once belonged to her mother. It was frayed at the hem and around the belt, but her only other robe was a thick terrycloth thing that would have melted her in the heat and humidity of July.

After cinching the belt around her waist, Courtney

opened the door and stepped out into the hall. The door to Jack's room was closed, and she found her thoughts skittering into territory better left alone. Courtney had not had a serious boyfriend since before the accident ten years earlier that had damaged her leg and killed her mother. Dates, certainly, though with the pub she rarely made time for them. And there had been a man a few years ago whom she thought might become someone special. That relationship had withered on the vine.

Now there was Bill. He meant a lot to her, and there was a serious attraction between them. They'd confessed as much to each another, but things had not progressed further, burdened, as she was, with the knowledge that Bill was not human.

How could she be involved with a man who was not a man? The question had lingered night after night as she tried to wish it away. Bill was technically an animal, and yet that did not make him any less the man she knew and cared for deeply. Or so she told herself.

But what about right now? she thought. *Behind that door, is it Bill lying there in Jack's bed, or is it the Prowler?* She knew that the creatures had to focus to retain human appearance, and wondered if that meant that during sleep they changed. Courtney chided herself for her thoughts, however. She knew that there was no man and beast where Bill was concerned. They were one and the same.

With her free hand she rubbed at her eyes, still burning from the rough night's sleep. Then she walked down the hall and into the kitchen. She was startled to see Bill sitting at the kitchen table, and let out a tiny gasp as she recoiled from the sight of him.

His eyes went wide in innocent dismay. "Wow. I know I look pretty scary in the morning, but I didn't think I looked *that* bad."

"No," she said hurriedly. "No, Bill, I just . . . the door was closed so I thought you were still sleeping."

He smiled. "That's a relief."

Courtney smiled in return. She hobbled to the coffee maker and poured herself a cup that he had made. Despite what Bill had said, Courtney thought he looked pretty good in the morning. He wore navy blue sweatpants and a New England Patriots T-shirt that was torn at the collar. His eyes sparkled.

"How'd you sleep?" she asked, unintentionally echoing her own thoughts from moments before. It made her self-conscious, and she glanced away from him.

"I did all right. Jack's mattress is hard, but it's comfortable enough. What about you?"

"Not so well," she confessed. "Worried about Jack, I guess."

His eyebrows shot up. "Oh, we're telling the truth, are we? Well, then I admit it, I slept pretty poorly myself."

"I'm sorry," she said quickly. "Is the bed too hard? You can sleep on the pull-out if you want. I'm sure Molly wouldn't mind."

Bill's smile was sweet and knowing. "I slept poorly because you were right on the other side of the wall. It was kind of a distraction, knowing you were curled up in there."

Taken aback, Courtney could only blink and stare at him.

The smile disappeared from Bill's face. "I'm sorry. I shouldn't have said that. I just . . . being here with you . . ." He looked a bit appalled with himself and ran a hand through his hair.

The overall effect of his awkwardness was decidedly charming. Courtney leaned forward and reached for his hand. She slipped her fingers into his and placed her other hand over his. Bill glanced up expectantly, still obviously uncomfortable with what he had said.

"It's all right," she told him.

"Now's not the time," Bill said. "We've got Jack and Molly to worry about, and the pub and all. Bad timing."

"Is there ever good timing?" she asked, half to herself and half to reassure him. She searched his eyes. They were the part of him that never changed, no matter how he appeared outwardly. "Anyway, I'm glad you told me that. It makes me feel good, especially when I've got that early-morning glamour thing going. Let's just not get ahead of ourselves, okay?"

With a deeply sincere expression, Bill nodded. "Agreed. Do me one favor, though?"

Squeezing his hand once, pleased by his response, she leaned closer to him. "Name it."

Bill grinned. "Sit up straight. I can see right down your shirt, and it's really distracting trying not to look."

"You're awful!" With an expression of mock horror

on her face, Courtney clenched a fist around the top of her robe and nightshirt and clasped it tight to her chest as she sat back and fixed him with a stern gaze.

"Why awful?" Bill protested. "I told you, didn't I? I could have just snuck a few peeks and never mentioned it. But that wouldn't have been very respectful, now, would it?"

Courtney narrowed her eyes and studied him, trying to hold back the smile that played at the edges of her mouth. The hot summer wind blew through the kitchen and the moon-and-stars clock on the wall ticked off a few seconds, until finally she just shook her head and laughed.

"What am I gonna do with you, Bill Cantwell?" she asked, a trace of her mother's brogue slipping into her voice.

"I wish I knew," Bill replied, no trace of flirtation in his voice, gaze locked upon hers. "The suspense is killing me."

"Why don't we start with breakfast? You can cook, can't you?"

"Are bacon and eggs all right?" Bill asked.

"It'll do," Courtney told him.

Bill stood up, went to the refrigerator, and began to putter around as he prepared to cook them breakfast. It was nice. *Very nice.* Courtney tapped the length of her cane against her knee, watched him, and was filled with wonder at the peculiar turns her life had taken.

Abruptly, as he put a pan on the stove, Bill stiffened. His eyebrows knitted together as he turned toward the window and sniffed the air. Then his expression went completely blank and he turned his attention back to the carton of eggs on the counter.

"What?" Courtney prodded. "What was that? What did you smell?"

The question broke down a wall between them. In the time since she had discovered he was a Prowler, they had never discussed it, either directly or indirectly. Now this seemingly innocent question put all the cards on the table. She was recognizing what he was, that he had senses far more acute than her own. Bill blinked in surprise, then shrugged.

"Nothing," he said. "Just smelled something nasty, that's all. Garbage truck going by, maybe."

He went back to cooking, and for a while, Courtney just stared at his back. Garbage pickup was on Wednesday. Bill knew that. Whatever it was he had scented on the wind, he didn't want to tell her about it.

As far as Courtney was concerned, that could mean only one thing.

Jack and Molly weren't the only ones in dangerous territory.

It was after eight o'clock when Jack came slowly awake. There was no air-conditioning in the room, and the morning was warm, the air close and moist. After a deep breath, he opened his eyes.

On the bed opposite his, Molly lay curled into a ball, wild red hair splayed around her head, falling over her face. Her green eyes were wide and watching him. Jack felt a rush of heat to his face as he wondered how long she had been doing so.

"Morning," he said.

"Hi," Molly replied, her voice a cracked, early-morning whisper.

"Been up long?"

"Not really."

"Was I drooling?" he asked.

Molly smiled. "Not much. I was just sort of lying here, thinking. You snore, by the way."

"No, I do not," he said, head still on the pillow, no desire to move. "What are you thinking about?"

"Pretending."

Jack frowned. "How do you mean?"

Molly's body unfurled beneath her covers as she stretched, catlike, eyes still on him.

"People pretend all the time, don't they?" she asked. "I mean, we pretend we're not afraid to die, or that we're not hurt when we are. We pretend we know so much; that we know everything, really. But we don't. We live in a world where things like Prowlers exist, and who knows what else, and we pretend not to be afraid of the dark."

After a moment's pause, Molly sat up in bed, hair tumbling over her shoulders, the covers falling away to reveal the soft sheath she had slept in. There was a sadness about her that belied the intensity with which she spoke. Apparently, she had been doing a lot of thinking this morning while she waited for him to wake up.

"God, Jack, we live in a world where what people

pretend to know—so they can hide their fear—is so huge that we can't even tell anybody what's real. Nobody will believe us because they're terrified what it would mean not to pretend anymore."

He was not at all sure what she was getting at, but Jack could see how grave Molly felt these thoughts were. Concerned, he slipped out of bed in the T-shirt and gym shorts he'd slept in to avoid any embarrassment, and went to sit by her.

"I can't argue with any of that," he confessed. "But we can't change the world, Molly. At least you and me aren't pretendin' not to know all that stuff."

Her smile was bittersweet. "Yeah. I guess."

What are you pretending not to know? he wanted to ask her. But he did not dare, for fear of what she might answer.

"You know what frightens me?" she went on. "When I think about it all, the ghosts and the Prowlers, and then I wonder—if those things exist, what else is out there? What if we've just scratched the surface of what's really there?"

Jack laid a comforting hand on her shoulder. The contact was electric, and he could see that she felt it, too. He thought she might have shuddered.

"Maybe you're right," he said. "But let's take one monster at a time, okay? Besides, I'm not afraid. I've got you watching out for me."

Her smile was uncharacteristically shy. "You're something else, Dwyer."

Molly stood up quickly, as if trying to escape the intimacy of waking up together. The sheath she wore was straight and featureless, but he still caught himself looking at her a little too long.

"I'm gonna jump in the shower," she said quickly. "Then we can grab some breakfast."

"Sounds good," Jack replied.

Molly gathered up her things for the shower and went into the bathroom without meeting his eyes again. Whatever was between them would remain unspoken. Artie's memory and spirit haunted the space that separated Jack from Molly, and so they would pretend, just as Molly had described, that those feelings did not exist.

But he wondered what else she pretended, if she was aware that her dead boyfriend's ghost watched over them.

He heard the shower turn on. A fog fell over his thoughts, a stillness with only a buzzing beneath the surface where all his questions and worries lay buried. Though it happened almost unconsciously, that expulsion of the concerns weighing upon him was the only way he could deal with them at the moment. His questions would be answered and his worries played out, but only over time.

A voice from behind him broke the silence.

"She's pretty amazing, isn't she?"

"Ah!" Jack lunged across the bed, rolled, and came up on the other side, heart thudding in his chest, lungs heaving with panic.

Artie Carroll's ghost was across the room, hovering

several inches off the ground. He looked as he had the night he died, his straggly blond hair down to his shoulders, his hooded sweatshirt ripped at the neck, hightop sneakers untied, the laces dangling beneath him, trailing on the floor. He had that innocent *who-me?* expression on his face, the one that had allowed him to get away with so much over the years.

"Damn it, Artie," Jack rasped, his voice sounding like the patter of water in the shower. "Don't *do* that! You scared the crap out of me."

The ghost held up both hands in a placating gesture. "Sorry, Jack, but think about it. What, am I supposed to knock?" He mimed knocking on the air. "Hel-lo?"

Jack's breathing had returned to normal, though his heart still tapped a rapid rhythm. He rolled his eyes at Artie's familiar tone and shook his head. The guy was impossible to stay mad at.

"Just . . . try to . . . manifest or whatever it is in front of me instead of behind my back, okay?" he asked.

"Right," Artie said, lips pursed doubtfully. "Like that's going to be less freaky for you. You're just gonna have to get a thicker skin, y'know? Why is it you strong guys are always the jittery ones?"

"I'm not jittery."

"Yeah, and politicians aren't corrupt. Actually, I wouldn't mind so much that they're corrupt if they'd just be more up front about it. Wear a 'for sale' button or something, y'know? If you're going to be greedy and sell your soul, stop being so afraid to get caught. They're all such babies about it. Talk about cowards.

Between the votes they've been paid off to cast, and the ones they cast 'cause they're too afraid of backlash from the religious right or whatever to actually vote how they think, I bet most of them don't ever cast a vote that really represents their own thought process. It's such a dirty business. No wonder there's—"

"Artie!" Jack snapped, his voice hushed, even though he was fairly certain Molly couldn't hear him over the shower.

The spirit's eyes widened, and Jack shuddered to see the eternal blackness within them. The rest of him was insubstantial. The morning sun passed through him, his body as gossamer as the curtains that hung over the windows. But those eyes . . .

"Sorry, bro," Artie said. "Just got carried away. Most of the folks over here in the Ghostlands don't have much patience with talk about their old lives, the world, y'know? Hurts too much to talk about what they've left behind."

Jack felt a stab of guilt, feeling as though he'd robbed Artie of the small pleasure of arguing. "Another time, okay? When Molly's not around, we can debate all you want."

Artie perked up. "Really?"

"Truly."

"Thanks, Jack. I mean it." The ghost's eyes darted toward the bathroom door. "So you and Molly . . . ?"

Jack stiffened. "Nothing, Artie. There's nothing going on."

Artie gazed at him with obvious disappointment.

"Come on. What am I, twelve? I've seen you guys dancing around each other like bugs trying to keep away from the backyard zapper. Just kiss her, already."

Horrified, Jack clapped a hand over his eyes and lowered his head. "Man, stop with that. She's your girlfriend."

When he took his hand away from his face, Jack saw that Artie was hovering only two inches away, close enough so that his fingers dragged through the ethereally cold nothingness that made up Artie's body.

Jack jerked back hard and his head hit the wall with a thud. He winced, but Artie moved closer. The specter's eyes had narrowed with anger and an abiding, aching sadness that hurt Jack to the core.

"Don't do that to me, Jack," Artie said through clenched teeth, angrier than Jack had ever seen him.

"What? Don't do what?"

"Don't talk to me like I'm *alive*." Artie turned and floated back across the room, his legs passing right through the bed. Once he had pretended to walk, but that had been right after he'd died. Now he simply drifted.

"Artie, listen—"

"No," Artie snapped, turning on him. "You do what you want, Jack. Do what your heart tells you to do. But you're my best friend. I expect you to watch out for Molly as best you can. Do I wish I could hold her in my arms and tell her everything will be all right?"

His voice seemed to drop an octave, to become hollow and distant and cold. The dark eyes swirled, with the eternity of the Ghostlands visible through them, and for the first time Jack was afraid of the ghost. He knew Artie could not hurt him, but there was a darkness in him in that moment, the sinister weight of death itself, that made Jack shiver.

"Of course I do," Artie whispered. After a moment, he looked up again. "But I can't do that, Jack. If Molly ends up with anybody else, it'll break my heart. But with you . . . I can live with that. I can even be happy for you. It's obvious you care about her, and I've seen the way she looks at you."

Jack sighed. He fixed his friend with a sincere gaze and shook his head. "We can't, Artie. You're still here to me. And Molly . . . I think she can sense that you're not really gone."

"But I *am* gone, Jack. That's what I'm trying to tell you. Molly knows it, too. It's pretty freaky that I have to be the one to tell you what any fool could see is happening with you two. Give it time, all right? See what develops. Don't let her end up with some jerk."

Jack took a deep breath and blew it out. "You're right about one thing. It's all pretty freaky. How the hell am I supposed to kiss her if I know you might be watching?"

The ghost shimmered, then flickered like the picture on a television set just before the power goes out. A sad look had come over Artie's features again.

"When you're right, you're right," he said. He floated toward Jack. "You've got my word that unless you see me, I'm not around. If I pop in and you guys are together, I'll bug out for a while."

"I really don't think you have anything to worry

about," Jack told him. "Nothing's gonna happen with us. I'm telling you. We've got too much between us."

Artie grinned at that. "We'll see."

Jack sighed. "Look, you didn't come here to talk to me about this. What's going on?"

"The locals—the dead ones, anyway—they're talking about the Prowlers. We already know from those ghosts you passed on your way into town that there's a pack in the area. But I did some more digging. It looks like they use the town as a home base and hunt around here. The strange thing is, they only started killing people *in town* recently. It's over some book apparently. I talked to the ghost of that mailman, Garraty? Tried to get him to manifest so you could talk to him, but he's still pretty angry about being murdered and all, keeping mostly to himself. I'll see if I can find out anything else."

Jack scratched at his chin. "Yeah. Thanks for that. What about the other local victim? Martin or Marlin or whatever."

The ghost drifted backward, toward the window. The closer Artie came to the sunlight, the more gossamer-like he became, until it was almost as though his whole body had been woven out of spiderweb.

"I've asked about him, but no one seems to know. Some think it's possible he's gone on already."

"Gone where?" Jack asked.

"To wherever he's destined to go. Those of us still here, we're the lost ones, Jack, or the ones who refuse to leave. The ones who have something keeping them from resting. People who die violently usually hang around for a while, clinging to the old world. Looks like Foster Marlin was the exception."

Jack thought about that. No Marlin. But at least the ghost of that mailman was still around. And if he and Molly didn't work fast, there would be more.

"All right. Thanks. Let me know if you come up with anything else."

He looked up at Artie but the ghost was staring past him, a wistful smile on his spectral features. Jack blinked and turned to find Molly standing in the open bathroom door, wrapped only in a towel. Her hair was damp and hanging across her bare shoulders in tangled skeins. She looked nothing short of extraordinary.

"Hey," Molly said quietly.

"Hey," Jack replied.

"You talking to one of them?"

Jack nodded.

"Let me just grab my clothes," she said. Quickly, Molly went to the dresser and made a small pile of the items she wanted to wear before hurrying back into the bathroom and shutting the door.

Alone again, Jack glanced up at Artie, who had a broad grin on his face.

"Told you," the ghost said.

"Told me what?" Jack replied quickly.

Artie rolled his eyes. "Oh, please. She could have brought the clothes in with her in the first place, Jack. Were you always this slow on the uptake, or is this a special case?"

Then the ghost dissipated into nothing, like the

momentary sheen of a rainbow in the spray of a back-yard sprinkler. Artie was gone.

"A special case," Jack whispered to the empty room. "Definitely a special case."

A few minutes later Molly emerged from the bath-room to rummage for her hair dryer. She wore a bright orange shirt that was cut above her belly button and white shorts. Jack offered her a smile that felt plastered on.

Dryer in hand, Molly stopped before going back into the bathroom. She studied him a moment.

"What is it? Did it tell you anything that'll help us?"

"Not really," Jack replied. "But it told me we were right about the Prowlers. They're here."

CHAPTER 6

The trees that lined Route 31 blocked out some of the harsh sunlight, allowing the breeze that rustled through the leaves to cool the air just a bit. It was a day that made Jack appreciate shade, not to mention the ocean breeze he usually took for granted, living so close to Boston Harbor.

That morning they hit the lobby of the Buckton Inn to find coffee, juice, and muffins on a sideboard against a far wall. There was no sign of Tina, just a gray-haired, stern-looking woman whose eternally pursed lips made Jack think of a prissy, tyrannical librarian he'd run into more than once at the Boston Public Library. Without a word, they collected what little the inn offered by way of breakfast and fled the lobby to escape the woman's intense scrutiny.

Jack drove them south along the Post Road, the way they had come the night before. In the passenger seat,

Molly spread a map out in her lap. They had pored over news reports of the mailman's death, and it looked as though Phil Garraty had been murdered on his route, just beyond the intersection of the Post Road—Route 31 on the map—and Route 219, which ran east-west just south of town.

They parked on the side of 219, fifty yards from the intersection with the Post Road. Jack spread the map on the hood of the Jeep and Molly stood still, apparently trying to get some sense of the place. From time to time, a car or an SUV whizzed by on 219, mostly headed east. East made sense to Jack. There wasn't much to the west except more towns like Buckton, more green hills and mountains.

Molly walked over and stood behind him, staring over his shoulder at the map. "I'm curious. What are we doing here exactly?"

"What do you mean?"

"What are we doing here?" she said again. "Exactly?"

"Just getting our bearings."

Molly stared at him. "The information the ghosts have given you is pretty clear. There are Prowlers here. A pack, though we don't know what size, exactly. But don't you think we should call Bill now? I really don't think we should try to take them on by ourselves."

His eyes widened. "Neither do I. Are you kidding? But Courtney and Bill have a lot on their plates already. We're keeping them posted, but I figure before we drag Bill all the way up here, we can at least try to figure out what's going on, see if we can't narrow down where the pack might have their lair. We might even be able to figure out who some of them are."

"And we're supposed to do this without drawing attention to ourselves?" Molly prodded.

Jack shrugged. "Basically. Look, the second we have any solid information or feel like we're in danger, we'll call him, all right?"

Molly seemed to roll that over in her head for a minute. Then she nodded. "Let's just be careful."

"Absolutely," Jack agreed. Then his attention turned back to the map. "Foster Marlin was killed in his home. Garraty was murdered out here, in the middle of the morning, while on his route. But the locals . . . the ghosts . . . they say those guys are the exceptions. Up until now, the pack hasn't hunted in Buckton. All the killings were in the mountains and other towns. If the information I got was right, they changed the rules because of some book that was stolen that they want back."

He had explained to her what Artie had told him, though without revealing it was Artie who had supplied the information.

"Doesn't seem like the smartest thing to do," Molly noted. "There have to have been ways for them to get the thing back without attracting attention."

"Maybe they panicked," Jack offered. He looked around at the trees and shivered, despite the heat. Though cars passed intermittently, they were pretty much alone out there. "Look, I don't know. I'm just trying to figure out what to do next."

Molly took a breath and reached out to stroke his arm once. "I know. You talked to Courtney this morning. Did she and Bill have any suggestions?"

"Other than 'don't get killed'?" Jack asked. He shrugged and walked along the Post Road a bit. "Not a whole lot, no. They both want to come to be with us, but there's the pub to be dealt with. I told them we'd be careful, to hold off until we really need them."

Molly rubbed the back of her neck, then leaned against the Jeep with her arms crossed, regarding him carefully. "So how are we supposed to figure out where the lair is?"

For a moment Jack felt at a total loss. The wind kicked up and blew the map off the hood of the Jeep and he ran to get it. Twice he bent to retrieve it, only to have it blow out of reach. The third time he stamped a foot down on it, then bent to carefully pick it up. The grimy print of his sneaker was smeared across the entire Buckton area.

Jack stared at the map.

"What?" Molly asked.

"We chart them. The corpses, I mean. We chart them out, and see if there's a pattern."

He went to the Jeep and rummaged in the glove compartment for a pen, then circled the spots where he thought the postman had been murdered, and where he thought Foster Marlin's house ought to be, based on the address he had gotten out of the phone book.

"Are you expecting help from Deputy Vance and the sheriff?" Molly asked. " 'Cause, no offense, but if you don't want to draw attention, asking about mysterious deaths and murders going back forty years or so is not the way to go unnoticed."

"They won't have any idea what we're doing until we have something solid to give them," Jack assured her.

"Then I don't get it," she said. "How do we find out the exact locations where all these people were murdered, where their bodies were discovered?"

Jack turned to her, aware that his smile had dissipated, his features now grim, but he felt unable to pretend with his emotions in front of her.

"We ask them," he said simply.

Eyes wide, Molly stared at him, then glanced around anxiously, as though aware for the first time that the lost souls of the dead were not there only when Jack saw them, but all the time. She took a step closer to him, one hand on the sun-warmed hood of the Jeep.

"You can do that? I mean, I thought you only saw them if they appeared to you."

"Not necessarily. Let's experiment."

Molly bit her lip and turned to lean against the Jeep, beside him. Jack closed his eyes and thought about Artie, and Father Pinsky, the priest the Prowlers had killed in Boston, and the other ghosts he had seen. He tried to force himself to feel that frisson of fear that always ran through him when his vision changed and he was able to see the Ghostlands.

"Hold my hand," Jack whispered, fingers reaching for Molly's. Something seemed to be tugging on him, and he wanted to hang on to her, as though she were his anchor.

"Hey," he whispered. "Anybody there?"

After a long moment he opened his eyes. Everything looked exactly as it had before. His mouth twisted with disappointment, and he glanced at Molly.

"Nothing."

"You can try again later. Let's have some lunch and maybe talk to some of the living instead," she said, trying to cheer him. "If we're casual enough, maybe it won't seem out of place."

Jack nodded. He pulled out his keys and jangled them in his hand for a second before he dropped them. They struck the pavement, and he bent to pick them up.

When he straightened up, he saw a battered old postal van rumbling along Route 31 to the intersection with 219. The van only paused a moment at the stop sign before starting across. A car came flying along 219 well above the speed limit, and passed right through the mail truck.

Through the postal vehicle, Jack could see the trees beyond. The thing was as insubstantial as smoke, even more so than most of the ghosts Jack had met. Behind the wheel was a man in his mid-forties who seemed nervous about driving that particular stretch of road.

"Garraty," Jack whispered to himself.

"What?" Molly asked.

He glanced at her for a moment, and when he turned back, the world seemed to invert. Jack's stomach lurched and he felt bile rising in his throat. His skin tingled, as though insects were crawling on him. Suddenly the world around him had become completely insubstantial, the Jeep, the trees, the road, even Molly herself were only specters of themselves, a phantom world.

The postal van that rolled toward him was completely solid. And Jack now saw that there were two passengers inside it. A U2 song, "Still Haven't Found What I'm Looking For," pumped from the stereo inside the van. Jack took a step forward and raised his hand, flagging down the van. Somewhere nearby he could hear Molly talking to him, but barely understood the words.

The van's brakes squealed as it came to a stop. A forty-something guy with a grim expression on his face stared at Jack as though he were a monster.

"You can see me?" he asked.

Jack nodded. "You're Phil Garraty?"

The postman blew out a breath. "Yeah. I just . . . I can't . . . how come you can see me?"

Jack didn't really have an answer to that. "A friend opened my eyes," he said. "But the way I've heard it, anyone can see the Ghostlands if they really want to."

Garraty shuddered. "That what it's called? The Ghostlands?"

Jack was barely listening. His gaze was on the figure in the passenger seat, an elderly man who sat with his limbs pulled in toward him, like a child who feared getting hit. The old man's expression was sad, yet somehow vacant.

"Wait. You're him, aren't you? The kid told me about you, the kid who talks all the time," Garraty said.

"Artie," Jack reminded him, happy that Garraty seemed to have at least begun to come to terms with his death. "I'm Jack. I want to find the Prowlers, Mr. Garraty. They're the things that did this to you. My friends and I want to stop them from ever doing it again. To do that, we have to find their lair."

Garraty's forehead creased and the edges of his mouth twitched with anger as he thought of his own savage murder. "Love to help you, son. Don't know what I can do for you though."

"This book that was stolen—"

"I'm no thief. Foster told me about the monsters, the Prowlers, but I didn't believe him. I carried the mail, that's all."

Jack perked up. "But who did you carry it to? Who did Foster send letters to?"

Garraty scowled. "Who didn't he? The man was a notorious crank. Always badgering people about painting their houses, keeping their dogs from crapping on the sidewalk. He acted like the whole town was his. Not many people were fond of Foster."

In the passenger seat, the old man began to whimper in a high voice, almost like an injured dog.

"Sorry I can't be more helpful," Garraty said.

"Maybe you can," Jack said quickly. "There are a lot of . . . souls around here, a lot of lost spirits whose lives were taken by the Prowlers. Hikers and people from out of town. I need to talk to them, or ask you to talk to them, tell me exactly where they were when they were killed. Show me on a map. It might help us find the lair."

A sparkle appeared in the black orbs that were Garraty's eyes. He sat up straighter now that he had a purpose. "I can do that, son. Nobody knows this area the way I do. I was the postman, you know."

"Any help would be appreciated." Jack stared past him again, at the old man, whose whimpering had risen in volume.

Suddenly the old man began to sing in that high, frightened voice. At first Jack didn't recognize the song, but after a moment he realized it was the theme from the old *Road Runner* show.

". . . if he catches you, you're through . . ." the insane ghost sang madly to himself.

"Who is he?" Jack asked, a pang of sorrow for the crazy old man spiking into his heart.

Garraty glanced at him as though he had not been aware the other ghost was there. Then his eyebrows went up. "Oh. That's just Kenny. He's the latest one they killed, but you won't get any help from him. Just keeps singing those old cartoon songs, then drifting off somewhere."

Jack shuddered as the song changed.

Then he frowned.

Jack, move!

It took a moment before he realized it was Molly, calling out to him. Jack turned toward her and saw the Ford pickup truck squealing around the corner, rocketing toward him.

He frowned. It was another ghost vehicle, a phantom Ford. *Why was Molly so freaked*, he wondered. Then he looked over at Molly. A phantom Molly. She screamed again and ran at him, and just as she collided with him, the world reversed again, everything taking on its true substance, its true flesh.

He went down hard on the pavement, with Molly on top of him and the Ford swerving to avoid hitting them. Even with the swerve, though, without Molly grabbing him, Jack knew he would have been hit. The pickup stopped a few yards along and a guy with scraggly hair and a beard leaned out the window.

"What the hell's the matter with you two?" he snapped in the deep Vermont twang so many of the locals had. Then he scowled and the truck roared out of there.

Jack was so engrossed in speaking to the dead mailman that he forgot he had been looking into the Ghostlands, and that, in that moment, the so-called real world would appear to be a phantom landscape to him. He had thought the actual truck to be a spectral one. Now he looked up at Molly, who was sprawled on top of him, eyes wide with fear.

"You scared the hell out of me," she said breathlessly.

He reached up and stroked the back of his fingers across her left cheek. "You saved my life. Thanks."

Molly smiled sweetly. "What else was I supposed to do? You have the keys to the Jeep."

Jack shoved her off him, both of them laughing softly, and they brushed themselves off. He glanced around, but there was no more sign of the ghostly postal van.

"What was that all about?" she asked.

"Help," he told her. "I think I've got us some help." As best he could, he explained his conversation with Garraty, and he described the disturbing sight of the old man's ghost.

"Another one," Molly said softly, a profound sadness filling her eyes.

Jack knew right away what she was thinking. "We can't start taking the blame, Molly. We're here to help, but that doesn't mean we'll be able to. Others may die. But if we can destroy this pack, other lives will be saved. We can only do what we can do."

"That sucks," she told him.

"Yeah. It does."

Molly held her hand out to him, green eyes flashing angrily now. "Give me the keys."

He did as she asked, and Molly went to the back of the Jeep, popped it open, and hauled the trunk with the weapons in it to the edge of the bumper. Jack was always surprised to see how strong she was.

"Hey," he said, going to her side but not doing anything to stop her. "Do you think that's a good idea? If we're caught carrying guns, we'll probably end up in jail."

Molly glanced at the pavement for a second, then turned to stare up at him, eyes intense. She shook her hair back and held his gaze.

"And if we're caught without one, what then?" she asked, voice steady, almost cold.

Jack couldn't argue with that. They each took a pistol from the trunk and then locked it back up, leaving the more serious armament for later. The other weapons would have been impossible to carry concealed anyway.

They got into the Jeep and Jack pulled a U-turn and headed back up the Post Road toward Buckton. A few minutes passed in silence, but just as the downtown area came into view, Molly slid her pistol into the glove compartment.

"Gonna have to figure out what clothes I can wear to cover that," she said. "Y'know, something that wouldn't look stupid in this weather."

"Me, too," Jack agreed.

But she was still staring at him. Out of the corner of his eye, he glanced at her. "What is it, Mol?"

Her eyes darted away a moment, then came back to rest on him again. "When you were talking to that ghost, I heard you say Artie's name."

It wasn't a question. Her words hung in the air between them, almost tangible. Jack did not look at her again, but kept his eyes on the road.

"Word gets around in the Ghostlands," he said, mouth dry. "They knew that I'd lost a friend to the Prowlers. That's all."

Molly said nothing.

Bridget's Irisk Rose Pub was just down the street from Quincy Market in Boston, a mecca for tourists. Jugglers and musicians performed for the crowds and street vendors peddled ice cream and cotton candy.

Parents bought their children brightly colored balloons, and young men bought their dates single red roses; both balloon strings and rose stems were clutched tightly in the hands of their recipients.

At nine o'clock that night, it was still eighty-four degrees and the cobblestoned streets around Quincy Market teemed with people. A perfect summer night for tourists and locals alike. Even the side streets were busy with pedestrians traveling to and from the garages and lots where they'd stashed their cars, or to the underground railway stations scattered around the area.

A lot of that foot traffic went along Nelson Street, the side road that passed right in front of Bridget's. It was barely wide enough for cars to pass in both directions. Once upon a time it had been run-down, but as Quincy Market became ever more popular, the storefronts had spawned successful businesses, including an Italian restaurant, a coffee bar, a florist, and a drugstore. Bridget's had been there before any of them, and it thrived by attracting a newer, younger clientele without alienating longtime regulars. An Irish pub and restaurant could not survive without its regulars.

Though, on nights like this—the pub packed shoulder to shoulder with tourists and young couples—the regulars either became disgusted and cut out early or never bothered to show up at all.

Bill Cantwell didn't mind. Not only did he like the chaos, the energy brought to the place by the young people, but he looked forward to such nights as a break from the most familiar faces at his bar. Not that he disliked them. In fact, most of the time he enjoyed their company. It was only that they were like most aging men who frequented pubs and bars—they shared their blues lavishly with others, but never took any of the advice they had asked for. It could be tiring.

The chatter in the restaurant was a dull roar, blotting out all but the conversation from the closest person. The waitstaff was harried, sliding sideways past one another to get to and from the kitchen and bar. The bar area itself was jammed with people waiting for tables, some of whom were unlikely to eat before ten-thirty or eleven, and who didn't seem to care at all.

Bill loved it.

A lithe girl with dark hair and vaguely exotic features had waited patiently for the crush at the bar to give enough for her to move forward. A couple of tanned, muscular guys hovered behind her, likely her dinner companions, Bill thought.

"Could I just get a hard lemonade, please?" she asked, all sweetness and light.

Bill smiled amiably and leaned on the bar, crowding some of the customers a bit. "I'm going to need some I.D."

"No problem," the petite brunette replied.

She reached into her pocket and pulled out a small billfold and a Rhode Island driver's license. Bill glanced at it, turned it over a few times, then handed it back to her.

"Nice job," he observed.

The girl frowned. "What do you mean?"

"I mean there are places people wouldn't spot that as a fake I.D., but this isn't one of them," Bill explained reasonably. He shot a hard look at the two guys behind her, and they wouldn't meet his eyes.

"It's no fake," the girl snorted. "I'm really twenty-one."

"License says you're twenty-two. Also, it doesn't say anything about you wearing corrective lenses. You've got contacts on. Try another place."

"I didn't have the contacts then," she scrambled, acting truly upset and casting quick glances over her shoulder at the guys.

Bill leaned forward and lowered his voice to a whisper just loud enough for her to hear. "Go, now, or I'll have to take that thing and destroy it, which is what I'm supposed to do. I didn't. But I will."

The girl gaped at him for a minute, then glowered as she turned and moved away from the bar.

"Damn, she was cute," muttered a customer in an expensive suit. "I'd have just given her the drink."

"She's a child," Bill remonstrated him.

"But a cute one," the suit replied.

Bill bristled, aching to slap the guy down, to hurt him, or at least to throw him out on his ass. The girl could not have been more than seventeen. It was monstrous for an adult to think about her in those terms. But they had had some odd incidents at Bridget's in the past few months, and the last thing Courtney needed was for her bartender to start slapping patrons around for having bad taste.

Bill poured three beers off the tap and slid them onto the bar. As he collected the money, he took orders for mixed drinks from a pair of fortyish women who had apparently escaped their husbands and children for the night. Old friends, by the intimate way they sat together. Bill could tell a lot about people just by the way they related to one another. And by scent. Scent told him a lot.

When Matt Brocklebank appeared at his side with an order for one of the tables he was waiting on, Bill sensed his distress immediately.

"What's up?" he asked the kid, brow furrowed with concern.

"Dunphy wanted me to tell you there was some guy out back asking about you," Matt said. He shrugged to punctuate his lack of further information.

"Out back meaning in the kitchen, or in the alley?"

Matt blinked. "Well, in the alley, right? I mean, nobody's gonna get in the kitchen doesn't belong there without Dunphy noticing him."

Bill nodded, heart quickening with anxiety. He had caught a familiar scent out the window early that morning—an animal scent—but had convinced himself it was not what he had thought it was. Now, though . . .

Nights as busy as this one, he always had a second bartender on. Bill strode over to Steve Meaney, who was drawing a fresh Bass from the tap, and threw his counter rag onto the bar.

"Cover for me a minute, will you?"

"Got it," Steve replied.

Bill went out of the bar and across the restaurant. He pushed through the doors into the kitchen and found himself in the center of a scene of such anarchy that it made the dining room and bar look downright orderly. In the midst of the cooks on the other side of the pickup counter, he spotted Tim Dunphy. One of the other cooks noticed Bill and tapped Dunphy on the shoulder. Tim glanced up, then pointed off to the side. Bill met him at the far side of the kitchen, near the door that led into the alley.

"What's this about a guy?" Bill asked.

Tim scratched at the back of his neck, then shook his head. "It was weird, Bill. I'm out there havin' a cigarette, takin' a break, y'know? This stocky little guy with a shaved head comes up, reels off this line how he's an old bud of yours, and wonderin' if you're livin' here now, like shackin' up with Courtney."

A chill ran through Bill. Tim shrugged, twisted his face up into a dismissive expression that had been mastered by Irish toughs from South Boston a hundred years earlier.

"Damn, y'know, that's not any of my business, and it sure isn't this guy's. I told him that, too. Asked him if he was such a good bud of yours why didn't he just go on in the front door. You're in there tendin' bar, right? I mean, what? He takes a look at me and thinks 'here's some bum from Southie with a peanut brain'? I'm not stupid, right? Guy's nosin' around about you. Thought you'd want to know."

"How long ago?"

Tim shrugged. "Five minutes, maybe."

With a frown, Bill glanced at the door to the alley. "Thanks, Tim. Don't mention this to Courtney, all right?"

"Yeah, all right. What are you gonna do?"

Bill blinked in surprise and looked at him. "If the guy's still out there, I'm gonna toss his salad."

The cook rotated his head around a bit, stretching and popping the muscles in his neck and shoulders. "You want me to watch your back?"

"Thanks," Bill told him. "But I got it." He held out a hand to Tim. "I owe you, kid."

Tim shook his hand once, firmly, then let it go. "Naw, man. That's how we operate, that's all." Then he turned and forged his way back into the cooking area, shouting instructions, snapping at cooks who had slowed.

Bill strode to the back door, hesitated only a heartbeat, then slammed it open. It clanged against the brick wall and the sound echoed out into the darkened alley. There was a commotion off to his left. Grunting, someone hustled up a fire escape a couple of buildings down and across the alley.

The hot summer breeze brought the scent to him, the same one he had caught that morning. The narrow slice of sky visible between the buildings was filled with stars, but not enough to more than dimly illuminate the dark alley. All three of the lights that normally burned back there among the Dumpsters and garbage cans had burned out. Or been shattered.

Bill sprinted soundlessly down the alley. He reached the fire escape in seconds and leaped to grab hold of the iron grate of the first-floor landing. Effortlessly, he scrambled up onto the web of black iron. Bill did not bother with the stairs, but climbed hand over hand, scaling the outside of the three-story metal structure in seconds.

He leaped to the roof and landed in a crouch, sniffing the air. His heart pounded in his chest, eyes darting about for any sign of his prey in the deep shadows of the night.

His prey.

A tiny smile flickered at the edges of Bill's mouth and he began to change. The flesh all over his massive body rippled and stretched as hair spiked through it from beneath. He stretched with it, as though he had been cramped in his human skin, and at last Bill stood on the rooftop in his true form. A snarl escaped from him, and his black lips curled back from a snoutful of needle teeth. As a human, Bill was a big man, broad-shouldered and imposing.

As a Prowler, he knew he was monstrous.

The entire roof was drenched in the scent of the Prowlers who had been hanging around, watching for him, asking about him. Him and Courtney. The thought of her in danger galvanized him into action. His ears perked, and he heard movement off to the right, a couple of rooftops away.

He rushed across the roof, silent as a whisper.

Hunting. It felt good.

But at the end of the block, when he ran out of rooftop, he realized that they had eluded him. Quickly, he backtracked to the nearest fire escape and found the scent heavy there as well. They were gone. He could track them by their scent. Could change back and pursue them almost anywhere in the city.

He trotted back to the fire escape he had originally come up. There would be a confrontation soon enough. For now, Courtney was his first and only priority. If they wanted her, they might try to draw him away like this to get at her. Bill was not going to allow that.

Dubrowski sat in the driver's seat of the ancient Mercedes and ran a hand over the stubble on his shaved hand. Beside him, Braun kept trying to lean over and look out Dubrowski's window to get a view of the roof. Dubrowski smacked Braun for the fifth time, but knew the moron wouldn't get the message.

"Aw, Doobie, what the hell'd you do that for?"

Braun rubbed his cheek where Dubrowski had struck him and glared. But Dubrowski knew he would do nothing. Though the two of them were among a small handful of survivors from Tanzer's pack, Braun had been very low in the hierarchy—Dubrowski much higher. Braun knew who among them was the superior warrior.

But that knowledge did not make Braun any smarter. Once again, he leaned over. Dubrowski sighed and rolled his eyes, a low growl building in his throat. This time, that warning was enough to get Braun's attention.

"Did you see him up there, Doobie?" Braun asked. "I

mean, I'm glad we got to the car before he hit the edge of the roof. If he'd seen us, I think he woulda just jumped on us. Cantwell's pretty pissed off, huh? He's a big one, too."

Dubrowski laughed. "He's rather large, yes, but don't concern yourself, Braun. Cantwell's a lap dog. Little more than a house pet. Dwyer and his sister probably paper-trained him. Whatever wild Cantwell had in him, I'd say it's been bred out. He's big, but he'll fall easy enough. We'll destroy him."

Braun laughed. "Exactly. That's exactly right, Doobie. Destroy him."

With a growl, Dubrowski backhanded Braun hard enough so that his head cracked the side window.

"Don't call me that."

CHAPTER 7

Saturday mornings at Travis Drug were usually pretty quiet. Truth be told, most mornings were pretty quiet. It was afternoons when Aaron Travis did most of his business. Every Saturday morning he spent a couple of hours straightening up and putting his new shipment of periodicals on display. Usually he did so with constant chatter from Kenny Oberst as background noise. Most mornings, Aaron griped about Kenny's incessant talk; the man had an opinion about everything.

That morning, however, when Kenny had not appeared by eight o'clock, Aaron grew concerned. The two old men had been knocking about together since the second grade. Kenny never showed up at the drugstore unless he was expected, and he never failed to show up when he was. Not without calling to let Aaron know.

Not ever.

Aaron phoned Kenny three times that morning, before, during, and after his racking of the periodicals. There was no answer at the Oberst residence. As ten o'clock came and went, he waited on a handful of customers, and in between he read the new *National Enquirer* cover to cover. He scratched at his scalp, where his white hair was thinnest, and cleared his throat. The sound echoed hauntingly in the empty store.

About ten-thirty, Aaron walked back to the magazine rack, convinced he had arranged the new shipment incorrectly. He favored his right leg, unwilling to rest too much weight on the left knee he had popped playing basketball in 1964. It only bothered him when he was trying to pretend nothing else was on his mind.

When he found himself reading the covers of women's magazines, he knew he had put it off long enough. Maybe too long. Anxiety simmering in the back of his mind, he swallowed hard and pulled the keys out of his pocket. They jangled as he went to the front, turned the sign around to CLOSED. He locked the door behind him and headed for the antique Dodge Dart he still drove.

Only minutes later he rolled the Dart slowly to a stop in front of Kenny's faded house. There wasn't any yard to speak of, but it still sorely needed attention. Aaron studied the yard in order to avoid consciously thinking about the house itself, and how quiet it all seemed.

Something itched inside his ear, and he stuck a finger

PROWLERS

into it and twisted it around. His knee ached the way it did before a heavy rain, though the weather report had said nothing about precipitation. After a moment's pause Aaron swallowed, his throat dry, then walked up to the front door.

It was open just a crack.

He rapped on the wood. "Kenny? You down with the flu or something?"

The words sounded downright foolish coming out of his mouth. He knew full well Kenny was not down with the flu. The old man could still answer the phone, couldn't he?

Aaron pushed the door open.

For a moment he only stared with wide eyes at what he saw within. Books were strewn all over the house, pages torn out, piled in stacks that reeked of urine. Furniture was shattered into kindling, the television had a hole the size of a basketball in it, the walls were spattered with blood. On the floor, near a pile of old videotapes, Aaron saw what he thought was a ruined eyeball, still trailing a piece of optic nerve behind it.

In the midst of the wreckage lay what remained of Kenny Oberst, who had been his best friend since before either of them could read.

During the time he'd served in the Korean War, Aaron Travis had seen a mother and child blown apart by a land mine; he'd seen soldiers cut each other down; he'd had to gut a man with a knife to save his own life outside a bar in Seoul. But he had never seen anything as savage and horrible as what had been done to Kenny.

"Oh, dear Jesus," Aaron whispered.

He put a hand up to cover his eyes and turned to walk out of the house, tears flowing freely down his cheeks. He limped to his Dart and climbed in, shuddering with the effort. Gravity dragged more heavily upon him now.

For the first time in his life, Aaron Travis felt truly old.

Molly sat exhausted on the floor of the forest, leaning against a tree, and closed her eyes. They had spent most of the previous day trekking along old hiking trails with bottles of water, chocolate-chip cookies, and a compass as the sum total of their supplies.

If she didn't count the guns.

At first, Molly had been sure they would get lost. Soon, though, she came to realize that as long as she was with Jack, she could never be lost for long. Not when he was constantly conversing with the lost souls who wandered the forests around Buckton. Many of those spirits who still lingered in the area had been victims of the Prowlers, and as the day had worn on, their sheer number had cast a pall over both Molly and Jack, a grim yet silent acknowledgement of the grisly murders that had occurred in the vicinity over the years.

Given what they had learned by Jack's contact with the dead, the pack had been hunting these mountains and the surrounding towns for decades. And yet, given that time frame, the unsettling numbers began to seem less outrageous, even modest. It chilled Molly to think in those terms, but the pack had been hunting here so long that it was amazing the death toll was not higher and that—as far as they knew—the Prowlers had never killed within Buckton until recently. They had clearly curtailed their activities in order to attract as little attention as possible.

Until now.

Molly figured that once they worked out why those patterns had been broken, it would not be too difficult to figure out who the Prowlers were. They had spent six hours the previous day putting together what she had come to think of as the ghost-map. After another dinner at the Jukebox Restaurant, they had both slept soundly, dreamlessly. This morning, after a quick breakfast, they had set out just after seven o'clock.

Now it was going on ten, and she needed a rest. Boston was a walking city, and she'd spent most of her life discovering it, but she now realized there was a significant difference between city miles and hiking miles, particularly in the ache that now throbbed in her legs.

It was cooler than it had been the day before, and she wore a light sweatshirt with a zipper up the front, mainly to cover up the gun that rested against the small of her back. Still, though, when the sun shone through the trees, it grew quite warm.

Molly heard Jack's voice. With her eyes closed, in that sliver of a moment, she was almost certain she heard another as well. Her eyes fluttered open and she saw Jack standing in a clearing where a ring of stones had once been used as a makeshift fireplace. A shaft of sunlight illuminated him as he stood there talking to the air around him, talking to nothing at all, talking to phantoms of people murdered horribly in these woods.

After a moment he sensed her eyes on him and turned toward her. A sweet, lopsided smile appeared on his face, and he muttered something to the spirits before striding through the trees toward her.

"How far do you think we are from the Jeep?" Molly asked.

"Maybe half a mile. Probably less," Jack replied.

"Want to carry me?" She massaged her calves.

"Be glad to," he said.

Molly unfolded the map in her hands and studied the red marks they'd made to indicate the locations of the murders of the ghosts Jack had spoken to. Though the spirits wandered the area, they did not stray too far from the places where their deaths had occurred. So far they—or, actually, Jack—had spoken to fifteen of them, not counting Phil Garraty, who had apparently paved the way with the other ghosts for Jack. The murders stretched back nearly seventy years, and all of them were in the surrounding area, but not in Buckton.

Though Jack was still communicating with various ghosts he encountered as they hiked around the area, they had begun to visit the actual murder sites marked on the map. Now Jack crouched down to look at the map with her. He pulled the red felt-tip pen from his pocket and marked a spot on the map, right in the middle of the most densely forested part of Pine Hill, not far from two other red marks. Molly frowned as she studied the map.

"Weird. That's the only cluster we've come across, those three."

"I noticed that, too," Jack replied. "Don't know if it means anything, but we should check it out. Two of the three who were killed there said they saw ruins, a chimney and stuff, like there'd been a house there once. That should make it easier to find."

Molly gazed up at him, putting on her most pitiful expression. "Today? I have to confess I was wondering if we could quit early, have a relaxing afternoon, maybe go to the movies tonight, if that place even shows anything that isn't in black and white."

"Hey," Jack protested. "There are a lot of good movies that were made in black and white."

"So, we're going to the movies?" Molly asked.

He laughed. "Sounds good. And I wasn't talking about today anyway. If there used to be a home there, it would have to be on surveyors' maps. That should make it a lot easier to find the exact spot. And it might be interesting to find out who owned that property."

Suddenly chilled, Molly stood and zipped her sweatshirt all the way to her throat.

"Let's get back."

A little past eleven o'clock they drove back into town, intent upon a trip to the town surveyor's office. Jack felt his stomach rumbling and regretted not having eaten something more substantial at breakfast.

"You up for an early lunch first?" he asked.

In the passenger seat, Molly had her eyes closed, a

content expression on her face as the sun shone through the window, warming her.

Is she sleeping? Jack thought. "Don't tell me I got you that tired out?" he ventured uncertainly.

"Hmm?" she moaned lazily. Her eyes fluttered open and she let her head loll against the seat as she looked at him. "Sorry, were you talking to me?"

"Who else would I be talking to?" Jack teased.

Molly raised an eyebrow. "Well, you never know, do you?"

Jack started to respond, then just laughed. "Touché."

Up ahead, he could see the theater marquee. Apparently the Empire made a habit of showing a new movie—or as new as they got this far into nowhere—and a classic as well, on different screens. The new film was not something that interested him, but the other was *Key Largo* with Humphrey Bogart. Buckton might be about as far removed from Boston as America had to offer, but there was something to be said for quaint.

"What's going on there?" Molly asked.

Jack slowed the Jeep and turned to see Molly pointing at a small congregation of people on the sidewalk. A police car was parked in front of the Paperback Diner, and he saw Deputy Vance on the sidewalk talking to a waitress.

"Good question," he said softly.

They parked the Jeep up the block, stashed the guns they had been carrying in the glove compartment, and walked back toward the diner. People were milling about, including a few whose faces he thought he recognized from around town. Quietly, without drawing attention to themselves, Jack and Molly merged with the crowd, and Jack tried to peer in through the glass door. Inside, he could see the sheriff and a number of people who looked like they worked there. The place was a mess, plates and books strewn all over.

A great many books. It suddenly occurred to Jack why they had called it the Paperback Diner.

There was a lot of whispered talk amongst the spectators. The waitress Deputy Vance was speaking to seemed very upset, and Jack wondered if maybe she was the owner.

A jostling in the crowd jarred him, and Jack turned to see that people had made way for a fiftyish man in dark pants and a button-down shirt with no tie. He was a kind-looking man with a ruddy complexion and an expression of concern on his face. When Deputy Vance saw him approaching, the lawman stood up a little straighter.

"What's all the ruckus, Alan?" the man asked.

"Morning, Mr. Lemoine," the deputy replied. He glanced back into the diner, and shook his head in confusion. "Just vandals, looks like. Probably kids. It's a crazy thing. Seems like sometime after midnight, somebody broke in and just tore the place apart. Ripped all the books down off the shelves but didn't steal anything, as far as we've been able to tell so far."

"Lemoine?" Jack whispered to Molly, frowning. "Why is that name familiar?"

Molly smiled. "Tina at the hotel? He must be her father."

Jack sensed a looming presence behind him and turned slightly to see a big, barrel-chested man leaning toward him.

"You got it in one, kids," the man said. "Are you nosy, or just observant?"

Though he smiled, a kind of dark energy seemed to flow off the man. He made Jack very nervous. But when he thrust out a meaty hand to be shaken, Jack took it quick enough.

"Bernard Mackeson," the man said. "I own the department store just down the street."

Jack and Molly introduced themselves. Mackeson eyed them both closely, even suspiciously, and Jack had to wonder if it was just the way Buckton residents treated anyone who wasn't a local, or if there was more to it than that.

Mackeson smiled, then moved on as though the encounter had never happened. He stood at the inner edge of the circle of spectators, eavesdropping—as they all were—on the conversation between Deputy Vance and Mr. Lemoine. Jack understood now why Vance treated the man with such respect. The deputy was in love with the guy's daughter; he had to be on his best behavior.

Lemoine scratched the back of his head and sighed. "A shame, isn't it? All that nastiness we see on television has finally started to make Buckton just as sick as the rest of the world. I never thought I'd see the day, Alan. Never thought I'd see the day."

Alan muttered something to the man, gave him a pat

on the back, and then Lemoine strolled off down the sidewalk in the general direction of Mackeson's store. For his part, the burly Mackeson remained in the crowd, paying no more attention to the man who had departed.

Someone in the crowd echoed what the deputy had been saying, repeating it for another who had just arrived. "Teenagers or something," the bystander said. "Though why they'd want to break in and throw all those books around and not even rob the place . . . I suppose it's probably drugs, isn't it?"

Jack blinked.

Books.

Suddenly he felt rather stupid. With a glance to make sure no one was paying particular attention to them, he leaned in toward Molly.

"I'm thinking this wasn't vandals," he whispered. "This whole thing is supposed to be about a missing book, right? I mean, that's why these three people were killed."

Molly nodded. "So this mess probably means someone thinks it's been hidden. And where else would you hide a book than with a bunch of other books?"

The crowd of spectators had thinned somewhat as people began to realize that no one had been killed or injured and nothing was stolen. They drifted back to their homes and jobs. As Molly spoke to him, Jack glanced up at Deputy Vance just as the deputy noticed the two of them.

Vance frowned.

After a moment he strode over to them. "Morning, you two. Tina tells me you were out hiking most of yesterday. Did you conquer the mountain or did it conquer you?"

Jack chuckled politely. "The battle still rages," he replied.

"What a mess in there, huh?" Molly said, referring to the diner.

Vance glanced over his shoulder, then back at them. He hesitated as if taking the time to talk to outsiders was not high on his list of priorities at the moment. Then he sighed.

"It's very sad. They were arranged just so and it's going to take a while to put all the books back in order. I told Trish, the woman who owns the place, that Tina and I would come over later and help out."

Molly warmed to him then. She patted his arm lightly. "That's sweet of you. We are pretty wiped out from yesterday and this morning, but if you think she could use some extra hands . . ."

Alan seemed surprised. His gaze went from Molly to Jack, and back to Molly again. "It's kind of you to offer. I'll mention it to Trish, see what she says." He paused, took a deep breath, and then gestured toward the store. "Nice talking to you, but I guess I'd better check in with the sheriff again. The way things have been going lately, people want to see us doing our jobs."

"It's got to be pretty unsettling, having all this stuff happen at once," Jack reasoned.

"No kidding," Molly agreed. "I can't imagine living

here, having no crime, practically ever, and then having three murders in a month and now this break-in, too. They must be freaking out."

Vance was retreating toward the diner, but he stopped and looked at Molly oddly. "Two murders. Don't make it any worse than it is," he told her.

Jack stiffened. *They don't know about the third murder yet.* He studied the deputy's face, but Vance seemed content to believe Molly had just misspoken.

"Sorry," Molly replied quickly. "I know it's a big deal here, of course, but in the city, two, three . . . that's sort of every night."

Vance rolled his eyes heavenward. "Thank God I never have to live in the city." Then he went into the diner.

On the way back to the Jeep, Jack glanced at Molly. "That was not good."

"It'll be all right," she consoled him. "I just got the number wrong. What, are they going to think *we* did it?"

When Alan walked back into the Paperback Diner, Sheriff Tackett was staring at him with a hard expression that unnerved the deputy. Tackett was a gruff, unforgiving man, but usually he was not openly hostile.

"Who were those kids?" the sheriff demanded, a cell phone clutched in his hand.

Alan blinked, confused. He cocked a thumb and gestured over his shoulder. "Those two? Just a couple of hikers from Boston. They're staying over at the inn. I talked to them when they checked in, and they were wondering what all this fuss was about."

"Hunh," the sheriff grunted.

Tackett stared out the window at Jack and Molly as they walked up the street. Alan knew that people in Buckton did not, as a general rule, like tourists very much. But the sheriff was usually more open-minded than that.

"People oughta mind their own business," Tackett muttered.

With a scowl, he turned to go. "This one's yours, Alan. I dusted for prints around some of the shelves and on the front door handle, but I'm sure we're going to get a bunch of nothing from that. Ask around, see if anyone noticed kids around last night or early this morning. You know the drill."

Alan stared at him.

"Are you having some kind of problem hearing me?" Sheriff Tackett asked, frowning angrily.

"Not at all. Just surprised you're leaving. Everything all right?"

Tackett paused, then strode over to stand only inches away from Alan. When he spoke, his voice was an angry whisper, but Alan did not think the anger was aimed at him.

"I'm pretty damn far from all right. The people of this town expect me to uphold the law. To keep them from getting murdered, for Christ's sake. I can't even keep some kids from trashing a diner, why should they trust me to find a killer?"

Alan shuffled uncomfortably. He did not have an answer.

Then Tackett leaned in even closer. "I'm going up to see Aaron Travis. Seems Kenny Oberst didn't show up at the drugstore today, so Aaron went to check on him.

"Kenny's dead. Aaron says it's the worst thing he's ever seen."

"My God," Alan gasped, eyes wide.

Sheriff Tackett started to walk away. Alan's mind reeled from the news of Ken Oberst's murder. *Another one*, he thought. *When is it going to stop?*

Another voice was in his head, though. A girl's voice. Alan frowned and called out to Tackett. The sheriff paused and walked back to him.

"The girl," Alan said. "The one you were just watching, with that other fellow? The hikers? We were talking about what's been happening and she mentioned three murders. Not two, three. It . . . it could have just been a slip of the tongue. That's what it seemed like—But . . ."

The deputy let his words trail off, uncomfortable as he was under the dark, suspicious glare of the sheriff's eyes.

"Could have been," Tackett agreed. "And it could be they know something we don't. People come from outside, they always seem to bring their own trouble with them. I still can't believe human beings can do this to other human beings, but you never know. We'll keep a close eye on these strangers, Alan. I get a very bad vibe off them.

"They just smell wrong."

CHAPTER 8

The lobby of the Buckton Inn was deserted when Jack and Molly hurried through the door, the air all around them was heavy with the possible implications of what they had learned. It was still early in the day, barely past noon, and Jack was troubled by how quickly things seemed to be moving.

Nobody was behind the check-in counter. As they strode to the stairs, however, the sweet sound of someone strumming an acoustic guitar drifted through the lobby to them. Molly turned to Jack, a curious frown creasing her forehead. Jack glanced into the small bar, where he had seen a piano before.

At a small circular table suited only for a couple of drinks, Tina Lemoine sat with a fat-bellied acoustic six-string and hummed amiably along with her own strumming and picking. Her fingers danced lightly across the guitar's neck as she searched for just the right chord. On the table were a tall glass of lemonade and a book, open and facedown, cracking the spine. Behind her, three tall windows let in the sun and the breeze that only swirled the heat around rather than lessening it in any way.

When Tina glanced at them, it was slow and deliberate. She did not interrupt her playing at all, as if she had known they were standing there all along.

"Help you guys with anything?" she asked, and her question had enough of a rhythm to it that the words were in time with the music.

Molly waved an apologetic hand. "No. We just . . . didn't know where the music was coming from. Sorry to interrupt."

"Just killing time," Tina revealed. "Someone's got to be around, but I get so bored sitting behind the desk."

"I can imagine," Jack said, mainly to have something to say as he drifted closer. "Hey, Tina, do you know if the Empire shows films in the afternoon, or just at night?" The book on the table in front of her, he could see now, was *The Turn of the Screw*.

The guitar thrummed beneath the motion of her hands as the song picked up speed. When she spoke now, it was between beats. Jack marveled at her skill.

"You're in luck," Tina replied. "There are afternoon shows Saturday and Sunday. What happened, did you overdo it up on the mountain?"

"You could say that." Jack waved to her as they went back into the lobby. "Thanks."

Upstairs, once they were in their room with the door

closed behind them, he let out a short sigh of relief and shook his head, still a bit taken aback by the developments of the day. Though nervous about carrying them around, they had brought their guns in from the glove compartment. Molly handed hers to Jack and he put them both in a drawer beneath his clothes.

"All right, so what do we have here?" he asked.

Molly studied Jack carefully, then raised one finger to her lips, though he thought it was a gesture of contemplation, rather than an attempt to hush him.

"Let me get this straight," she said. "You want to go to the movies this afternoon?"

Just the tone of her voice made Jack smile and chuckle. Molly, however, did not seem to appreciate his amusement. His grin disappeared and he scratched his head idly.

"Let's come back to the movies in a minute, okay?" he suggested. "This other stuff is more important."

Molly nodded once, emphatically. "My point." Then she shook her head slowly, a self-effacing smile surfacing. "Sorry. I'm just . . . I feel like we should have been able to stop this last one, you know what I mean? We come up here, poking around, like there's something we can do, but we couldn't save this Mr. Oberst."

The pain and confusion in her voice stopped Jack cold.

"This isn't our town, Mol. No matter what happens, we can barely scratch the surface around here," he told her. "But that doesn't mean we can't help. If somebody here knows what's really going on, they're not gonna tell us. We could just pack up and go home. And that's what I'll do if you want me to."

"Oh, no," Molly said quickly, shaking her wild red hair back over her shoulders. "We're not going anywhere."

Jack nodded, paused a moment in his pacing. "All right, then. Good. So, what do we know?"

Lips pressed together in a tight line, Molly let herself flop back on the bed and she stared at the ceiling. After a moment she cleared her throat.

"The spot on the map where there was a cluster of victims, and supposedly some sort of ruins, seems like the best place to start looking for the lair," she replied. "From there we can check the other murder sites we haven't visited yet. The vandalism at the diner probably means the ghosts were right about this book that was supposedly stolen from the Prowlers. The vandals didn't take anything else, so it stands to reason that they made that mess because they had to be looking for the book."

"My guess is they didn't find it or they wouldn't have had to trash the whole place," Jack added. "Also, if they killed Oberst and trashed the diner all in one night, they're either not afraid of getting caught . . . or there are more of them than we thought."

Molly wrapped her arms around herself and shuddered. "I don't like either option." Her gaze locked on Jack's. "So, what next?" she asked at length.

"Next, we call Bill, get him and Courtney caught up. Then we have lunch, and then head over to the surveyor's office and look into those ruins. Tomorrow we hit the mountains again, try to have a look at them and at other locations we think might be their lair."

"Courtney won't like us getting that close without Bill," Molly reminded him.

"Who says we're going to get close? We might not even find the right place. But if it makes you feel better, I'll lay the whole thing out for them and get their feedback."

Molly nodded slowly, considering. "All right. So what do we do tonight?"

"You wanted to go to the movies, get our minds off of all of this."

Molly rolled onto her side on the bed and stared at him. He could see that she was spooked, that the speed with which things had begun to happen around them had also unsettled her. And he did not blame her.

"I'm not sure anything would get my mind off this. Not until we're on the way home."

"Hey, it's Humphrey Bogart," Jack reasoned, his tone light.

"Oh, well, that makes all the difference," Molly teased.

"It does!"

Silence descended upon the room. They stared at each other for several long moments before Jack went over to the phone between their beds. Jack dialed the number at Bridget's Irisk Rose Pub. Bill was more likely to be down at the bar already than to be up in the apartment. On the third ring, a female voice answered. It took Jack a second to place it as belonging to Kiera Dunphy.

"Kiera, it's Jack," he began, then forged on before she could ask him if he was enjoying his trip. "Can I talk to Bill?"

Molly stood up from the bed with a creak of springs and he could feel her eyes on him as she went to the bureau to click on the television. The volume was low, but he could hear the *pop-pop-pop* of her changing channels.

"Jack?" Bill said as he came on the line. "What's happening up there?"

There was something odd in Bill's voice, a tension Jack hadn't heard before. Certainly, Bill was worried about them—that had been evident all along—but this was something different.

"What's going on down there?" he countered.

The bartender paused for a second or two before responding. "Nothing. Business as usual. Did you find what you're looking for?"

"Yeah," he replied, still concerned by Bill's tone. "Yeah, they're here. In force, I think. There's been another killing."

He explained how they had gone about creating their map, and that they were going to be out searching for the lair the following day. Jack was fairly certain Bill was going to insist that they wait for him, and at this point, he was certainly not going to protest. But when he finished, there was only silence on the other end of the line.

"Bill?"

The bartender cleared his throat and it sounded almost like a growl. "I don't want you to do anything until I get there, but I can't come right now, Jack."

The words chilled him. "Why not? What the hell's going on?"

"Give me twenty-four hours. Forty-eight, tops. Then I will be there. You two can lie low for a while, go sightseeing or something if you want. Go up to Lost River Gorge; that's up there somewhere. It's amazing. Trust me."

"We should come home," Jack said quietly, all sorts of dark and ugly images forming in his mind.

"No," Bill almost snapped. "No, don't come home, Jack. That would be bad."

A cold fist clenched in Jack's gut. "Jesus, Bill. You've got more down there." It was not a question. "Courtney . . ."

"You trusted me to watch over her, Jack. I'm doing that."

"Jesus," Jack whispered again. He leaned over as though he might be sick and put a hand to his forehead.

He felt the bed shift as Molly sat down behind him. She laid a hand, long fingers gently reassuring, on his shoulder.

"Twenty-four hours, Jack," Bill said. "Just keep your head down. Don't do anything stupid. I'll take care of business here and then I'll be up."

Several courses of action occurred to Jack in a heartbeat, but he dismissed them all. It was not that he did not trust Bill to protect Courtney—despite what Bill was. It was that Jack felt that it was *his* responsibility to keep his sister safe. That particular emotion had been with him since Courtney survived the accident that had taken their mother's life. It was not going to be easy to shake.

Jack was about to insist, when Bill spoke again.

"I think you'd be walking into the line of fire if you came back right now. But if I don't deal with it in the next twenty-four hours, you can come home then, all right?"

"All right," Jack agreed, voice thick with emotion. "I don't think I could handle it if anything happened, Bill."

"I know," Bill replied. "I know."

They said their good-byes and hung up. Slowly, still shell-shocked, Jack turned to Molly. He opened his mouth to explain but she held up a hand to forestall him.

"I think I've got it," she said, sympathy and warmth in her eyes. "So, Humphrey Bogart, then?"

"Yeah," Jack agreed slowly. "First, though, I think we need to have a talk with Maria Von Trapp downstairs."

Alan felt as though the whole world were turning upside down. It may not have been the worst day of his life, but it was certainly the strangest. He thought it was almost perverse that the weather was so damned beautiful on a day when so many dark things were taking shape in Buckton.

Though he knew the sheriff's expectations—and

those of the townspeople—meant he ought to be out questioning people to try to find a single witness who saw something useful, Alan had stopped at the inn first to see Tina.

He needed to see her, if only to remind himself that there were parts of his life that could not be tarnished even by the ugliest business.

As she strummed her guitar, he sipped a lemonade he had poured himself from a pitcher, and listened to her play. It soothed him. Just watching the way her fingers moved, the expression of peace, of bliss, on her features, he felt better. Alan Vance was a law officer, but he had to remind himself sometimes that he was also just a man. He could only do what he could do.

"Hey," he said, voice low.

Tina looked up and stopped playing immediately. He leaned toward her and she lifted her chin so that he could kiss her. Their lips grazed sweetly, and then he kissed her again, with more passion.

"You're a good man, Alan," Tina whispered.

His heart felt lighter already.

"Oh, I'm sorry. Are we interrupting something?"

With a start, Alan turned to see Jack and Molly standing just inside the bar area. Jack looked uncomfortable at having walked in on them, but Molly—who had spoken—had a mischievous smile on her face.

Alan wasn't in the mood. "As a matter of fact—"

"Not really," Tina interrupted. "Just commiserating. Alan's having a bad day at work."

"They know," Alan said quickly. "They saw the mess

at the diner." He stood up and hefted his gun belt on his hips, then mentally cursed himself. Tina always told him he looked like a cartoon deputy when he did that.

"What can I do for you two?" he asked.

Jack scratched the back of his head. "While we were hiking yesterday, we ran across what was left of a house. It's a cool spot, so we thought we'd try to picnic there today, but couldn't find it. That's half the reason we came home early. We were worried about getting turned around. Anyway, we thought we'd look up the property so we could be sure to find it again. We'd do that at the surveyor's office, right?"

Alan chuckled. "In a town this small? The survey map books and all of that stuff is in a room at the library, but they close at one o'clock on Saturdays." He glanced at his watch. "You've got fifteen minutes."

The reaction that news got out of the two city kids surprised Alan. Both of them grimaced as though the information was much more important to them than just a place to picnic. He studied them a bit closer and realized that both of them seemed edgy. Even more so, he thought, than might be expected given the events of the day.

"I don't suppose they're open Sundays?" Molly asked.

"Sorry," Tina said.

"Not that big a deal, I guess," Molly said. "Oh, one other thing. Are there any good bookstores in town?"

"There aren't any bookstores in town," Tina said. "Nearest one's in Dunning, about fifteen minutes from here. Maybe twenty."

Molly frowned. "So, other than the diner, there's nowhere in town to get books?"

"Just the library," Alan supplied. "But that doesn't help you this afternoon."

Though there was still something off about Jack and Molly—and he kept Sheriff Tackett's instructions to watch them in mind—Alan knew he had better get on with investigating the break-in at the Paperback.

"I guess that's my cue," he said, then glanced at Tina. "As long as nothing *else* happens, we're still going to help Trish later on?"

"I'll be there," Tina promised.

Once more Alan waved good-bye to her and then started for the door. Behind him, he could hear her begin to play guitar again, picking out the first notes of an old song by the Eagles, "Hotel California." On his way out, he caught Molly's eye.

Something sparked in his mind, and he stopped.

"By the way," he told her, "you were right. We had a third murder just last night. A local guy. Ken Oberst. He was old, but people were fond of him."

"That's awful," Molly replied quickly. "I'm sorry to hear it."

"Still no idea who's behind it, huh?" Jack asked.

Tina played as if none of them were even there.

Alan sniffed. "We're getting there," he lied. "Only a matter of time."

A few minutes after Deputy Vance left, Molly and Jack stepped out of the inn. On the sidewalk, they hesitated.

"I feel like we've hit a dead end," Molly confessed.

"Today at least," Jack agreed. "We'll have to find that place just based on the map we've got. We're going to have to start our expedition early tomorrow. It may take a while."

Molly nodded, deep in thought.

"What?" Jack asked.

She gazed at him. "If there's nowhere else to buy or borrow books in this town, and that diner was ransacked last night for the reasons we think, it seems to me it's only a matter of time before they hit the library."

"Might even be tonight," Jack suggested.

"If there's nowhere else for them to look, and they didn't find what they wanted, it stands to reason. Alan said they think the place was vandalized sometime after midnight."

Jack let out a long breath. "I think we're going to be up late tonight."

The Buckton Public Library wasn't much to speak of. Once upon a time it had served as the headquarters for the Town Council and the Historical Society, but sometime in the late 1950s that had changed. In truth, despite attempts to modernize as much as possible, many of the books in the library—a round building of stone and glass—were leftovers from that era.

Still, on the nights her father had to work late, Janelle Meredith found plenty to entertain herself. It was funny, really. She did not like school at all—tests, teachers, whole boring classes filled with stuff she had no interest in—and yet she loved to learn. The library was like a treasure trove, filled with fantasy stories as well as those that were true. Though Janelle liked novels, she liked history and geography the best, learning about the world and the past.

Her teachers were always after her to study harder. The problem, as they saw it, was that Janelle did not apply herself to the things she was being taught. As Janelle saw it, however, the problem was simply that they were not always teaching her the things she wanted to learn. On the other hand, Mr. Giordano, who was her history teacher, grew frustrated with her because she always wanted to know more about a topic than he was willing to teach.

Secretly, she suspected it was because he did not know any more than he had prepared to lecture about.

It was summer now, which was a wonderful relief. All she had to do was make it through her senior year in high school, and then she could leave Buckton behind and find a college where they had real teachers.

That Saturday night, when most kids in town were either at a party or the movies, or at the Pizza Bubble, Janelle had opted to hang around at the library. Not only did it mean she could spend a couple of hours roving through the stacks, but she got to spend some time just hanging around with her father.

Ned Meredith was the athletic director at Buckton Regional High. He had started out years before— Janelle wasn't sure how many, but she knew it was a lot—as an assistant football coach. Back then he had picked up the second job of cleaning and maintenance man for the small library. These days he probably could have gotten by without the extra money, but it was his responsibility. And he knew how much Janelle enjoyed the time they spent together with the stacks of books all to themselves.

During the school year, he coached football games on Saturday morning, spent the afternoon with his family, and saved his duties at the library for the night, and Janelle often accompanied him. When summer came, Ned didn't have to coach, but he kept his schedule the same, regardless.

They didn't really talk much while they were there. Ned had his work to do, and Janelle was lost in a world of discovery. From time to time she would call out to him, insist that he come have a look at some book or other that she had unearthed.

That night, she lay sprawled on the carpeted area in the ancient history section, entranced by a book about the three hundred Spartans at Thermopylae. There was something so tragic, yet so romantically heroic about that bit of history that when she was finished, she poked her finger into the book to hold the page and then rose to go find her father.

I wonder if he knows this story, she thought.

Almost on cue, she heard the sudden whine of the enormous machine he used to clean the tile floor out by the front desk.

With an excited smile, Janelle walked a bit faster. She

went out of the stacks toward the center of the library, where a pair of ten-year-old computers, which represented the entirety of Buckton's involvement in the cyber age, sat. There were enormous old wooden cabinets that still contained a card catalog, though the library had also finally created a catalog on computer.

Janelle brushed past them, book in hand. The whine of the buffing machine grew louder as she approached, and it reminded her very unpleasantly of a dentist's drill. When the carpet ended and the tile began, it was cold beneath her bare feet, and she wished she had not left her shoes back in the stacks. She wore a T-shirt and cutoff denim shorts, and with the chill of the floor rising up her legs, she suddenly found that her whole body was cold.

Over the whine of the buffer, she could hear her father whistling an old rock song she vaguely recognized. She passed the enormous checkout desk on her right, and then her father came into view. The foyer of the library was dimly lit, and the moonlight streamed in through the wide glass doors at the front, and the line of windows that went around the circular building.

Ned Meredith wore a pair of light gray overalls and black sneakers. He was a thin guy, with round glasses—not at all the picture of the average athletic director, Janelle suspected. But her dad was in excellent shape, and he was reportedly merciless on the field. The buffer was a heavy piece of equipment, but he almost seemed to dance with it as he moved it across the tile floor.

"Dad!" Janelle shouted.

Over the hum of the machine, he did not hear her at first, so Janelle walked over and tugged on his arm.

"Dad!"

Ned gave a little jump of surprise as he glanced back to see his daughter gazing at him impatiently. He reached down to click off the buffer.

"What's up, 'Nelle?"

She grimaced at her childhood nickname, but had long since given up trying to break him of the habit of using it. Instead, she lifted up the book to show him the cover.

"I was just reading the coolest story. These Spartan soldiers—"

Thump!

Janelle frowned, glancing around for the source of the noise.

"Now what the heck was that?" her father asked.

Just then Janelle's gaze fell upon the double glass doors at the front of the library, and the trio of faces beyond them. Animal faces, shaggy creatures down on all fours with long snouts and glowing eyes, each pair a different color: blue, green, orange.

With a tiny gasp, Janelle stumbled backward a step. Her breathing came fast and her heart raced. She pointed at the doors, even as she glanced around and saw that there were more of them at the windows on either side of the entrance.

"What the hell . . ." her father muttered.

"Daddy, what are they?" Janelle whispered.

"Not a clue," Ned replied. But he puffed out his

chest and took two steps toward the door. He waved his hands out in front of them as if he might whisk them away.

"Scat!" he shouted.

The strange beasts, which had been on all fours, stood up suddenly on two legs. Like humans.

Janelle heard her father cursing under his breath.

Then the glass shattered as the monsters moved in after them.

CHAPTER 9

Window fans hummed all through the apartment above Bridget's Irisk Rose Pub, providing little relief from the hot, damp night. A summer did not go by without Jack's asking Courtney why they had central air in the restaurant downstairs, but not in the apartment. She always told him that it was an additional and unnecessary expense, something they needed to avoid to stay afloat in the restaurant business.

Nights like this, she regretted her frugality.

Of course, at the moment, the heat was the last thing on her mind. Or, rather, it was merely a distraction so that she did not have to think about how quickly her control over her life was slipping from her grasp. Courtney Dwyer's life was usually nice and predictable. This had been a bad year for predictability.

Though she could not see the clock from where she lay on her bed, tangled in the sheets, Courtney thought it was close to ten o'clock. Downstairs, the late dinner crowd was just finishing up. The hostess, Wendy Bartlett, along with reliable Tim, would have things completely under control. The bar might be a bit hectic, however, as Bill had the night off.

Bill was next to her, stretched out on her bed, skin glistening with moisture from the humid night. Courtney was cradled in the crook of his arm, her head upon his chest, listening to his heart beat.

Fast.

Too fast.

The beat of his heart seemed odd to her, abnormal . . . inhuman. And yet she could not decide if this was because he *was* something other than human, or if she were manufacturing this detail to remind herself of that fact.

Eyes closed, she breathed in the smell of him, and a smile played at the corners of her mouth. Time and time again, a little voice inside her tried to remind her of his true nature, as if it ought to bother her. But each time, she found that she did not care. Whatever else Bill was, he was a man of integrity and passion, loyalty and strength.

And yet, he was *not* a man.

In her mind's eye, Courtney relived a tiny moment from an hour or so earlier. She had come up from the pub and found Bill standing by the windows in the living room that looked down on the busy street below. When he had glanced over his shoulder at her, there had been a kind of fire in his eyes that blazed brightly for a moment before subsiding. Then he had smiled warmly.

"Hey" was all he'd said.

Then the words spilled out of her mouth, and Courtney still was not quite sure where they had come from. She had certainly not expected them.

"I think I'm going to turn in early tonight," she had said, voice catching in her throat. Butterflies had swarmed in her stomach as she laughed a small, nervous laugh.

"Want to come along?"

Now she laid her cheek on his chest, and sighed with amazement at her forwardness, at this recklessness that had arisen in her without warning. It felt good, but it was also terrifying.

"What are we doing?" she whispered to him.

Bill stroked her face, pushed her hair back over her ear, and bent to kiss the top of her head.

"If you don't know, then I sure don't, either," he confessed. "But I hope, when you figure it out, you don't decide it was wrong."

Unsure how to respond to that, Courtney gazed up at him. His eyes were wide and bright in the darkness and the heat of the bedroom. She burrowed closer to Bill, enjoying the heat of his body despite the temperature in the room. The air from the fans blew across their skin, and she shivered, though she doubted the breeze had anything to do with it.

In the years since the accident that had crippled her and killed her mother, Courtney Dwyer had never felt safer.

Bill tensed suddenly.

In the same instant a loud crash came from the room she used as an office.

With blinding speed, he was out of the bed, crouched on the floor of her bedroom, nostrils flared as he sniffed the air. Courtney's heart hammered in her chest and she sat up, sheet pulled up to cover her body.

"What is it?"

His eyes ticked toward her, head moving in short jerks, a predator on the hunt. A shudder went through him and when he spoke, she thought his teeth might have grown longer. It also seemed that there was more hair on his chest, and Courtney doubted that was her imagination.

"I don't suppose you'd be willing to hide in the bathroom," he said, voice a low growl.

Courtney frowned, appalled by the idea. She inhaled deeply, sitting up straighter on the bed, making it clear to him that, bad leg or no, she was determined to take care of herself.

Bill reached out a thick, powerful hand to her. "Come on, then. Stay with me."

Sliding off the bed, she tried to grab for her clothes.

"No time," Bill told her.

When she glanced at him again, he held her cane in his huge fist. Courtney took it from him and clutched the sheet around her as best she could as she followed him out into the hall. The crash in the office had been followed by at least one loud thump, possibly more.

It occurred to her that it could be an ordinary burglar, in which case Bill's appearance might cause them trouble. Then she recalled the way Bill sniffed the air, and Courtney realized that there was no guesswork on his part. Bill's animal senses had already identified the intruders.

Outside the door to the office, he glanced at her with regret in his eyes. Then he turned his back to her and began to change. Courtney could not help it. She recoiled in horror. It was the second time she had seen Bill change, seen him reveal the true face beneath his human guise, but he had been clothed before. This time she could clearly see the fur forcing its way through his skin. What disturbed her most, however, was the snapping sounds made by his jaw bones as they extended into a snout. With a shudder she tried to compose herself, not wanting him to see her react.

She knew what he was, but had convinced herself she was all right with that. Now, being there with him . . . he seemed so huge, hunched over slightly, as he sniffed the air. Courtney did her best to hide it, but she was just as afraid of him as she was of whatever had climbed the fire escape and pushed in the window fan there. It hurt, and though she realized that it was the only sane reaction, she felt disappointed in herself.

At the moment, though, it was hard to remember that this thing was her friend, her lover. Bill glanced at her, eyes narrowed. He sniffed at *her* now, and Courtney knew that she could not hide her fear. She began to speak, to try to communicate what she felt, but he held up an enormous hand, a claw-tipped finger to his nose.

This monster was shushing her. The absurdity of it calmed her, at least as much as possible considering the situation.

Anxiously, Courtney glanced around at the other doors off the hallway. If they had come, there was no way for her to know how many of them there were.

Bill would know.

He hesitated just out of sight of the open door. Then he turned to her again, needle teeth gleaming, pointed ears twitching for the slightest sound. He leaned toward her and she felt his hot, wet breath on her throat. Courtney closed her eyes.

"Trust me?" he asked, his voice barely a whisper.

Her eyes snapped open and she stared into his . . . and her fear disappeared. The eyes were Bill's. Courtney nodded. She trusted him.

He opened the door and grabbed hold of her arms. Then he spun her around and, propelled her backward into the office where the Prowlers waited to tear out her throat.

Courtney screamed as her bad leg gave out beneath her and she tumbled to the floor, rolled over several times, and slammed painfully into the legs of her desk.

There were two Prowlers, slavering thick drool that spilled upon the floor as they sprang at her. Courtney screamed again. Even as terror struck, so did the heartbreak of what Bill had done.

He . . .

Before she could finish the thought, Bill was there.

The two Prowlers had leaped at her simultaneously.

Bill moved so quickly that Courtney's eyes could barely follow him. His huge arms were raised, and he brought them down in a savage swipe of murderously long claws that tore through fur and flesh. Both of the Prowlers roared with agony as they sprang away from him. One leaped on top of Courtney's desk and the other rolled into a corner and began to rise, grievously wounded.

The stench of them was awful. Courtney was trapped, pinned to the floor beneath them even as the battle raged. Blood spattered around the office as the one on the desk leaped at Bill. The intruder's claws grazed Bill's chest, drawing a bit of blood.

Courtney winced.

But Bill had let the Prowler get that close for a reason. He was bigger than these other two. Stronger and faster. When the intruder clawed him, both of Bill's hands clamped on the sides of the creature's head and he twisted with such ferocity that the Prowler's neck broke with a sound like splintering wood.

The corpse flopped to the floor beside Courtney, and she saw that Bill had twisted so hard that the head was turned around backward, the flesh ripped in a long gash. He had nearly torn the monster's head off.

Courtney's stomach convulsed and bile rose in her throat. Only the terror of the moment, the fact that it was not over, kept her from throwing up.

Chest heaving with deep, snarling breaths, Bill stood over the other. The monster reached behind his back and drew his hand forth again, smeared with his own blood.

He glared at Bill with bright green eyes. "Didn't think you still had the wild in you. Never figured you to be so nasty . . . so fast . . ."

"I know you," Bill growled. "Dubrowski."

The injured Prowler stood a little straighter. "It was a long time ago, Cantwell. You were a coward even then."

"Is that what you call it?" Bill mused.

He stood a little straighter, then, and for the first time, Courtney could see some of the man in the monster. Then it was gone, subsumed within the Prowler, the savage beast.

Bill's claws flashed down again. The injured Prowler blocked one of Bill's arms, but missed the other, and a quartet of deep furrows was torn into his chest. Again the beast roared.

Bill grabbed hold of Dubrowski with both hands and slammed him against the wall hard enough to knock a framed print off its hook. The frame hit the ground and glass shattered. The injured beast snapped at Bill, jaws clamped around his wrist, fangs digging into flesh.

With a hiss of pain, Bill slashed the Prowler's face.

This time Dubrowski did not roar.

He shrieked.

Courtney winced at the horrible brutality of it and felt tears begin to brim at the corners of her eyes.

"Jasmine sent you," Bill snapped at the monster who was bleeding all over the floor. "Where is she?"

The other Prowler laughed, a sound almost like choking. Bill rammed him against the wall again, and a window cracked with the impact.

"Where?" Bill roared.

No more laughing. The Prowler wiped blood from his face and glared balefully at Bill, not even glancing at Courtney, who lay sprawled on the floor only half a dozen feet away.

"We haven't seen Jasmine since the night your little friends killed Tanzer, traitor. She ran. Only Braun and I were faithful enough to stay behind, to wait for a chance to end the lives of the ones who killed the leader of our pack."

Dubrowski sneered. "The word from the other packs is that Jasmine has been running since then, trying to find a place to rest, to rebuild. Last I heard she was headed to the sanctuary in Vermont to rest up before coming back for you."

"And you were thinking to beat her to it, establish primacy over the pack," Bill said, a clear spark of understanding in his eyes.

Courtney got it now. They wanted to lead the pack. This Dubrowski did. And they would have bought themselves that leadership with the blood of the people responsible for Tanzer's death.

She shuddered.

Then something else occurred to her. *The sanctuary in Vermont.*

"Bill? Vermont?" she said quietly.

He stiffened, black lips curling back from his fangs, and leaned in toward Dubrowski. "Where is this sanctuary in Vermont? What town?"

"No town. It's in the mountains," Dubrowski

replied, again wiping at the blood on his face. "As though I'd tell you the name of the town anyway."

Courtney glared at him. She pulled herself up to a seated position, leaning on the desk and beginning to rise.

"Buckton," she said.

Dubrowski twitched, unable to hide his surprise at the mention of the town's name.

"Damn it!" Bill roared.

The injured Prowler took that moment of distraction as an opportunity to break Bill's grasp and lunge for his throat. With a snarl, Bill slapped his hands away as though his opponent were beneath notice. He loomed over Dubrowski, grabbed the bleeding creature by the human clothes he still wore, and took two strides before propelling Dubrowski through the half-open window, shattering the glass.

The monster fell thirty feet to the pavement in the alley below in a shower of glass. When Courtney had managed to retrieve her cane, she moved around the fallen fan—which the Prowlers had pushed in to gain entry—and went to the window to glance down at the broken body below.

Bill had been here to protect her. But Jack and Molly were on their own. She turned around to find that Bill had withdrawn inside the human disguise within which he lived most of his life. He stood naked before her, dressed in an illusion of vulnerability that she doubted she would ever truly believe again. How that would impact her feelings for him, she had no idea.

"Call Detective Castillo," she said quickly. "He'll get

rid of these bodies quietly. I'm going to call Jack and warn him."

"I'll leave for Vermont as soon I board this window up," Bill told her. "I think you're safe now."

"Safe as I'll ever be."

The moon hung low, just above the mountains, peeking in on them around every curve in the road. It was already nine-thirty and Jack was glad finally to be doing something he felt was constructive. He and Molly had spent the afternoon at the movie theater, then had a late dinner at the Jukebox. Though he knew that the Prowlers were unlikely to move on the library until long after dark—if they did so at all—and it would not have been practical for them to have come to the library earlier, the hours had passed slowly for him.

The headlights picked out a narrow road on the left and a wide blue sign with the words Buckton Regional High School. The library was just next to the school.

"Here we go," he said as he slowed for the turn.

Molly had been almost completely silent since they had left the restaurant. Now she let out a long breath.

"Maybe this isn't such a good idea," she said. "Are you sure we should do this?"

"No. Did I sound sure?"

That earned him a smile, but only a very half-hearted one.

"Bill's going to be here tomorrow night," Molly continued. "Maybe we shouldn't be doing this without him."

The road up to the school passed a small lake on one side—barely large enough to make the upgrade from pond—and he gazed at the body of water briefly. Buckton was a nice town. Old New England the way that most of New England had forgotten how to be. It was a shame that the Prowlers had to ruin it.

"Jack?" Molly prodded.

He braked slightly, the Jeep slowing as they glided around a long curve in the road.

"We could wait," he agreed. "Maybe they won't come at all. We could be totally wrong. And even if we're right, it may not be tonight. But if we're right about their reasoning here, hitting the library is the obvious next step."

Hands gripping the steering wheel, a chunk of ice in his gut, he glanced at Molly. "I've gotta do something, y'know? We spent the whole day sittin' around, and I can't do much more of that. Let's just check it out, see what we can see."

Molly did not respond. He glanced at her again and found her staring at him.

"What?" Jack asked, an edge in his voice.

"Whatever's going on, Bill will protect her. You know that."

"Yeah," he agreed. "I know that."

Molly's expression was sweet and gentle, and he regretted having snapped at her.

"I can hold my own, Jack. I've done it before," she began.

"I don't doubt that," he replied quickly.

Molly waved his words away. "I know you don't. What I'm telling you is that I'm with you, all the way. But I'm afraid that the reason you don't want to wait is that you're so worried about Courtney and Bill that you're looking for something to worry about. We need to be careful, here."

"I'd never—" Jack began, but he bit off the denial. After a moment he exhaled. "Maybe there's something to that. But I think we need to find out as much as we can. If the book is here, and they get it, we might never find them. I need something to take my mind off things in Boston, yeah, but that doesn't mean this doesn't need to be done."

Molly reached out and touched his arm, then drew her hand away. "I just wanted to make sure."

Slowly she opened the glove compartment and removed the gun she had placed there earlier. Molly held the weapon in her hands and did not put it down again.

Buckton Regional High was all cement and faded brick and glass windows. There were houses scattered along the road, and a few beyond it. Several other official-looking buildings were within spitting distance of the school, and one of them was a circular stone structure.

"The library," Jack said softly.

The trees were farther back from the road here, and the heavy moon cast the night with an eerie, surreal illumination. Enough, in fact, that to Jack it felt like they were on some massive movie set.

He turned into the library parking lot.

"Jack, look!"

The large glass doors of the library and several of the windows were shattered. Their theory had proven itself correct, but Jack was not sure he was pleased.

"But it hasn't even been dark that long," he said, mostly to himself. "I never thought they'd come so early."

"Me, either," Molly agreed. "But it's really remote down here, not a lot of homes. I can't believe they beat us here. I thought we'd be up half the night."

"Let's check it out," he said.

He put the Jeep in Park and they got out quickly. He went around the back, keys jangling, intending to get something with more stopping power than the pistols they carried.

"They're still here," Molly whispered. "They're coming out."

Jack ran around to her side of the Jeep to see that several Prowlers had come out the front door and were already loping around to the side of the library and heading for the forest and the mountains beyond.

As they watched, others emerged. One of them carried a girl over his shoulder. At first Jack thought she might be dead or unconscious, but then she began to scream and beat at her captor.

Before Jack could stop her, Molly raised her pistol and fired once into the air.

"No!" Jack shouted, but it was too late.

The Prowler holding the girl stopped to glare at

them. Even from a hundred yards away, Jack could see him sniffing the air, getting their scent. Others ran out of the library as well, and they began to gather on the lawn, some of them moving across the grass toward the parking lot.

"Get in the Jeep!" Jack said.

"But the girl—"

"There are too many." He had counted at least twelve so far, including those who had run into the woods.

Molly backed toward her door, gun in both hands.

Several of them hesitated. One, his muzzle dark with something Jack suspected was blood, snarled at the others. The one carrying the girl glared at them a moment, then turned and ran for the forest. One by one, most of the others in front of the library followed.

Two were left behind. A pair of Prowlers, snorting and slavering. They charged across the lawn toward the parking lot. Jack tested the weight of the keys in his hand, glanced through the back windshield of the Jeep at the crate Bill had loaded in there, and knew that he did not have enough time to get to those weapons.

Ninety yards away.

Not even enough time to get into the Jeep.

Molly took a step back.

"Too late," Jack told her. "If we run, or try to get to the Jeep, they've got us. Stand your ground."

Seventy yards.

He pulled the pistol from the clip at the small of his back. It slid out quickly, and the weight was good in his hands. Side by side, he and Molly lifted their guns.

She fired first.

As though they sensed the shot before she took it, the Prowlers darted out of the bullet's path.

Impossible, Jack thought. Or, at least, it was impossible for them to have dodged the bullet. They must have seen her aim, gauged the trajectory . . . how close would they have to be before that trick wouldn't work?

Forty yards.

"Wait," he said. "Don't waste your clip. When I tell you, you shoot mine and I'll shoot yours."

"Jack . . ." Molly said, voice revealing her terror.

It matched his own.

"You know," growled one of the Prowlers, "I usually don't like to eat this late."

Twenty yards.

Just what I need. A monster who thinks he's funny.

Ten.

"Fire!"

He twitched his aim over to fire at the Prowler lunging at Molly, and squeezed the trigger four times in rapid succession. The beast dodged at least one, another went wild, but two bullets ripped into his chest, stopping his momentum. He dropped dead.

Jack flinched as he turned to face the one coming for him.

He was on its back, limbs splayed wildly, part of his head missing where a bullet had shattered his skull.

"I didn't even hear you firing," he whispered in relief and amazement.

Molly went to him and her arms slipped behind his back in a light, quick embrace. "What now?"

Jack swallowed hard. "The girl. Molly, I . . ."

"I know," she said. "We can't just leave her to them."

Together they went to the back of the Jeep. Jack unlocked the crate and flipped the top open. Though they had retrieved two pistols from the large chest before, the two of them gaped at its contents. Two rifles. Three pump shotguns. Boxes of ammunition and clips. Half a dozen small round objects Jack suspected might be grenades. At least five semiautomatic pistols, though he thought there might be more. And an assault rifle, a small thing with a long clip jutting from its belly and a metal stock stretching out behind it.

Molly took a deep breath and let it out noisily. "Most of this stuff I can't even imagine using. I mean, I couldn't aim a rifle, and I'm sure as hell not tossing explosives around. I'd kill us both."

Jack nodded slowly. After a moment, he reached into the crate and withdrew a long, mean-looking pump-action shotgun. He cracked it open and found that it was fully loaded. Satisfied, he slung the weapon over his shoulder and reached back in for another, which he handed to Molly.

"Anyone can fire one of these. Aim in the general vicinity of something, and you'll hit it," he told her.

"All right," she said, though somewhat reluctantly.

For one long moment Jack stared into the chest again, wondering if he should bring the assault rifle or a grenade or two. But he was no more confident than

Molly of his ability to use either without killing them both.

"Artie would hate this," Molly said suddenly.

Jack froze. He swallowed hard and stared at the guns, glanced at Molly, and found the sight of her bearing arms very disturbing. This was wrong. Guns were nasty, brutish things. But then, what choice did they have?

"I think he'd understand, given the circumstances," he quietly assured her.

Molly frowned. "Do you really think so? The way he felt about guns?"

Jack reached into the Jeep and shut the crate, locking it up. "We're not killing anyone, Molly. Not even aiming a gun in the wrong direction. We're after monsters just like the ones that killed Artie.

"Trust me. He'd understand."

There was no way he could tell her that he had had that very discussion with Artie's ghost.

Fortunately, Molly did not argue it further. She slid her pistol into the clip at the small of her back and held the shotgun in front of her with both hands. Jack slammed down the back of the Jeep and they set out across the parking lot, moving as fast as they could.

"This is suicidal, you know," she told him.

"Then why are we going?" Jack replied.

They did not speak for quite some time after that, for they both knew the answer. They could not just leave that girl to the Prowlers. Behind the school, they found a trail that led up into the forest toward the mountains. It was possible, of course, that the Prowlers had simply gone through the trees, headed in another direction entirely.

But it was also possible that they were following the path. And Jack and Molly had nothing else to go on.

Together they jogged along, peering into the darkness for any sign of the monsters' passing, listening intently for some sound that would indicate the girl was still alive.

CHAPTER 10

Sirens pierced the night, and emergency lights cast the trees on either side of School Street in a flickering, ghostly red and blue. Alan Vance ground his teeth as he trailed the ambulance up toward the school. Tina had met him at the Paperback as planned, and they had worked for hours to help clean up the mess the vandals had left behind. Then, a little after eight, Tina had started to get a migraine and headed home. Alan had been moping about it, wondering if she really did not feel well or if she was angry with him for something, when the sheriff had called.

Shots fired down on School Street, near the library. One of the neighbors had called it in. Alan had run out to the car and sped toward the scene. At the center of town he had fallen in behind the ambulance, tires squealing a bit as they raced around corners. On the way to the scene, the sheriff had come over the radio, shouting at them all to hurry.

The ambulance hit a speed bump ahead as they raced past the high school. A pang of nostalgia for simpler times came unbidden to Alan's heart as he glanced over at the darkened building. Then he realized that compared to this, they had all been simpler times.

Ahead of him, the ambulance turned into the library parking lot without signaling. Alan tapped the brakes, then turned to follow, engine revving as the car swung in behind the ambulance. The other emergency vehicle bumped right up onto the library lawn, no longer blocking Alan's view of the scene before him.

The lights inside the library blazed, the whole building lit up. The front doors were shattered, some of the windows as well. The sheriff's patrol car was skewed at a crazy angle across the lot, door open and blues flashing. There was another vehicle in the lot, however.

A green, somewhat weathered Jeep Cherokee Laredo.

It took him only a moment to recognize it as the vehicle driven by Jack Dwyer.

"You've gotta be kidding," he muttered to himself. But he knew there was no joke involved. The kids had asked him about the library earlier that same day. The sheriff had been suspicious of the two teens from Boston the moment he had laid eyes on them. Now it looked as though that suspicion was going to be borne out.

Alan's tires grabbed the pavement as he laid on the

brakes, then jumped out of the car. Sheriff Tackett jogged across the lawn toward him, leaving the wounded face of the library abandoned for the moment.

That was the second alarm that went off in Alan's head. Sheriff Tackett did not pick up the pace for anything, ever. Yet now the man's slightly rounded face was grave and determined. He had his gun out, held down by his leg, as he came over.

"What's going on, Sheriff?" Alan asked, thinking the question made him sound like a dimwit.

"Ned Meredith's been murdered," the sheriff said, a twitch in his left eye revealing his tension. John Tackett did not get rattled easily, but he was rattled now.

"Mr. Meredith?" Alan asked, heart sinking. The dead man had been a football coach at Buckton High when Alan was there.

"The library's been ransacked, Ned's blood is all over the place. I found a backpack and some things belonging to his daughter, Janelle. I think she was here, but she isn't now."

Alan hung his head. "Oh, God."

The EMTs were running across the lawn toward the school when the sheriff called after them.

"Langer!" he shouted at the man who was senior among them.

Both EMTs turned.

"I hereby deputize both of you. The man in there is already dead. He doesn't need your help. I do. Secure that crime scene and don't let anyone in until I get back."

"Get back?" Alan asked. He stared at the sheriff, wide-eyed. "Where are we—"

"Did you see the Jeep?" Tackett snapped.

"Well, yeah—"

"It belongs to those kids you told me about today. You know, the ones who knew there had been a third murder before we did? Well, this is number four, and I have a hard time believing it's a coincidence that their vehicle is here? The hood was still warm when I arrived. They can't have gotten far."

Suddenly Alan understood what the sheriff was planning, and he held up both hands in protest. "Sheriff, I don't know if this is the best—"

"I'm going, and I need backup, so you're going," he told Alan. "Ned's dead. He's not going anywhere. The way I've got it figured, maybe these kids—if they're the ones doing this—have Janelle up there in the woods."

"It's night," Alan said. "How're we—"

Tackett suddenly turned on him, rage in his eyes, face contorted so that for a second he looked almost inhuman. "Think of the girl, Alan!" he snarled. "I've been walking the trails back there my whole life. They can't have more than ten minutes on us, and they don't know this mountain. Now, let's *go!*"

The sheriff spun and walked away, and for a long moment, Alan just stared at his back. Then he ran to his car and pulled the flashlight out of the glovebox. There was one main trail that led up from behind the library into the mountains. In high school, he and some of his buddies had gone up there dozens of times to drink beer or make out with girls, so he knew the path well enough. But off that path, there were dozens of narrow trails. Alan thought it would look kind of silly if he and the sheriff got lost up there.

The sheriff . . . Alan stared at Tackett's back as the man jogged across the lawn of the library toward the forest. There had been something in his tone, something in the way the man had eyed the woods, that unsettled Alan. What had happened in the library was nasty, but it was a bit premature to blame it on Jack and Molly just because the Jeep was there. The kids had been poking around, sure, but for all they knew, those two could be in danger as well.

Weird, Alan thought.

Then he trotted toward the tree line.

Behind him, inside Jack's Jeep, a cellular phone began to ring, but there was no one there to answer it.

In the alley behind Bridget's Irisk Rose Pub, Bill Cantwell threw a suitcase in his trunk and slammed it shut. He glanced over at Courtney, who stood in the open back door of the restaurant with a cell phone to her ear. Bill could tell by the dismay on her face and by her scent that there was still no answer.

As he walked back around to the driver's door of his huge, aging Oldsmobile, Courtney clicked a button on the phone and then held it at her side. She came out into the alley to stand by him.

"Nothing," she said, voice hollow with fear for her brother.

"They're all right," Bill promised, though it was only a guess.

"Then why aren't they answering?"

His only response was to retrieve his keys from his pocket and unlock the door.

"Bill."

Her voice caught him, all the emotion in it, the confusion making his heart ache. Bill turned and went to her. But he did not reach out for her. Did not try to embrace her.

"It's hard," he said. "You seeing what I really am. It puts a lot of distance between us."

Courtney glanced away. "It does," she admitted. "I don't live in the world I used to. This is all new, and pretty terrifying."

Finally she raised her eyes.

"It's going to take some getting used to," Courtney revealed. "But I can't pretend, can I? I can't go back to being ignorant like everyone else. We'll deal with it. We'll *evolve.*"

Bill smiled. "We can do that."

He slid behind the wheel of the Olds, started her up, and rolled down the window. Courtney bent down to gaze in at him. Neither of them had any idea what he would find when he got to Buckton.

"Bring them home," she told him.

After only a moment's hesitation, Bill nodded.

While he drove off, she stood in the alley and watched him go, arms wrapped around herself as though it were the dead of winter.

It was quarter to eleven on a Saturday night in the middle of July, and even that late, it was well above eighty degrees.

The whole forest seemed alive.

Jack and Molly were city people, born and raised. Unlike some of their friends, they had spent little time out of Boston, hiking or camping or rafting. Now as they hurried along the trail that cut through the forest, ducking low-hanging branches and jumping over dead-fall, Jack felt as though the woods around them were allied with the Prowlers.

This is the wild, and we are intruders.

He gripped the shotgun tighter and watched the ground before him as best he could, knowing that a wrong step could cost him. He felt eyes upon him from the trees on either side of the path. It might have been only paranoia, but he would not rule out that the Prowlers were lying in wait.

One of them, at least, had their scents. Jack knew that meant the monster could find them any time now.

Fortunately, the wind through the trees was coming down off the mountain, and thus their scents would not carry to the Prowlers ahead of them. Of course, the beasts would likely hear them coming; their senses were far more acute than those of humans. But Jack could not worry about that, could not even think about it. He knew that he and Molly would not be able to look at themselves in the mirror if they did not try to save the girl.

A few minutes into their trek, a scream tore through the woods, and something rustled in the underbrush off to the left. Jack tried to convince himself that it was just an animal, something harmless. He froze on the path and glanced back at Molly.

"They're not on this path," she whispered, her eyes were wide as she gazed into the darkness for some sign of the Prowlers.

Jack nodded in agreement. He had hoped they would not have to go through the trees. They would make even more noise, and the going would be much slower. There was nothing to be done for it unless they were willing to turn around and go home.

It was too late for that. Too late for going back.

Molly touched his shoulder. Their eyes met and he knew that she felt the same way. His heart raced even faster, but he reminded himself how much more terrified that girl must be. Molly gripped her shotgun with both hands once more.

Together, they stepped off the path and into the trees.

Folded in his back pocket he carried the area map they had marked up on their explorations of the area. They had no flashlight, and he doubted he could have read it by the light of the moon. On the other hand, he was far from certain he would be able to figure out where they were at the moment even if he had had enough light to read it by.

The forest was not as dense as Jack had expected, and the going was easier than he feared, but there were plenty of branches to brush by and twigs that snapped underfoot. Any hope he had of catching the monsters unaware was dashed by those tiny noises.

As they jogged through the woods, the air close and humid and far too warm, they were careful not to catch their feet on stones or roots. Horrid sounds came down to them at odd intervals: another scream or two, a howling laugh that sounded much too close, the swish of something moving in the dark nearby. Their eyes had now fully adjusted to the moonlight, but the trees stood out in silhouette, more like paper cutouts than actual growing things, and once again Jack had the impression of being on a movie set.

But the fear, that was real. And that made it all real, no matter how eerily false the world around him appeared.

Those black silhouettes that made up the woods could have hidden anything. Their depth seemed endless. Jack almost wanted to close his eyes, but he dared not. A branch scratched his right cheek and he felt a thin line of blood drip from the cut. The smell of pine needles and of wild things was strong.

Several times they passed places where the stink of animals was almost overpowering, and Jack wondered if the Prowlers had marked those spots.

They had been moving through the trees for at least ten minutes when Molly tapped his arm. Jack flinched then, and he let out a long breath when he glanced at her inquisitively.

"I don't hear anything," she whispered.

A cold shroud blanketed him suddenly, heavy and cloying. He knew she was right. There had been no audible sign of the Prowlers for over a minute. Either they had lost the monsters, or the girl was already dead.

"Damn it," he cursed, voice so low the warm breeze seemed to steal it away.

Jack let out a frustrated sigh and turned to peer into the forest ahead of them.

The monster stood between two trees, almost as though it had been there all along and he had only now noticed it. It was the large Prowler with reddish fur who had carried the girl over his shoulder. The one who had scented them, marked them with a glare.

"Don't lose faith now," the monster said. "You've almost got us."

Without even raising the weapon, Jack fired the shotgun. The Prowler bolted to one side behind a thick maple and the blast peppered the tree bark. The creature darted around in the woods just out of the edges of their vision. It was fast, despite its size.

It was playing with them.

"You two are just determined to get killed, aren't you?" the monster asked, voice guttural and cold.

Jack shivered. He pumped another round into the shotgun's chamber and backed two steps toward Molly. A quick glance at her was all the communication they needed. She turned her back to him and they began to make their way forward, back to back, watching every tree, every pocket of blackness left unilluminated by the moon.

"Just give us the girl and we'll leave you alone," Jack said aloud, relieved to find that his voice did not reveal his fear.

The Prowler laughed. It was a sickening sound, like bones snapping. "Truly amazing. Who do you think you are?"

"We're the ones with the shotguns."

Molly bumped against him slightly. "We're the ones who killed Owen Tanzer."

Silence in the trees. Jack smiled to himself. *Way to go, Molly.* That had unnerved the monster, he was sure of it.

"We'll just be going, now," Jack said. "Up, I mean. There's a girl up there we're going to take away from you."

"You can't go up there," said a voice from the trees. "It's sacred ground." Jack tried to get a fix on him, but the voice seemed to roll across the ground like mist.

"Sacred?" Molly asked. "What do Prowlers hold *sacred?*"

"Sanctuary," it replied. "This place has been a haven for all our kind for ages. Once before we were driven out, and now your kind threaten its purity again. You steal our past, our legacy."

"We stole nothing," Jack said grimly, tensed and expecting the monster to attack at any second. "Just give us the girl."

"Stole . . ." Molly muttered. "Jack, he means the book."

The red-furred beast snarled. "What do you know of the book?"

Something swept between two trees ahead of him, and Jack's finger twitched on the trigger, but he did not fire. No waste. Not now. Not when their lives could depend on it.

"Jack!" Molly cried.

With a sudden rush of fur and gleaming teeth, a pair of Prowlers hurtled at them from either side. Jack swung the shotgun toward the monster lunging in from his left. The trigger was tight, and when he pulled it the kick of the shotgun drove him back a step and he stumbled, nearly fell. It was little more than sheer luck that the blast tore a chunk out of the creature's chest, spattering fur and blood and flesh on a fat tree trunk.

Two echoes resounded through the trees, and he knew that Molly had fired as well. Jack pumped another round into the chamber and spun to see that the second Prowler was slumped against a tree as though he were drunk. He swayed there, holding on to a branch, and his head rolling on his thick shoulders, eyes turning toward them.

One eye, at least. The other, along with part of his face, had been erased by the shotgun blast. He stumbled away from them, and Jack and Molly were both in such shock at its appearance that neither of them even attempted to shoot it again. Instead, they stood back to back, shotgun barrels scything the darkness as they searched for some sign of the one with red fur.

It was gone.

"We should be dead," Jack whispered.

"Speak for yourself," Molly replied breathlessly.

But Jack knew that was just talk, that she understood as well as he did that if Red had stayed to back up the other two, they would be just two more ghosts in these mountains. Twice in a handful of seconds Jack had gotten lucky with his life on the line. He took a long breath, realizing that he could not count on any more luck tonight, that he might well have used up his entire share for the year.

Things whispered in the trees, maybe bats or owls or other night birds. Maybe chipmunks, skittering off at the sound of the weapons thundering. Maybe just the wind.

Every sound, every tiny noise made Jack twitch. His chest heaved as he tried to catch his breath. His eyes darted toward Molly every second or two, and he wondered if she felt the same way he did, if she could read his mind.

Stupid. It was stupid to come up here. They had no place here, a couple of city kids trying to play hero, save a girl's life. They should have let it go.

Then he snarled silently and cursed himself for even allowing the thought into his head. No way could they have turned around and gone home after they had heard that girl screaming.

The barrel of the shotgun wavered in front of him as he turned around, nervous that the huge, red-furred beast who had spoken to them might appear again at any moment.

"Let's go," he told Molly, no longer whispering. No longer worrying about the attention they would draw.

The shotgun blasts would have pinpointed their location for anyone who cared to listen.

Ignoring the things that seemed to flit about at the edges of his peripheral vision, Jack pushed his way uphill through the trees. Uphill. That was the way the Prowlers did not want them to go. Of course that was the way they had to go. Molly followed him at a quick pace.

"Keep your eyes open," she said. "He's not gone."

Jack knew it, too. He could almost sense Red somewhere nearby, breathing hard, hating them. Could almost smell the creature.

Branches scratched at his arms but he forged ahead, steadily moving uphill. Something was different about the landscape up there. Jack narrowed his eyes and realized that there was a clearing coming up. Thrusting up from the ground, he could see a dark, straight silhouette against the sky. A moment later he realized it was a crumbling chimney.

Jack stiffened. *A chimney. The ruins the ghosts talked about.*

"Come on," he said, voice falling into a whisper again. "I think we've found what we've been looking for."

Then a figure appeared out of the trees, just at the edge of the clearing.

On instinct, Jack pulled the trigger. The figure slapped his hands to his gut and stumbled backward, and Jack felt a frigid tendril of fear wrap around his insides as he realized it was a human being.

"What are you shooting at?" Molly hissed quietly behind him.

Jack blinked.

The figure he had shot was still standing. And through it, he could still see the crumbling chimney. Jack rushed forward to find the ghost of Artie Carroll glaring at him angrily.

"Why the hell'd you have to shoot me, man? That was totally not cool," Artie instructed him.

"You're already dead," Jack whispered.

He glanced awkwardly at Molly, who had run into the clearing after him and was swinging the barrel of her shotgun around anxiously. The last thing he wanted to do was have a long conversation with Artie right now.

Artie shook his shoulder-length blond hair out and lifted his chin petulantly. "Yeah, no kidding, Mr. Sensitive. But it's still freaky getting shot at."

"Sorry," Jack said. "But, y'know, maybe now's not the—"

"Yeah, yeah. I know."

The phantom turned to look at Molly, who was still on alert, scanning the clearing, ready to fire. Molly shot a questioning glance at Jack.

"If there are ghosts here," she whispered, "can they tell us if we're alone?"

In Artie's endlessly black eyes, Jack saw that the ghost still loved her. No matter what he said, he probably always would.

"I wish you hadn't brought her up here," Artie said.

"Wasn't up to me," Jack replied, a bit miffed.

Artie smiled. "Yeah. Yeah, I guess you can't really tell her what to do, can you?" Then the smile faltered and the ghost stared at Jack. "Word got to me that you were in trouble."

"Could use some help," Jack admitted.

With a nod, Artie pointed up, above Jack's head, into the trees. "Might want to start by shooting that big bastard up there."

Startled, Jack turned and swung the barrel upward. Red was crouched on a thick branch that jutted out into the clearing, staring down at them. When Jack noticed him, the Prowler roared and leaped out into empty space.

The shotgun cracked, echoing all through the clearing.

Red flailed and then hit the ground face-first, hard. After a moment, the huge Prowler twitched and started to rise. Molly waited until he began to snarl and climb to his feet before blowing out his spine.

"That's my girl," Artie's ghost said admiringly. Then he turned to Jack. "They left this one and a couple of others behind to kill you. Didn't want to, either. There's a lot of death here. It's a special place for them, I think."

"Yeah. So we heard." Jack gazed around the clearing. The foundations of an old estate jutted up from overgrown grass and scrub brush. What remained of a road ran off away from the spot where they now stood. The chimney looked like a strong wind would knock it over.

"Look familiar, Molly?" he asked.

She nodded. "Like you described. Where the cluster of deaths was on the map."

"Not much of a lair," Jack said. "But a meeting place, maybe."

"Sacred," Molly replied. "That's what the thing said. It's sacred."

Artie had begun to drift across the clearing, the mist where his legs ought to have been shimmering as though blown by some invisible, otherworldly wind. Jack wanted to ask him why it was that sometimes his legs seemed fully visible, and other times they were just wisps, but now was not the time.

"We should go, Jack. This girl . . . I don't think we're going to find her. I think they're gone."

Jack glanced over at Artie—who stood in the ruins of the old homestead with his head bowed, looking down sadly at something Jack knew he did not want to see—and he knew.

"They're gone," Jack agreed. "You're right about that. But the girl . . . they didn't bring her."

The light went out of Molly's eyes then. She closed them, took a few tiny breaths, and then shook her head. "How are we going to stop them?" she asked, as though pleading for an answer.

"I don't know," he said softly, and hated himself for not having a better response.

He walked over to where the specter of her boyfriend stood over the dead girl. Jack glanced up and was startled to see almost a mirror image by that chimney. He and Molly stood side by side. Before him, he saw Artie standing next to the ghost of the murdered girl. He whispered comforting words to her, but Jack could not hear what they said, nor make out the words from the movements of their lips. And he thought that was probably for the best. Maybe it was not his place to know what words would comfort the soul of a dead teenage girl.

The two phantoms moved away from the chimney. Moonlight passed through them both, and the shadows of the trees and the chimney and the swaying brush fell through them. *More insubstantial than the shadows and the moonlight*, Jack thought. How this girl, now dead, would deal with it, he had no idea.

Phantom tears streamed down her ghostly face.

And yet Jack did not feel the horror of her death, the tragedy of it, the loss, until he heard Molly's tiny gasp and glanced down to see the ravaged corpse at their feet. The girl's body was torn up, bones snapped and exposed, stomach ripped open and organs strewn about. Teeth had savaged much of her body, parts of the organs were missing.

"Oh, God," Jack whispered.

But it was Molly who really began to pray, whispering in earnest, for the poor girl's soul to pass on without memory of the torture she had endured. Jack glanced away from the dead girl to see that there were tears on Molly's face as well.

"Monsters." She turned her gaze upon Jack. "They really are monsters, aren't they? All along, I've been thinking they're just animals. We hunt them down like we would dangerous bears or wolves, but they're not just some ancient species we never knew about. They're monsters. They're evil."

Jack nodded again as he slung his shotgun over his shoulder. "We—people, I mean—can be evil, but not like this. They know what they're doing, and they love it. It's what they live for."

Molly turned away from the dead girl. "Why didn't they kill us? Why did they just leave us here? The odds were in their favor."

"Maybe they didn't want to lose any others," Jack suggested. "Keep the pack intact, y'know? Maybe they'll just wait for . . ."

"A time when we're not armed. Not ready," Molly finished for him.

Artie appeared suddenly beside him, and Jack started, swearing out loud. "Don't do that!"

"Do what?" Molly asked.

"Sorry," Jack told her quickly. "Just . . . just got spooked, that's all."

He made no attempt to hide the fact that there was still a ghost with them. But he edited his words and actions, almost unconsciously, the way he always did when that ghost was Artie.

"Maybe they had other things in mind for you," the specter suggested.

The words were ominous. Jack glanced around for the dead girl's ghost, but she was gone. His gaze came to rest on Artie again, but he could not look for long at those eternal eyes.

"What are you—"

"You don't have time to run," the ghost said. "Just wipe your prints off the guns and toss them. You're about to have company."

Jack's mouth hung agape for a second or two. Then Artie told him he should hurry. With a muttered curse, Jack turned to Molly.

"Someone's coming," he said as he pulled off his shirt. "We've gotta wipe down the guns and get rid of them."

Even as Jack started to do just that with his shotgun, Molly was shaking her head.

"But . . . we could just run."

"He said we don't have time. Too much noise. They'd catch us," Jack told her. His voice had dropped to a whisper. They had no way of knowing how close the newcomers were.

Molly did not ask who "he" was.

Jack used both hands to fling the shotgun into the brush on the other side of the chimney, then lifted the pistol and clip out and did the same thing. Molly used the bottom of her long shirt to clean her prints off the shotgun, then dropped it at her feet. Jack picked it up, using his shirt, and tossed it for her.

Molly had just pulled out her pistol and belt-clip when a flashlight beam caught them both where they stood.

"Police!" shouted a voice. "Throw down the weapon and both of you put your hands up."

Jack's heart sank. It was the sheriff. They stood over

the ravaged corpse of a teenaged girl. Molly had a gun in her hand. She tossed it away as Sheriff Tackett and Deputy Vance approached across the clearing. Jack and Molly both put their hands up.

The body, he thought. A tiny sigh of relief escaped him. They had a dead Prowler on their hands, and another in the woods. Two or three more down by the school. No way could the sheriff think they were involved in any of this.

Then Jack glanced over at the edge of the clearing where they had left the dead body of the massive, red-furred Prowler, and his heart went cold and silent. He stopped breathing.

The monstrous corpse was gone.

CHAPTER 11

The Buckton police station was a stone and mortar affair with a bit more flair than many of its 1940s contemporaries. The town hall, with which the police station shared a parking lot, was a much larger structure that made the junior building appear to be a carriage house in comparison. It was small-town America at its finest, with a memorial to locals lost in America's wars right in the center of a small green island between the buildings.

Any other night, with the stars shining above and a few lights still burning in both buildings, Molly would have thought it was quaint.

But she was not in the mood for quaint.

Unlike so many of the kids in her Dorchester neighborhood, and even some of the students she had gone to Catholic school with, Molly Hatcher had never been handcuffed before. She had never been arrested until now. A twisted, sarcastic voice insinuated itself into the back of her head. *At least you did it up big,* the voice said. Molly knew it was her own sub-conscious, trying to make light of her situation. But she wasn't going for it. Suspicion of murder; possession and discharge of unlicensed firearms. Nothing light about their predicament at all.

And the only weapon they had at their disposal was the truth.

Molly and Jack had remained silent on the short ride back to downtown Buckton and the police station. Their eyes met several times, but Molly found that her throat was dry and did not think she could speak even if she had any idea what to say. They rode in the back of the sheriff's car, and the man's eyes almost burned in the rearview mirror, with the flash of streetlights strobing across the windows, reflecting into the interior of the car.

Deputy Vance had followed in his own car, and that gave Molly the tiniest spark of hope. Though he seemed a bit odd, and possibly not very bright, she liked Deputy Vance.

The sheriff, on the other hand . . . she was not even certain he was human.

As soon as the two patrol cars came to a halt in the parking lot, Molly and Jack were hustled into the station as though there might be reporters lurking around, ready to ask questions. Or, she thought, even some sort of co-conspirators waiting to break them free. She only wished she had some co-conspirators.

In the movies and on television, the police always split up the suspects to question them separately, see if their stories could be shaken. Molly figured Sheriff Tackett didn't watch much TV because he marched them right down the hall on the first floor to the back of the building with the pure anger of his physical presence alone.

Molly was first through the door. The room was about fourteen feet square with bars on the windows and a long wooden table in the middle with five metal chairs around it. The table itself had been defaced over the course of years by pens, pencils, pocket knives and markers—even a few burns from lighters—so that it now looked like the average truck-stop bathroom wall.

"Sit down," the sheriff ordered. The first words he had spoken since getting them into the car.

Jack bristled at the instruction. Molly watched as he turned on the two officers. Vance laid a hand on his nightstick, but there was a frown on his face that said he didn't understand any of this. Molly thought that was good. If he did not understand, maybe he would be willing to listen. Tackett, though, was another story. When Jack stood up to him, the sheriff only smiled thinly, like he wanted Jack to do something stupid.

"Hey," Molly said, voice soft, cracking from lack of use.

Jack glanced at her, then sighed. "You gonna take these cuffs off?" he asked the sheriff.

Tackett hesitated a moment, then nodded for Vance to release them. The deputy's keys rattled as he unlocked the handcuffs.

"Have a seat," the sheriff instructed.

The metal chairs scraped on the linoleum floor as they sat down.

The window beyond the metal bars was open and a sweet summer-night breeze blew into the room. Tackett turned and pulled the door shut, closing all four of them in the room together, and the wind died. It became still in the room, and Molly could almost feel, almost smell, the tension. Deputy Vance leaned against a wall, his arms crossed.

Sheriff Tackett was a man past his prime, his gut protruding over his gun belt, his mustache hiding his upper lip in a drape of steel gray, his hair receding. But despite that outward appearance, he fixed them in a piercing gaze as though his eyes might leak acid at any moment.

With a sudden movement that made Molly flinch, Tackett pulled out a metal chair and sat down in it. He slumped a little, but regarded them with cruel indifference. Jack did not flinch. He just waited.

"So, you're tourists?" Tackett asked.

Jack sighed and glanced at Molly. He shrugged slightly, as if to tell her it did not matter what they said.

"Yes," Molly replied. Her eyes ticked toward Deputy Vance, who gazed at her with open curiosity.

Tackett grunted. "Tourists. But you knew Kenny Oberst was dead before anyone else. Except maybe Kenny. You're up in the woods, loaded for bear—"

"Those guns weren't ours," Molly interrupted. "Those others you picked up, I don't know where they came from. But the one I was holding when you came into the clearing? I had just found it on the ground and picked it up."

Deputy Vance stepped away from the wall. He walked across the small room scratching his head, but he did not look at anyone, only at the bars across the window.

"We heard shots. A lot of them. That's what drew us to you," the deputy said. "No one else was in that clearing except you and the dead girl. But let's set her aside for a second. What do you think we'll find when we tow in your vehicle and search through it?"

Jack glared at him, turned his head to stretch his neck muscles. Molly heard a pop from his neck and shivered.

"We get a phone call, right?" Jack asked.

"Right," the sheriff replied. His smile was nasty. "But not just yet."

"I want a lawyer," Molly said quickly.

"Don't we all?" Tackett replied. "You'll get one. But first we're just chatting a little. You two don't mind, right? I mean, you're just tourists. You didn't do anything. Didn't fire any guns. Didn't murder Ned Meredith and his daughter."

Jack crossed his arms and glared at the sheriff. It was a contest. Neither of them was going to give an inch. Molly turned to look at Deputy Vance again, and she could sense him sizing her up. He was not as dim as she had thought. In fact, she was beginning to think he was a lot smarter than anyone would guess, and a lot better at his job. That might be their one hope.

"We didn't kill anyone," Jack said, voice cold and emotionless. "We went up there to save that girl's life. Risked our own lives."

"And you did this unarmed?" the sheriff asked quickly.

Jack frowned, about to argue the point, but then he realized what the sheriff had done; he had almost gotten Jack to admit the guns were theirs. That was a charge that would stick, no matter what else happened. Jack gave the sheriff back an eerie mirror image of his creepy smile.

There's something so shuddery about the sheriff, Molly thought. *As though, at any moment, he might lose it completely.*

"He was a friend of yours, this Ned?" Molly asked.

Tackett's face reddened. He stared at her as though he would hurt her. "Yes. You could say that."

Vance sat on the edge of the table. "What were you two doing at the library after hours anyway?"

Jack grinned at him. "Getting frisky."

Molly blushed and looked away.

Vance waved the words away. "Bullshit. You two aren't a couple. You told me that yourselves. And even if you were, you've got a room at the hotel. So, again, what were you doing there?"

Slowly, Jack reached up to scratch his head. Then he stood up from the table and walked toward the barred window in the back. He glanced out at the stars.

"We got lucky," Jack said, back to all of them. "We were driving around, just checking out the town. It's nice up here, but I don't have to tell you that. We went down the wrong road and drove into the library lot to turn around. We heard screaming, glass shattering, and we got up to run toward the front doors just as they came outside with the girl. I'm guessing her father was already dead inside. They ran off with her into the woods, and we followed. Her screams led us to that clearing, but by the time we got there, she was already dead."

"And these mysterious killers, they had the guns?" Tackett asked, nearly spitting with his disgust at what he perceived as an outrageous lie.

"They tried to kill us. They missed. We got lucky, I guess," Jack replied. Then he turned and glared at the two lawmen. "If you could call this luck."

Tackett stood and stalked across the room toward Jack. The sheriff glared at him, tried to force him to make eye contact. Finally Jack turned to meet his penetrating gaze.

"You killed the girl," Tackett said, voice cold. "You killed Kenny Oberst. And I'm wondering if you have an alibi for two other recent murders up here."

Jack sneered at him. "For Christ's sake, Sheriff, even you don't believe that. So why do you have us locked up in here?"

"Why don't I believe that?" the sheriff asked, incredulous.

Molly's eyes lit up. "The blood."

"What?" Deputy Vance asked.

"There's no blood on our clothes," she went on.

Then she turned to gaze at Jack and the sheriff, and knew it was true. "If we had killed that girl, we'd be covered in her blood. We're not."

Tackett's nostrils flared and he lifted his chin slightly. Then he reached into his pocket and pulled out a folded map. "I found this in your pocket, Jack." He unfolded it.

Molly cringed. On the map were all the marks they had made when charting where the Prowlers had left the corpses over the years. It was a map of where murders had been committed in the area around Buckton, going back decades.

"I'm not going to ask what the x's are just yet. For now, answer me this. These three," he pointed to a small cluster on the page, "they're at the old Bartleby place. That's where we arrested you. Want to explain that?"

Deputy Vance stepped up to study the map, then glared at them both. "They told me they'd stumbled on that place hiking the other day, and were trying to find it again so they could have a picnic there."

Jack only glared at them. "There's no blood on us, Sheriff. How do you explain that?"

"Maybe I don't have to. You're in this. You were the only ones there. And I know those guns were yours. You can't even tell us what these killers supposedly looked like."

A shiver went through Molly, but Jack only laughed. He walked back to the chair, shaking his head, and sat down again. When he glanced up at the sheriff and Deputy Vance again, the almost perverse smile was still there, but his eyes were filled with pain. This was the Jack she knew, the boy she had been through high school with, the one who had worked so hard and lost so much and never been anything but good because he didn't know how to be anything else.

The moment he revealed that pain within him, Molly knew that he was going to do something stupid.

"Jack—" she began, trying to caution him.

But all caution was gone from him.

"You never asked us," Jack said. His eyes went from Tackett to Vance, and then back. "How come you never asked us before this? What they looked like, I mean. I'm guessing it's because you already know."

Molly stiffened. She had her own suspicions about the sheriff, for a lot of reasons, but she doubted that bringing them up was the wisest thing to do.

Especially if they were true.

The gray box of a room seemed to grow smaller around them. Tackett crossed his arms and stood officiously over them. Deputy Vance glanced back and forth between his boss and his suspects with an expression of utter confusion on his features. But it was clear he sensed that something unusual was going on here. A weird energy crackled in the room.

"Jack," Molly began again. "Maybe now's the time for that lawyer."

"Y'know," Sheriff Tackett observed, arms crossed over his belly, not even bothering to tuck his shirt in where it had slipped out of his pants, "I'm not sure your boy here wants a lawyer."

"What good would it do?" Jack replied harshly.

But Deputy Vance was still stuck on Jack's comment about the killers. He cleared his throat, scratched his head, and hefted his gun belt around his hips. It was something he did from time to time, Molly had noticed, and she wondered if it was his way of reminding himself of his authority.

"What about these supposed killers?" the deputy prodded. "I don't like the sound of what you're suggesting, Jack. Maybe you want to elaborate on that?"

Molly was startled when Jack turned to look at her. His smile faltered as he reached out and took her hand.

"Talk to them, Molly."

"What's the point?" she asked, surprising herself. "They had to have found the bodies, which means they're just playing with us now."

Deputy Vance stiffened. "Bodies? More than one? What are you confessing to here?"

Jack closed his eyes to shut them out. Molly realized he was trying to figure out a way out of this. Swallowing hard, she leaned forward on the graffiti-scrawled wooden table and gazed at the deputy. She ignored the sheriff.

"The killers you're looking for? They're covered in fur and have snouts and mouths filled with sharp teeth. Wild animals, Alan, but as smart as we are, maybe smarter."

Deputy Vance blinked, and a bemused grin appeared on his face. "Prowlers," he said. "You're talking about Prowlers."

Molly's mouth dropped into a little O, and Jack's eyes snapped open.

"You know about them?" Jack asked angrily. "Then what the hell are we doing here? Why aren't you out there hunting them down?"

Tackett started to laugh. His face grew red and he bent slightly at the waist, shaking his head in amusement.

"You two are something else," he said.

Vance did not seem as amused. He frowned as he studied first Jack, then Molly. Finally he sat down across from Molly and gazed at her intently.

"Miss, the Prowlers, they're just legends," he said. "They're like . . . like the bogeyman, up this way. Everyone's heard the stories, but only children believe them. You hear the occasional story from a hunter. Don't go into the woods alone or the Prowlers will get you. And certainly there have been run-ins in these mountains with bears and bobcats. But Prowlers are no more real than Bigfoot or the Teddy Bear Picnic. Now I'll be honest with you. I know you're involved in this thing somehow, but I'm not convinced you're killers. I don't think the sheriff's convinced, either."

"Deputy," Tackett growled in a warning voice.

Vance ignored him. Molly's respect for him went up by leaps and bounds because of that.

"But you've got to give us something more than 'the bogeyman did it,' " the deputy finished.

Jack stared hard at him, hard enough to draw Vance's attention. For several seconds, their gazes met in silent combat.

"Alan," Jack said, voice low and controlled. "They're real. We killed two of them at the library. Then two, possibly three more in the woods up near that clearing. They killed the girl and her father, and Kenny Oberst, and Foster Marlin, and Phil Garraty, too. Something's been stolen from them and they want it back."

"Those are the bodies I was talking about," Molly said calmly.

Silence fell over the little room, but a dark energy seemed to connect the four of them, a circuit that ran from person to person, a circuit of suspicion. Molly wished Jack had not mentioned the Prowlers until they had a lawyer, if ever.

There were only two possibilities. First, that the sheriff and his deputy had no idea the Prowlers were real, in which case talking about them would only make the lawmen think she and Jack were out of their minds. Second, that Tackett and Vance knew and were somehow involved, or even Prowlers themselves.

Molly's throat was dry as she finally accepted that the second possibility was the most likely. After all . . .

"Where are the bodies?" Tackett demanded.

He had put voice to the biggest question in Molly's mind.

"What?" Jack asked, growing angrier.

"These monsters you say killed all these people. There should be corpses at the library and in the woods. Where are they?"

Jack slumped back in his chair, at a loss. But Molly's mind was swirling with the implications of the ques-

197

tion. She knew she ought to keep quiet, but found the words spilling out.

"You moved them," she said.

Tackett glared at her, arms dropping to his sides as he nearly shook with anger. "What did you just say?"

But she ignored him. Instead, Molly looked at Deputy Vance. The shock on his face was something he could not hide. She believed he was not in on it. Therefore, he was their only hope.

"They could have dragged the bodies away from the woods near the clearing. I'll buy that. But we chased them up into the forest after the whole library thing. They left those corpses behind. Who was the first person on the scene at the library?"

Vance glanced at Tackett, and Molly knew.

With a sigh, she nodded. "I thought so."

Tackett slammed a hand against the wall and it shook the room. He was overweight and aging, but he was still very strong. Molly was not surprised.

"Damn you, girl," the sheriff thundered. "Both of you. You're talking about legends and monsters. I'm talking about the real thing. People have been murdered. As far as I know, you don't have any alibis for the vandalism at the Paperback Diner or at the library, or for any of the murders. No alibis except each other. You were at the scene. You were armed with unlicensed weapons. I found you with a corpse at your feet. Now maybe you ought to start talking about what's really going on here, otherwise I'd say you're screwed."

Molly and Jack exchanged a single glance. They sat

in silence a moment. Deputy Vance seemed more than agitated as his gaze ticked from one to the other and back at the sheriff.

"Can we make our phone call now?" Jack asked, all sweetness and innocence.

Deflated, Tackett threw up his hands. "Sure, kid. Call anyone you want. Make it count, though. We don't like murderers around here."

Again, Molly ignored Tackett. She turned instead to Deputy Vance. She raised her hands and stood up. Twirled in a circle, like she was showing off her gown on the red carpet on Oscar night.

"Look at me, Alan. Look at Jack. That girl was ripped apart. You see any blood on us? Any at all?"

Tackett grunted once. "Alan, let them make their call and then put them in a cage. I'm going for a little walk, clear my head. When I come back, you can head home."

As he left, all three of them stared after him in silence.

Not long before midnight, inhuman things gathered in the sprawling home of Bernard Mackeson. It was an old Federal colonial that had stood there as long as any of the other structures in Buckton, on an expanse of grassy hill where the trees seemed almost to have retreated from the home out of apprehension rather than having been cleared. The Mackeson place stood back a quarter mile from the main road, invisible in its crescent of woodland, and yet still keeping the wild at bay.

Or it would have, had it not invited the wild in.

In an enormous front parlor filled with antiques and leather, the Alpha sat in a high-backed chair in front of a dead fireplace. The sounds and scents of the forest swept in on the breeze, and he shivered with pleasure almost unconsciously. For this was no time for pleasure.

His world was falling apart.

Wearing a human face and human clothes, he glanced around at the members of his Pack, who had gathered in the room. Young and old, they sat on sofas and leaned against walls and stood in doorways, waiting for him to speak, waiting for his guidance. That was what it meant to be Alpha.

And yet, now, somehow, he felt as though he were letting them down. He should have been with them at the library; because he had not been, things had gotten complicated. There were other ways to deal with them, neater ways, but they were still too complicated. Simple was always best.

Still, the journal was the priority. If he had never written that history . . . but there was no use wishing. It had come to blood and death now, and perhaps that was for the best.

The Alpha wondered for the first time if he might not be too old, if someone else should not challenge him for the mantle of the lord of the pack. Curious, he cast his gaze upon each of them in turn, eyes catching theirs.

One by one, they all looked away.

The Alpha felt tired. Yet not one of them seemed able to do what must be done. Only he.

The world was falling apart, and only he could put it all back together again. He resolved himself, in that moment, with only the light of the moon and stars seeping through the windows to illuminate them. The Alpha vowed to himself to save the Pack, no matter the cost, no matter the bloodshed. Buckton had been a sanctuary to all of their kind for a century. But if the sanctuary itself had to be destroyed, even that was not too high a price to pay for the sanctity of his Pack. A new sanctuary could be created in another location, but only if the Pack survived to create it.

Sadness revealed itself on his false human face as he leaned forward in the antique chair. On the carpet lay their dead, five members of the Pack who would not hunt again. Jellison had died only twenty minutes ago, after a long struggle to survive the shotgun blast to his head. It was not to be.

He wanted to weep for each of them, but did not. What he owed to them was vengeance.

"How to explain this," he sighed to himself.

The Pack let out a collective sigh, perhaps of sympathy, or perhaps merely of relief that he had finally spoken. Some of them transformed, as if unable to control themselves, revealing their true forms—the wild, the beast within.

Though Jellison and two others among the dead would not be missed, or even recognized, by the people of Buckton, the other two would not go unnoticed. One was Juliette Bleier, who had taught mathematics at the high school.

The other was Bernard Mackeson himself.

It might be days before anyone noticed the absence of Mackeson—whose large, red-furred corpse was matted with dried blood—but when Juliette did not show up to teach her summer school students, questions would be asked. Her disappearance could be explained, perhaps. Covered up.

But the Pack could not afford any more losses.

"Who are they, these children?" he snarled. "I know their names, but what are they doing here? How can they be so unafraid?"

They all stood a bit straighter then, but none dared to answer. None of them *had* an answer.

"The journal is still missing," the Alpha growled. "Now these children arrive, and they appear to know far more about us than we do about them. It makes me wonder . . . maybe *they* have the book. We will find out more about them. Find out if they do, indeed, have the book. Then we'll make them tell us, one way or another."

The Alpha rose from the chair, flesh tearing away to reveal the monster beneath. He growled, the anger and pain coming from deep within him.

"If we have to tear apart every human in this place, we will have that journal. We will protect the Pack and the purpose of this sanctuary, even if it means the destruction of the sanctuary itself."

What the hell are you doing, Alan?

It was about the twentieth time he had asked himself that question. He had tried desperately to go to sleep. The sheriff had been gone over an hour. When he came back, he told Alan to go home and get some rest, that he'd sleep in the jail overnight, a job they always split up when they had prisoners. Which wasn't very often. Alan had been relieved not to get that duty.

But he had been unable to sleep.

Where's the blood? The girl, Molly, had spun around like it was prom night. But she had been right. No blood on either one of them. No way could they have killed the Meredith girl. She and her father had been torn apart, just like Foster and Garraty. Just like Kenny Oberst. Chunks torn out of them, organs ripped out, bones snapped and scraped as if by teeth.

Animals. All along a little voice in his head told him that these were murders, perpetrated by a person or persons more savage than anything he could ever have imagined. Because animals wouldn't have attacked Phil Garraty's van like that. Wouldn't have trashed Kenny Oberst's house, or the diner or the library.

Prowlers.

Whenever he had closed his eyes he had seen Molly Hatcher's eyes. Jack Dwyer's anger and sadness. He had recalled the way they had looked at the sheriff, as if he were the criminal and not the other way around.

Prowlers couldn't be real. Alan knew that. Sure, at the age of seven, he had believed in them wholeheartedly. Even imagined he had seen one of them out his parents' basement window, loping through the woods one night. But they weren't real. Like Bigfoot, or the Loch Ness Monster, they were modern myths.

And yet . . . the savagery of the murders, the strength of the killers, the things these kids said and did, the guns, their appearance at the library . . . the only way Alan could truly make sense of all of it was if he did the one thing he could not possibly imagine doing.

Believe.

Now he found himself in an impossible place, trapped between knowing it could not be true, and beginning to believe that it might be. The question had kept him awake, the image of Molly spinning, untouched by the blood of the dead girl had haunted him until he had gotten up from bed, dressed, and driven back out to the library.

What the hell are you doing, Alan?

It was a fine, warm July night, but he was cold as he trekked up through the woods. The flashlight beam was strong and wide before him, and he easily found the place he and the sheriff had diverged from the path upon hearing the sound of gunfire up the mountain.

What are you doing?

Investigating, he told himself. *I'm investigating.* Yet it was ironic, Alan thought, that he was up here at all, traipsing around the woods at one o'clock in the morning in search of some evidence that Molly and Jack's story was true.

If he did not believe in it at all, he would never have come.

But if he truly *did* believe them . . . he would never have come, would never have had the courage to return to the forest around Buckton.

Now, as he pushed through the trees and the night sounds of the woods came to him, Alan found himself believing more and more and wondering if he should not go home, go back. Return again in the morning, when his imagination might not be so likely to run away with death and legends. In his present state of mind, filled with fear and wonder and curiosity, he was just as likely to see a windigo or some wood sprites as to find evidence that Prowlers existed.

It was more than fifteen minutes of brisk walking later, through trees and underbrush, that he emerged into the same clearing. He would never have been able to find it again, save that there were still trails in the woods, though not commonly used by hikers or teenagers these days. Both brands of forest-wanderers tended to stick more to the path most traveled.

It would have been much simpler to drive up there. The coroner's truck had made the trip up to the ruins of the old Bartleby place with only some damage to the shocks and suspension. Alan could have taken his cruiser over that same overgrown terrain. But that was not how the kids had done it, and he wanted to try to follow their trail as best he could.

There had been no dead monsters in the woods.

In an odd sort of way, he found that disappointing.

In the clearing, he first made his way to the ruins from which they had retrieved the girl's body. There was blood soaked into the ground there in the circle of police tape, but that would tell him nothing. The flashlight beam shone like a searchlight down upon the area around where her body had been discovered.

His breath caught in his throat.

There, upon a pile of shattered brick, was a tuft of fur.

Could be nothing. Just an animal. Any animal, really.

Mind struggling not to leap to conclusions, despite the dark influence of the night and the dread that began to build within him, Alan made a circuit of the clearing. Molly and Jack had said they had killed one of the Prowlers just at the edge of the clearing.

Alan smiled. Of course they had not admitted to owning the guns, but the implication was there that they had shot the creatures.

The flashlight beam cut a wide swath across the grass and brush, but there was nothing there. Three-quarters of the way around the clearing, and he had found nothing. Alan had begun to feel the tight knot of tension in his chest unraveling.

He did not know what was really going on around here, but to think it could be some kind of monsters was just . . .

"Ridiculous," he said aloud.

But his voice cracked and sounded absurd even to him. For in midthought, he had stumbled upon something. The flashlight beam caught a splash of something on the ground. Only a dozen feet from the place he had come into the clearing there was a broken tree branch, and beside it, a dark pool of blood soaking into the ground and the brush.

There was reddish fur there as well, little tufts of it on the grass.

Alan closed his eyes a moment, but when he opened them, though his flashlight beam wavered in his hand, the evidence was still there. Something had been killed on this spot. Something with fur. Something large, judging by the way the brush had been crushed beneath its weight.

Something glittered in the light and he bent to poke through the brush. He retrieved a shell casing from a shotgun.

Up this close, the blood was a deep crimson. Alan reached out to dip a finger into it. He raised it to his nose and inhaled, hoping it would prove to be something else, but the copper scent confirmed it. Blood.

It can't be true, he thought.

But he knew, then, that it was.

Something shifted in the darkness behind him. Twigs snapped.

"You shouldn't've come up here again, Alan," growled a deep voice. "Should've left it alone."

The voice sent a shiver up his spine and everything inside him seemed to let go. The fear came up in him full force, and he was not even breathing as he turned around. Alan did not dare to lift his flashlight. He did not want to see more than the moon and stars would show him.

For that was terrifying enough.

It was rows of razor teeth, and eyes that seemed to glow in the starlight. The thing's muscles rippled under its fur, and it seemed almost to be mocking him.

"You could run, you know," the Prowler said almost kindly.

As if a switch had been thrown, Alan came alive. He spun around, dropping his light, and sprinted toward the edge of the clearing. His breathing sounded impossibly loud in his ears. He reached for the weapon at his belt, unsnapped the gun, and drew it from its holster.

He felt the thing's hot breath on his neck, heard it loping after him.

He would be killed.

Alan turned, raised his gun, and fired once as he fell.

Then the monster was on top of him, cracking his ribs. His throat was torn out in a single gulp and his blood fountained onto the scrub brush. Then his chest was opened and his heart ripped out.

C H A P T E R 12

Tina always felt small in John Tackett's office. When she was a girl, her father had visited Tackett from time to time, mostly to talk local politics. Boring talk, but Tina had been thrilled just to have her father take her along, and to have the sheriff's office to explore. There was an antique globe in one corner, not far from the a table upon which the sheriff almost always had a vase of fresh flowers. Tackett's penchant for flowers had seemed odd to her, even as a child. She wondered if he kept them around because he enjoyed the scent, or if he felt it took some of the edge away from his status and demeanor.

For Sheriff Tackett's demeanor had always had an edge.

This morning that edge seemed to have been worn away.

"Tina, we'll get to the bottom of this. I promise we will," Sheriff Tackett told her.

His eyes were crystal blue sky, not a trace of tears, but the way his lips were pinched together beneath his thick mustache revealed the emotion roiling in him. The rage and the grief. Or, at least, that was the way Tina interpreted his expression.

She saw herself reflected in his eyes, her hair a scraggly mess, eyes raw and red, mascara-stained tears on her face. Tina did not want to see that face, did not want to acknowledge her reflection. She closed her eyes tightly and more tears squeezed out to run down her cheeks. Though it was at least ninety degrees, she shivered and hugged herself tightly.

"Why'd it have to come to this?" she whispered, voice cracking with grief. "What the hell was he thinking, going up there by himself?"

Tackett encircled her with his beefy arms. The aroma of his deodorant was strong and sweet and it gave her a little comfort, like cotton that had just been ironed. Her tears stained his shirt. Tina let out a long breath, coming to terms with the horrid truth of that morning.

Alan . . . her Alan . . . was dead.

He had never been a dynamic individual, but he was a good man, sweet and sincere, and he had loved her. Tina knew that as long as she lived, she would never really be able to forget the pain of the news of that morning, under the harsh sun. Sheriff Tackett had caught up with her outside the Inn.

That morning, when she went to assess the damage to the library, Lavinia Murray had been surprised to see

Alan Vance's patrol car in the lot. After an hour or so with no sign of him, she had called the sheriff's office. Tackett had immediately feared the worst, and a trip up to the ruins where they had arrested Jack and Molly the night before had led to the grisly discovery.

"It's not fair," she whispered.

Tackett gazed at her, a grim expression on his face. "No. No, it isn't. I've been to see Alan's mother already. You might want to go over there, now, Tina. She may need help making plans."

The edges of Tina's mouth lifted as if to smile, but the ache in her heart would not allow it to be truly born. She knew that the sheriff figured that she and Mrs. Vance would both need to do some crying, and that they could lend each other support both needed. She also knew he wanted her out of his hair so he could continue his investigation.

"Thank you, Sheriff," she said, wiping at her eyes. There was a hollow place inside her, but she knew there was no going back.

The phone on his desk rang and Tackett gave it a hard look, as though he might shoot it. He gave her an apologetic shrug and went over to answer.

"What is it, Alice?" he asked. Alice Tyll was the department's receptionist.

As the sheriff listened, Tina began to wander around his office. He was a man who liked things neat and orderly, and yet that effort seemed to be undone by the number of knickknacks he had. Little antique picture frames, animals carved out of wood, and other odds and ends adorned the cabinets and bookshelves. Tackett was an enigma, and always had been.

"Tell him he'll have to wait just a little longer," the sheriff muttered into the phone. "If you have to, tell him what's happened. Maybe he'll understand better. Just tell him to wait."

Tina let her fingers slide over the spines of the old books on the sheriff's shelves. His taste in antiques included books, and she wondered if some of the things up there were first editions. They must have been worth a great deal of money, if they were.

Her fingers stopped on a cracked, leather-bound volume with no title on the spine. With a small frown, she slid it off the shelf. The cover was also blank.

Curious, she flipped the book open to find that it was handwritten in an elegant scrawl, the words all seeming to bend to one side as though in a breeze.

Tina recognized the penmanship, and a chill ran through her.

"Sheriff, what's this?" she asked.

He seemed not to have heard her. "No, Alice. Just tell him to . . . hold on." Tackett put a hand over the phone and glanced at her. "I'm sorry, Tina, I have a visitor I'm not going to be able to put off. Can you let yourself out?"

The sheriff was watching her closely, out of concern. She glanced again at the writing in the book, then closed it and reluctantly slipped it back onto the shelf, wishing she could have taken it with her. In her grief and rage over Alan's murder, nothing made sense to her anymore.

"Of course," she said. "I'll talk to you later."

"I'll call as soon as I have any new information."

Tina thanked him and left the office. She had parked in the lot behind the building, so she went out the rear door.

Less than a minute after Tina left, Tackett gave Alice the okay to let the visitor in. The man who stepped into his office was tall and broad-shouldered, rugged-looking in that needed-a-shave-two-days-ago sort of way.

"I'm Bill Cantwell, Sheriff. We spoke on the phone this morning. You've got some friends of mine locked up, and—"

"I know who you are, Cantwell. Saw you play for the Patriots ten or twelve years ago. You were good, but they lost too many yards to penalties from you roughing up the other teams," Tackett declared. "In case my receptionist didn't tell you, Mr. Cantwell, we've had a rough morning here."

"I heard about your deputy, Sheriff. You have my sympathies. But you're holding my friends in connection with some murders that I'm guessing are similar to what happened to your man last night. Which means they haven't done anything. They've been in jail all night and all morning, sir. I'd like to ask you to let them out now."

Every joint in Jack's body ached with an echo of the discomfort of the night before. It had taken him more than an hour to fall asleep on the torturously uncomfortable cot provided in his cell. His mood upon waking had been quite dark, but he did not blame the sheriff for his discomfort. It was jail, after all, not a hotel. But their predicament was worrisome, to say the least. While they lingered in jail, the monsters preying upon the people of Buckton still roamed the land.

The night before, Jack had used his one call to telephone the pub, only to have Courtney tell him Bill was already on the way. Ever since dawn, he had been waiting for Bill to arrive and get them cut loose somehow.

It was almost noon when Tackett came to let him out of his cell.

"You're free to go, Dwyer," the sheriff grumbled, eyes empty and gray as the sky just before a storm rolled in.

Jack wanted to ask why, but thought better of it. When the sheriff released Molly from her cell at the other end of the corridor, however, she had no such hesitation.

"There's been another killing, hasn't there?" she asked. "That's why you have to let us go."

The sheriff turned to her slowly, like the straight man in an old vaudeville act. It was unnerving to see, and for a moment, Jack thought he might hit her.

"Deputy Vance," Tackett said bluntly.

"Oh, no," Molly replied, a hand flying to cover her mouth. She turned to Jack, gaze weighted with guilt and sorrow.

For a second Jack thought she might offer condolences. He felt some obligation to do so himself. But in the back of his mind was the suspicion he had been nursing since the night before . . . that the sheriff himself was a Prowler. With that lurking in the back of his mind, he could not bring himself to offer any kind words at all to the man. Molly, too, kept silent, and he imagined her reasons were the same.

Sheriff Tackett walked the two of them up to the front of the building where Bill was waiting.

"Are you going home soon?" Tackett asked, glaring at them.

"Not sure," Jack replied.

"Come talk to me first if you plan to leave," the sheriff commanded. "I think you know more about what's really happening here than you're telling me . . . and not that crap about Prowlers, either. The real thing. If I thought I could make those weapons charges stick in court, I'd hold you here."

Molly stiffened. Her hair was even more wild than usual, tangled and dirty, and she pushed it away from her cold, sad eyes as she turned on the sheriff.

"Why don't you?" she asked him. "You never even got a chance to impound and search Jack's Jeep. Did you even search our room at the inn?"

"Molly, maybe this isn't the time?" Bill suggested.

But it was too late. The sheriff turned on her, anger making his mouth and nostrils twitch as he tried to control himself. The storm had come into his eyes at last.

"Miss Hatcher, why don't you keep your mouth shut?" he snapped. "I know those guns were yours. I know you probably have more in your vehicle. But I've got a situation here that sort of takes precedence. In a bigger town, you'd be screwed right now. But I'm just one man. Count yourselves lucky and get out of my sight."

Her mouth dropped open and she seemed to be formulating some response when Jack and Bill ushered her out of the police station. At the door, the sheriff stood and glared at them until they had all climbed into Bill's huge Oldsmobile in the dusty parking lot.

Jack was in the backseat. When Molly swung the heavy door shut with a loud thump, she turned to give him a withering look. Bill started the engine and it roared to life.

"What?" Jack asked, uncomfortable under Molly's gaze.

"You should have said something," she told him.

"What did you want me to say? He's right. If we leave this town without spending any more time in jail, I'd say we're pretty lucky."

Both of them looked to Bill for his input. The burly bartender guided the car along the main road. After Jack gave him directions, he turned down the road that would lead to School Street, where their Jeep was still parked in front of the library.

After a long moment, he seemed to sense their attention upon him and glanced over. A grim smile appeared on his features.

"What next? That's the question, right?" Bill asked. "Funny. You two usually figure out what's next without much help. Why all of a sudden are you looking for suggestions?"

Jack frowned. It was a good question. "This isn't our territory. It's like, out here, in the middle of nowhere, there could be a Prowler behind every tree. Back home . . . it's just easier to kick ass and take names when you know where to run if it goes down ugly."

"Sounds like you've already figured out the next step," Bill noted, both hands on the wheel.

"Kicking ass and taking names," Molly said softly. "And maybe not even the names part."

"So where do we start?" Bill asked.

"The sheriff," Molly said quickly. She rolled down the window of the car and sweet summer air blew in. "He's a Prowler."

"Is he?" Bill asked, frowning.

"Isn't he? You should know. Didn't you get a scent off him?" she prodded.

Bill contemplated the question a moment. Then he shrugged slightly. "He has some pretty aromatic flowers in his office. And even out there in the foyer. There's a Prowler around that office. Probably him. But I'd be lying if I said I was sure."

"I think we need to go on the assumption that it *is* him," Jack put in. "Hate to say it, but those gun charges could have been pretty bad. Especially if he searched the Jeep. Maybe it's true he just doesn't care right now. Or maybe he wanted to let us out, wanted us to be roaming around."

In the front seat, Molly turned to look at him, eyes haunted. "You mean, so they could kill us?"

Jack did not answer. He did not have to.

"We killed a couple of them at the library last night," Molly told Bill. "The sheriff was the first one there, but when Deputy Vance got there, the bodies were gone. The sheriff had to have moved them. He was only a couple of minutes behind us, and the Prowlers were all ahead of us."

Bill turned on School Street, jaw set in a grim line. "Sheriff of a town like this. What better position to be in if you're the Alpha of a Prowler pack? You decide what evidence gets paid attention to, and if a couple of hikers disappear, you get to play dumb without the law poking their noses in. It makes a nasty kind of sense."

Jack felt his sadness over Deputy Vance's death mingle with his fear for himself and his friends and grow into a new resolve. This could not go on any longer. Now that Bill had arrived, it was time to act.

"We're going to have to go forward assuming the sheriff's one of them," he said. "That's bad because he knows all about us, now. But it's good because we know where he is. We've got a lot of questions, and now we know who to ask."

"He's not going to want to answer," Bill reminded him.

"It's too late for what he wants," Jack said gravely. "Now it's about what we need to stay alive. What really pisses me off is that they can move during the day if they want to, but we can't exactly raid the police station in broad daylight. Tonight, though—tonight, we go after answers."

He turned to gaze out the window at the passing

trees and his stomach grumbled. "In the meantime, is anyone else hungry?"

Hate flowed through Tina, trying to fill her up, and she let it in if only because it helped to force out her grief. Dust rose up from the dirt road that cut across her father's farmland as she drove toward his house. The house she had grown up in. Off to her left a tractor was stopped in a cornfield, probably broken down. Several hands were standing around staring at it as though it would fix itself. As the sound of her engine reached them they turned to wave, almost in unison.

Daddy, she thought.

A tear slipped down her cheek.

Her lips curled up in a soft growl.

The moment Sheriff Tackett told her what had happened to Alan, she began to rehearse the confrontation that was about to come. Now, though, as she drew closer to the huge, rambling farmhouse, she knew that she would never be able to speak those rehearsed words.

The tires bounced through ruts in the dirt road, and then she was there, the house looming up in front of her. Tina hit the brakes, threw the car into park, and killed the engine. She sprang from the car and hurried toward the door. By the time she reached it, she was running.

"Daddy!" she shouted as she tore the door open and rushed into the foyer. "Daddy!"

"In here."

The voice came from the sun-filled parlor to the left of the front door. It had been her favorite room as a child; her mother's favorite room. Until her mother had died. Now, even from the corridor, she could see her father in the antique rocker that sat in the far corner, its back to the windows. His face was partially in shadow, his gray hair turned halo-golden by the sunshine streaming in around him.

"*Henri Lemoine,* you are a monster," she said, pronouncing his name with the accent of his native French.

"Christina," he replied softly, gazing up at her with an expression of sadness that she almost believed.

Tina shuddered and shook her head. "No, Daddy. You killed him! You killed Alan, or had one of the others do it for you."

Her father stood at last and crossed the room toward her. "Christina," he said again, reaching out for her. "He gave me no choice. Alan was always a curious young man. Things had progressed too far. It would have been impossible to erase what he had seen from his mind."

Though fury rippled through her, made her want to change, to give herself over to the wild, Tina refused to allow it if only to deny him that one small thing. He would have wanted her to give reign to the beast within her, but she would not. Just as Henry Lemoine now wore his human face in an attempt to mollify his daughter's sorrow.

"Don't try to tell me that Alan was responsible for his own murder!" she yelled. "You killed him, you old bastard. You animal!"

"Yes, I am an animal. And yes, I had him killed. But he left me no choice."

Fuming, her chest heaving with her rage, she slapped her father across the face, long nails scratching him and drawing blood. Henry touched the wounds and then licked his own blood from his fingers.

"You could have prevented it, you know," her father said.

A chill went through her. Unable to believe she had really heard those words, she shook her head. "What are you talking about?"

"I tried to talk to you about what was happening, but you did not want to hear it. Ever since you came of age, daughter, you have vexed me whenever possible. You embraced the human world, spurned your heritage here, this sanctuary for your kind. You left us—"

"I went to college!" she shouted.

Henry nodded sadly. "And you only came home because your mother was ill and I promised to buy you that old hotel. But I did that to keep you close to the Pack, hoping that one day you would see that you were mistaken. That one day you would become part of the Pack again, that you would at last understand the importance of sanctuary and the dream behind it. Even when you became involved with a human, I indulged you."

"I loved him," Tina whispered, on the verge of fresh tears.

Her father scowled. "He was kind, Tina. But he was *human*."

She turned away. All she wanted now was to run, to leave her father, his precious sanctuary, and all the Pack behind forever.

"None of this would have happened if you had not broken your own rules and started killing the people in town. We lived among them so long and they never knew, not for sure, that we were real. Then you throw that all away in a matter of weeks."

Henry let out a long sigh that sounded more like a rumbling growl.

"You would understand if you had been willing to let me speak to you of this before. I tried, Tina. Do not forget that. And you turned me away, shushed me. Will you listen now?"

She did not respond, only kept her back to him. But she listened. He spoke to her then the way he had at bedtime when she was a child, as though they sat around the fire and he shared with her the great wisdom of his ancestors. Which was, she supposed, true enough in his mind.

"Once, the Great Packs roamed all the continents of the world, sometimes at war with one another, sometimes at peace," Henry Lemoine told his daughter. "But as humanity evolved, they spread like a forest fire. Soon there were so many that the Packs found *themselves* hunted. The early humans had been prey, but over time, they became the enemy.

"The Packs splintered, internecine war erupted over the hunting grounds that were free of the taint of humans. But the humans kept coming, spreading their influence. Over the course of thousands of years, we evolved the ability to appear human, we adapted. But by then it was too late. There were thousands of tiny Packs spread across the world, mostly in the dark, forgotten corners where few humans congregated.

"During the twentieth century, many broke off from the Packs and hid themselves away within human society, became part of it. When there was no loyalty between the surviving packs, nor even any real communication, there was no society. Without that, there was no responsibility, from one of us to the other.

"Sanctuary was created as a response to that, a place where we could come to rest, to be safe, to consider our place in a society that barely existed any longer. Rogues or renegades, no matter what their Pack affiliation, or if they had no affiliation at all, they are welcomed here. They can join the Pack, or stay for a short while, living in the mountains, in the wild, as their ancestors did.

"The sanctuary is a sacred thing, a memorial to the greatness we achieved in the past and a testament to our belief that we can reach those heights again. Society is the answer. Together we can return to the glory of an almost forgotten age.

"But only if we do so quietly."

He paused then. Tina swallowed hard and turned to face her father. She still did not understand what any of that had to do with the Pack's breach of its first law. They had killed people in Buckton, where they lived, drawn attention to themselves.

"Christina," Henry said gently, "when word came to

us about what had happened to Owen Tanzer and his pack, we mourned. But they were foolish. Tanzer forgot that this is *their* world now. If the land is to be returned to us, we will have to muster our strength quietly. It took thousands of years for things to evolve into what they are now, and it might take thousands of years to reverse them.

"This sanctuary was meant to set an example. Serenity and caution are necessary if the dream it represents is ever to come true, but knowledge is equally important. If it could take thousands of years to usurp the humans, then that knowledge will need to be passed along."

Again, her father paused, and there was weight to his silence.

"I wrote it down. All of it. The history I know from oral tradition, the experiences of my own centuries of life, the purpose and philosophy of the sanctuary. I wrote it all down in a journal."

"Oh, my God," Tina gasped, one hand flying to her mouth in astonishment.

A journal. She had meant to ask her father about the book in Tackett's office, the scrawl of his handwriting, but in her grief over Alan's murder she had not yet gotten around to it.

"That's what this is all about?" She stared at him, horrified. "You're not even hunting. You're killing all these people, folks I've known my whole life . . . Alan . . . You killed Alan over this *journal?*"

All the love and warmth went out of her father then. He glared at her, cold and savage. "It's a shame you wouldn't listen to me before. You might have kept him out of it. But now we've done what we had to. If that book ends up in the wrong hands—"

But Tina wasn't listening anymore. Her hands fluttered in the air as though she could brush the horror away, and she turned and stormed out of her father's house without another word. As her feet hit the dirt, she let the tears flow freely, and when she slid behind the wheel of the car, she slumped over the wheel and sobbed.

Tina Lemoine was not a fool. She knew what she was, what they were, her kind. But she had never really felt a part of it. Her father was right in that she had come back to Buckton after college because her mother was ill, dying, and because he had promised to buy the inn for her. But she had stayed because, in the end, Buckton was her hometown. These were her people.

And they were dying because for her father's pride, for his arrogant insistence upon creating a legacy that would live on after he was gone.

Tina wiped her tears away and started the car. She did a quick U-turn and took off down the road, dirt rising up in clouds again from the road. The hands in the field were still standing around staring expectantly at the dead tractor, though one of them had climbed up on top of the machine and seemed to be taking the engine apart.

She did not see if they waved this time. She was not looking.

Tina would leave Buckton and never return. After

this was over, she was going to stay as far away from her father as she could, for the rest of her inhumanly long life. But she would not leave until she had put a stop to these killings, and she realized now that it was within her power to do that. Her father's journal was in Sheriff Tackett's office. She had no idea if Tackett knew that, but she was determined to retrieve it, and end the violence that was tearing her town apart.

Once the journal was in her hands, it would be over, and then she would leave Buckton—the sanctuary—and the pack behind.

C H A P T E R 13

It was dusk and the waning sunlight gave way to the stranglehold of darkness without a whimper. Slow, inexorable, the night swept in. The afternoon had gone by painfully slowly. Several times, they had discussed not waiting, simply going after the sheriff right then and there. But wisdom had prevailed—such things were better done under the cover of darkness.

They had eaten lunch at the Jukebox just before two o'clock, then wandered through the few shops in town that were open on Sunday. Molly had been impatient for a shower, and Bill and Jack accompanied her back to the inn before dinner. Their fears had gone unspoken, but they were unwilling to leave her alone, even for an hour.

By the time they had sat down for dinner, they had run out of the energy it required to pretend at being carefree. They had eaten, mostly in silence, and then returned to the inn to await nightfall.

And now it had come.

Molly sat in the back of the Jeep with a pair of 9mm handguns clipped to her belt at the small of her back and the remaining pump shotgun on the floor at her feet.

Crazy, she thought. *The whole world is crazy.*

The window was open, and the night air was hot and sweet. A bit of sweat trickled down her throat and chest and it felt strangely cold to her, as though her every nerve were reaching out, examining each sensation.

This was not the first time she had gone knowingly into danger. In some ways, this was simpler. There was only the one monster to contend with. And yet, this was the first time she had had this much time to prepare for it, to roll it over in her brain as though it were a hard candy in her mouth that had to be worked at to surrender its flavor.

Danger had a flavor all its own. And though it terrified her, Molly would not turn away. She was bolstered by her hatred for the Prowlers. It gave her strength.

Jack shut off the headlights as they rolled into the lot behind the Town Hall. The police station was partially dark, but the light in the front reception area and several at the side windows were still burning. They were counting on the receptionist, Alice, to work only set hours. With Alan Vance dead, that meant that, if Tackett was in there, he was probably there alone.

"Things must be quiet," Bill said. "Looks like he's still here."

"Yeah," Jack agreed. "Or he's waiting for us."

Molly swallowed hard. She did not like that idea. Not at all. Jack killed the engine and they got out slowly. Molly reached back into the Jeep for the shotgun. Given that she had very little experience with weapons, the shotgun was the best weapon for her. Big bang, a lot of damage on a wide radius.

Bill carried a small canvas bag in which he had placed the tiny grenades that had been in the crate in the back of the Jeep. Jack had three nine millimeters, one in each hand and one clipped to his belt at the small of his back. Bill had identified the other gun in the crate as a twelve-year-old assault rifle, but they all thought it wisest to leave it right where it was.

What they were doing was crazy enough without a weapon like that in the hands of someone who had never fired one before. Bill claimed to know how to work it, but then, after all, he hardly needed one.

The wind seemed to die quite suddenly as they slipped along the front of the building, trying to stay out of sight. What breeze there had been dropped away, and Molly felt too warm, as if the air itself was stalking her, the humidity preying upon her.

At the door, Jack moved ahead. Molly and Bill were side by side and she could feel the raw, animal power emanating off him. He was tensed and ready, and suddenly she understood the word *wild* in a way she never had before.

Molly was concerned that the door might be locked, but Bill pulled it open and ushered them in. Jack went first, arms bent up close to himself, guns aimed at the ceiling. Back to one wall, he slid quickly up the corridor to the first junction. Molly breathed a sigh of relief when there was no reaction within. That meant that they had been right about the receptionist; she would hate to have terrorized the woman. After a moment, she followed Jack into the building, shotgun held up straight the way Bill had shown her. She watched as Jack ducked his head around the corner, then turned back to nod wordlessly before continuing along the corridor.

As she was about to pursue him, Molly felt Bill's powerful grip on her shoulder. Alarmed, she spun to stare at him, wide-eyed, now extraordinarily aware of the beat of her own heart in her eardrums, the rise and fall of her chest with each anxious breath. He slipped past her, made it clear to her that she was to take up the rear. Ahead, Jack moved quickly, almost stridently, down the hallway toward the door to the sheriff's office. It stood open, a soft golden light coming from within, a counterpoint to the harsh overhead illumination in the hall. Bill caught up to him a second before Molly did, and tapped him on the shoulder.

When Jack turned to look at them both, his eyes were wild, and Molly realized exactly how frightened he was, scared for himself, for them, and at the idea that they might not be able to stop the Prowlers. She knew him well enough to realize the latter scared him the most.

After a moment Jack let out a long breath and stepped back just a bit to let Bill go in ahead of him.

Unarmed.

Bill pointed at each of them in turn, the gesture taking in their weapons, maybe emphasizing their importance—or not, Molly could not be sure—and then indicated that Jack should go to the right inside the door and Molly to the left.

They both nodded.

One hand up, Bill ticked off three fingers.

Then he strode into the sheriff's office. Jack darted in behind him and to the left, both nine millimeters raised.

Molly swept into the room and leveled the shotgun. The sheriff was behind his desk, paperwork all over the place, a cup of soup at the edge with a plastic spoon in it, still steaming from the microwave. The large, potbellied man's eyes were hard and angry, but not afraid. He began to rise, reaching for the gun at his hip.

"Put your hands on the desk, *now!*" Jack shouted.

Incredulous, the sheriff froze, but he did not comply. His hand was only inches from the weapon that rested in its holster.

Molly pumped the shotgun once, directed its barrel toward him.

"Do it, Sheriff," she said. Her voice sounded cold to her, distant. But there was a reason for that.

Something was wrong here. Something just did not feel right about any of this.

With a grunt, the sheriff did as he had be instructed. He bent slightly over the desk, palms out flat. His eyes darted to each of them in turn and then went to Bill, who had not said a word.

"You're interrupting my dinner," he said gruffly. "The paperwork I could do without. But my soup's going to get cold."

"Who eats soup in this weather?" Bill asked, almost as though he were amused by it all.

"Thought I might be coming down with something," the sheriff revealed.

Jack glared at Tackett, then glanced quickly up at Bill in confusion. He dangled the gun in his left hand down at his side, but kept the other aimed directly at the lawman.

"Where's the lair?" Jack demanded.

The sheriff exhaled loudly. "What the hell are you talking about?" he snapped angrily. His furious gaze was on Jack now. "You want to kill me, rip me up like you did the others, not much I can do to stop you. But where does it go from here, boy?"

"Don't try to play with my head!" Jack roared. He took two steps in toward the sheriff and aimed the gun at his head. "I want to know where the lair is. There isn't going to be any more killing."

"I'm relieved to hear it," Sheriff Tackett replied.

A growl began to build in Bill's chest. All the shouting and tension seemed to be rocketing along toward a violent crescendo, but until Molly heard that wild sound from Bill, she had felt almost powerless to stop it.

No more.

"Stop!" she snapped at Jack.

He turned to look at her, confused.

Molly stepped toward the sheriff, her shotgun aimed

at a vague place perhaps two feet to his left. If she had fired then, the only thing she would kill was a potted plant or the file cabinet beneath it.

"Change!" she yelled, voice quavering with nerves.

He's got to be, she thought, almost crying inside. *He's got to be one. If he's not . . .*

But even as the thoughts skittered through her mind, Molly could see in the sheriff's eyes that he had no idea what she was talking about. Everything clicked together in her head. Paperwork? Soup for dinner? And he was mystified and infuriated by their intrusion.

"Oh, God, Jack, he's human," she whispered. The barrel of her shotgun drooped toward the floor.

"He can't be," Jack replied. "I mean . . . he let us go. And who else could have moved those bodies? He was right behind us. It doesn't make sense."

Bill grunted loudly and blinked. Then he moved toward the sheriff, who seemed to shrink away from him slightly. Bill sniffed the air near him, and Molly saw him deflate a bit as he stepped back.

"Molly's right," the big man said without glancing at Jack. "There've been Prowlers in here, but with all the flowers, I couldn't separate out the scent right off. But he's human."

"Oh, hell," Jack groaned. Both guns lowered now, he backed up and leaned against the wall. "What've we done?"

Slowly, the sheriff stood up. "Why don't you put the weapons down, all of you, and we can try to make sense of what you're going on about."

He kept his hands in front of him, making sure they all saw that he was in no rush to reach for a weapon. Molly stared at Bill, hoping for some solution from him.

"Sheriff, listen," Jack began, raising both guns again. He aimed them toward the back of the office, but it was clear to all of them that he was ready for a fight. "We told you our story before. It's the truth. I know you don't believe it, but think for a second. What else makes sense? If we were the people you're looking for, would you even still be alive?"

But Tackett was angry. His nostrils flared and he studied Jack closely. "Put the weapons down, kid. Then we'll talk."

Jack sighed. "Don't be an idiot."

The sheriff actually cracked a smile at that one. "*I'm* an idiot? Look at the three of you. Illegal possession of firearms. Trespassing. Assault on a police officer. Give me time, I'll come up with more."

"The Prowlers are real," Molly said, her voice barely above a whisper.

The clock ticked on the wall. Behind her, Molly could hear Jack breathing hard. The sheriff's chest rumbled, and she thought maybe he really was fighting a cold, as he'd said. The smell of his soup, French onion, filled the room.

"I'm sorry. I just don't believe that," the sheriff said at last. He kept his gaze locked with hers, granting her at least the respect of not looking away. "Frankly, Miss Hatcher, I think you three have seen too many movies. You're all a bit off. Lay the weapons aside now, and I'll be as kind as I can with the charges. But there will be charges."

Molly turned away, heartsick. What were their options now? They could surrender and go to jail, or cuff the guy and become fugitives. Neither was much of a choice. But if they were incarcerated, there would be no one else out there to combat the Prowlers.

Filled with dread and confusion, she walked to Jack and stared at him. "What do we do?"

Jack let his shoulders sag and he stared for a moment at the ground. They were well and truly screwed. What they were doing was difficult enough without having Sheriff Tackett as an enemy. Jack was at a loss. The guns in his hands felt heavy and more than a little silly. With a shake of his head, he lifted his eyes and met Molly's expectant gaze.

After a moment Jack chuckled softly. "This is stupid."

"Won't get an argument from me," Sheriff Tackett declared, an impatient expression on his face.

"What?" Molly asked. "What've you got?"

Jack shrugged. He couldn't believe he'd been so foolish. "Proof. We've got proof, Molly."

Then he glanced over at Bill, no longer amused. "Show him," Jack said gravely.

Bill twitched and stared at him in astonishment. Jack understood. He knew he was asking something terrible of his friend. One of the fundamental survival instincts of a Prowler insisted that he never reveal his true nature to a human who was not prey. Even Jack and Courtney and Molly only knew because Bill had saved their lives.

It was even more important for someone who was attempting to live in the human world, to live, essentially, as a human being.

But Jack could see any no other way out of the situation they were in. They needed Tackett as an ally now.

"We don't have any choice," he said, hoping Bill heard the apology in his voice.

The burly man nodded grimly, took in a long breath, then stepped up to the sheriff; he towered over the man. "Sheriff Tackett, you don't have a weak heart, do you?" Bill looked angry, and he looked mean.

"You threatening me, mister?" the sheriff asked, misreading Bill's intentions.

"Not at all."

The sheriff frowned. Maybe there was something in Bill's voice that unnerved him somewhat. Whatever it was, he took a step backward and studied Bill a bit more closely.

It happened all at once, and Sheriff Tackett's eyes bulged out. Bones cracked and popped in a change much more swift than those Jack had seen other Prowlers perform. Bill's face altered, fur sprouted through the skin all over his body, his jaw elongated, and his teeth thinned and multiplied into rows of tiny razors. His ears were pointed and jutted upward. What had been skin now flaked away.

"Jesus," Tackett whispered.

He staggered backward a few steps and unconsciously clapped a hand over his chest, as though his heart might actually stop. Then the sheriff fumbled for his gun, and drew it out of the holster.

With a single, fluid motion, Bill reached out, grabbed him by the hand, and removed his gun. The enormous, brown-furred Prowler walked over and put the sheriff's gun on the far side of the man's desk, and then just left it there.

"You . . . you're one of them," Tackett muttered, staring in fear and amazement.

As they all watched, Bill changed back. It took perhaps a second longer than the first change. Jack knew that extra moment was necessary because this change was more difficult. The first had been simply revealing the beast within. This one required the biological manufacture of skin and the alteration of bone structure . . . the rebuilding of a façade.

"I'm a Prowler, yes," Bill said, voice thick with his reluctance and anxiety over where this would all lead. "But I'm not one of them, not the way you mean. The ones who've been preying on this town? There have been dozens of disappearances and killings in the mountains around here that might have been Prowlers. I don't hunt anymore. Haven't for a very long time."

Tackett stroked his mustache and stared at Bill, tilting his head first this way and then that, as though trying to see the magician's trick that had made the transformation possible. But it was no trick.

"That's a comfort," the sheriff said dryly.

Jack was about to step in when Molly beat him to it. He breathed a sigh of relief. It would be better coming from her. Tackett seemed to trust her, at least a little.

"We thought you were one of them. The Alpha, actually," she explained. "That's the pack leader."

Tackett leaned against his desk and stared at the three of them incredulously. "Should I be flattered?"

"In a way," Molly replied awkwardly. "The thing is, you've got to know that we're not it. We're not who you're looking for. We need your help to figure out who in this town isn't what they appear to be."

The sheriff's gaze moved back and forth between Molly and Bill. Jack knew that he was barely on the man's radar at the moment. Molly was the one forcing him to think logically in the presence of a monster. Or, at least, a being Tackett could only see as a monster. Bill wasn't, but even Jack had a hard time coming to terms with that fact, and they were practically family.

Idly, Tackett wandered back to his gun. Jack could have shot him, then. Bill was fast enough to attack and tear the weapon from the man's hands. But the time had come for the chips to fall. Nobody moved as the sheriff lifted his gun off the edge of the desk. He gazed at it a moment, and then slid it into his holster.

"All right," he said, a rasp in his voice. "What've you got?"

Almost in answer there was a soft thump somewhere down the hall.

"Sheriff?" a female voice called.

"Damn it," Tackett muttered. "Your weapons." He glared at them and it was obvious he meant they should hide them.

Jack stuck one of the 9mm pistols in his rear waistband,

next to the third that was in its clip there. The second he placed on a shelf beneath a stack of file folders. When he glanced over at Molly, she had taken up a position near the window, and Jack could see her shotgun leaning against the wall under the curtains. The breeze billowed them slightly, and he hoped it didn't draw attention.

A second later it was too late to worry about it.

Tina Lemoine stepped into the office. There were tears on her cheeks, and angry streaks of mascara ran like war paint down her face.

"Sheriff?" The frightened woman glanced around at the others gathered in the office and frowned in confusion. But she did not let her surprise distract her very long.

"Tina, what happened? What's—"

"I was attacked," she told him. "Two men, snarling at me like animals . . . they chased me."

Tina gripped Tackett's hands in her own, clearly becoming more self-conscious about those around her. She glanced at them, as if she felt foolish. Jack's heart went out to her. Then she frowned deeply and stared for a long moment at Bill, as if she had suddenly recognized him from somewhere.

"Where?" Jack asked.

Tackett glared at him. Then he turned to Tina and rephrased the question, speaking softly.

"Where did you see them, Tina?"

"Out behind the inn," she said. Once again she looked at Bill, oddly distracted from her own plight, and she shuddered slightly.

"Tina!" said a stern voice from the open doorway.

They all turned to see her father, Henry, standing in the hall. He still carried himself with a dignity and an air of power that Jack had seen in wealthy men before, but at the moment Henry Lemoine looked rattled.

"This was a mistake," he told his daughter. "Come away, now, before you say something you will most certainly regret."

Jack frowned, confused but also repulsed by the questions in his head. What was it Lemoine was afraid his daughter would tell the sheriff? What had he done to her?

"No, Daddy, don't do this," Tina pleaded. "You don't understand. All I wanted was to get the journal back, to stop all of this."

Her father froze. "You mean it's here?"

Tina nodded slowly. Her father began to smile, but his expression faltered and he sniffed the air, then turned to glare at Bill.

"Now, look, Henry," Tackett interrupted. "I'd really like to know what's going on here. Tina just said she was attacked, and—"

"Who are you?" Henry Lemoine demanded, staring at Bill.

Then he sniffed the air.

Jack understood then. "Molly," he said, voice hushed. "Get over here."

But she had caught on at the same time, and she edged closer to the shotgun where she had propped it against the wall.

"Your journal?" Bill said. "That's the book your pack has been killing civilians to get back?"

"What the hell's going on here?" Tackett snapped, a bit of panic creeping into his voice as he glared from Bill to Henry to Tina.

"The old man's the Alpha," Jack explained. "Looks like his journal fell into the wrong hands. All this time they've been trying to get it back, killing anyone who may have had it. The way Tina's acting, my guess is Foster Marlin stashed it here because he figured if anything happened to him, you'd find it eventually."

Jack watched as Tina glanced over at the bookshelf on the other side of the room, confirming his suspicions. The journal was here, in the room with them.

Henry Lemoine began to laugh. "Not bad, young man. That's pretty much how I've got it figured as well." Lemoine didn't look tired or anxious anymore. As he laughed, his voice became deep and throaty, and silver fur began to sprout all over his body.

The sheriff cursed loudly. Though he'd seen a similar transformation a moment before, this was a man he'd known most of his life.

Then Tina began to change as well, tears on her face. "It shouldn't have come to this," she said, but her voice was low, as though she had already surrendered to the conflict she knew must come next.

One of the windows shattered and Jack glanced out to see a crowd of terrifying figures silhouetted in the dark.

The Prowlers were coming in.

C H A P T E R 14

It was as though the world hesitated a moment, as in the eerily calm eye of the hurricane, just before the calamitous, primeval force of the storm crashed down upon them.

Molly cursed loudly and snatched up the shotgun. She turned her back to her friends and the two Prowlers who had first come in. She was counting on Jack and Bill to protect her. The two windows in the outside wall of the office were showering glass shards and splinters of frame down onto the carpet, and Prowlers were leaping in through the ravaged openings.

Somewhere nearby, she thought she heard music playing. Light, sweet jazz with a bit of melancholy. It made her want to laugh, crazy as that would have been.

Molly's finger tightened on the shotgun's trigger as the two Prowlers nearest her lunged forward. She fired,

and a monstrous face was erased in a spray of blood
and fur and bone. The blast killed the one and caught
the other in midleap, peppering his torso with shot and
dropping it to the carpet.

A third was already inside, and he glared at her war-
ily as she pumped the weapon again. In quick succession, two bullets punched through his chest and
slammed the beast back into the opening, blocking the
way for a moment.

Molly glanced around and saw Sheriff Tackett standing behind her, eyes dark, expression grim.

"Time to go, young lady."

The growling, that was what unnerved Jack the
most. It welled up around him almost as though the
ground were ready to split, a volcano struggling to be
born. But it was not that. This was the sound of the
wild, the sound of bloodlust.

Bill Cantwell, a man he trusted, a man his sister
cared deeply for, stood beside him, snarling with rage
and menace. But Bill was not really a man. Only
moments ago he had proven it to the sheriff, and now
he had changed again. Saliva dripped from his gleaming
fangs, his black nose sniffed at the air, and he danced
from one foot to the other, staring down the others,
ready to break them, to make them bleed, to tear at
their flesh with his jagged maw.

The silver-furred Prowler Jack suspected was the
Alpha and the dark-furred female—*Tina, it's Tina*, a voice
within reminded him incredulously—started toward

them, both snarling with a savagery that stole from him any memory of how benevolent they had seemed only moments before. He had been trying to make sense of Tina's entrance and he was certain now that she had been trying to avoid this moment. But now that it had become inevitable, she stood by her father's side.

Part of the Pack.

"You've caused a lot of trouble, boy!" the Alpha growled at him.

Jack's fingers closed around the nine millimeter he'd slipped loosely into his belt before. Almost unconsciously, he drew it out, aimed, and fired one round between the two creatures.

"It isn't over yet," he said coldly.

The weight of the gun was warm and welcome in his hand. The thing was awful, the insidious power of the weapon, but it was also the only chance they had to survive.

A loud shotgun blast echoed off to his right, but he did not dare turn his eyes. Sheriff Tackett had rushed to aid Molly when the invasion had begun, and he had to rely on both of them to protect themselves, at least for the moment.

The Alpha leaped at Bill, claws slashing down. Henry Lemoine's human appearance was misleading. He seemed slim, slouched, even old. Lemoine was larger by far than he'd appeared, and age had not slowed him. His claws swiped toward Bill's throat and would have torn it out, a killing blow, if Bill had been one second slower.

With a thunderous roar that Jack felt in his gut and his bones, Bill deftly turned the attack aside, then lunged forward, driving Lemoine back. The two of them went down in a tumble, clawing and biting.

With feline grace, Tina moved toward him. Then she paused, not threatening, not attacking.

"I'm sorry," she growled.

Then she lunged at him.

Jack fired three times, hitting her twice. One bullet tore through her shoulder and spun her around, the other punched through the side of her head.

"So am I," he muttered with regret, remembering her human fingers strumming an acoustic guitar.

With one last glance at the dead creature, he grabbed up the second nine millimeter he had placed on the shelf earlier. When he turned, he saw Bill lift the Alpha over his head and slam him hard against a bookshelf. Wood cracked and books tumbled down. With that eyeblink of a respite, Jack glanced over toward the windows. The sheriff was there, shielding Molly from the new onslaught from outside as he fired four quick rounds at the monsters silhouetted in the windows.

"Tackett! Let's go!" Jack shouted.

The sheriff glanced back quickly, but hesitated. Molly did not give him a choice. She grabbed him by the arm and hauled him away. Jack caught her eye, saw the iron courage there, and knew they were going to be all right. They had to be.

"Bill!" Jack shouted. "Get us the hell out of here!"

"Let's go!" Bill roared.

The enormous Prowler led the way, bounding powerfully for the door. Jack and Molly followed, with the sheriff bringing up the rear. Tackett fired twice more into his office as they ran out into the corridor.

Then the sheriff swore. He was out of ammunition.

Jack was barely paying attention. Down along the corridor, the front door was wide open and six or seven Prowlers were already inside. The animals froze a second when their prey lurched out into the corridor. Then they started forward. A snarl started low, building as it was joined by each of them in turn until they formed a savage harmony.

Molly stopped short, leveled the shotgun, and blew a hole in the one second from the left. The one in front reached them, but Bill was there. With a single, darting motion, his claws tore out the monster's throat. Blood fountained from the wound as it went down.

Jack slapped one of his guns into the sheriff's hand, then reached around to snag the third nine millimeter he'd clipped to his belt.

With a gun in each hand, he fired at the Prowlers even as they rushed in. Two of them were hit, wounds popping open in their chests like firecrackers.

"Back there?" he snapped at the sheriff, tilting his head toward the rear of the building, where the cells were.

"Not that way," the man replied quickly, firing into the crowd of monsters as even more slipped in through the front door. "Follow me."

"Bill!" Jack cried out to his friend.

Molly had fallen back beside them. She pumped another round into the shotgun's chamber, and almost as one, the four of them surged forward, toward their attackers instead of away.

But only for a heartbeat or two.

The side corridor they turned into was narrower and seemed to dead-end at the door to another office. As they ran down it, the Prowlers screeching and calling out in triumph as though they believed their prey cornered, Jack felt fear spike up inside him. Unlike the sheriff's large office, or even the main hallway, there was no room to fight here.

His heart raced. His throat went dry and he gritted his teeth as he hustled after Molly and the sheriff. Bill was bringing up the rear as they ran past multiple doors on both sides of the hall.

Jack stared ahead at the door at the end of the hall, and a horrible certainty filled him, that the door would not open. That they would be cornered.

Then the sheriff slammed into the door, twisted the knob and nearly tore it off the hinges. On the other side was a kind of conference room with a long wooden table in the center and a broad picture window on the far wall.

The sheriff glanced back at Jack.

"Got it!" Jack shouted. "Bill, the door!"

They were all inside the room and Bill slammed it shut, twisted the lock on the door, and threw his weight against it. It splintered as Prowlers crashed into it from the other side, hard enough to shake Bill.

The sheriff was already at the table and Jack joined him. He tossed his guns onto the wood and bent down to push. The legs scraped the floor, but it slid grudgingly across the room to slam against the wall right under the window.

"Molly!" Jack glanced around to see her leveling the shotgun at the six-foot-wide, multi-paned window.

"Got it!" she shouted.

The shotgun roared.

The picture window exploded out into the night, leaving jagged edges of glass jutting from the frame.

But it was enough.

"Go, go!" Bill yelled behind them.

Molly went first, scrambling up onto the table and leaping out into the darkness. Jack said a silent prayer that there were no Prowlers waiting. As the sheriff followed Molly, Jack grabbed up his guns.

"Bill!" he snapped.

The Prowler let go of the door and in three long strides had leaped up on top of the table. He grabbed hold of Jack, hauled him up, and then the two of them dove out through the jagged maw of glass side by side.

They tumbled on the grass.

Molly and Tackett were already up, guns aimed into the darkness. Inside the conference room they could hear the door give way with a crash of breaking wood. Jack hesitated.

"There are too many of them, Jack," Molly said quickly. "We need room to breathe."

It pained Jack to do it, but with a single glance back

at the sheriff's building, he ran. All four of them went together, sprinting around the front of the building, where at least a dozen Prowlers milled about, battering at windows in a kind of animal fury that was irrational, savage, and inhuman.

Beasts, Jack thought. *That's all they are. Not evil.*

But they *seemed* so evil.

Mainly 'cause they want to kill us.

The sheriff's patrol car was all the way around the other side of the parking lot. The Jeep was closer. Jack slapped the keys into Molly's hand. With her in the lead, they ran diagonally across the lot toward the Jeep as the Prowlers began to lope across the pavement to intercept them.

Tackett paused, took aim, and put a round through the right eye of the one in the lead, blowing out the back of his skull. He went down, tripping up a couple of the others.

"Back off!" the sheriff commanded.

They did not listen. But at least they slowed down a bit, perhaps wary of his marksmanship. Jack fired a few times at them as well, and one of the bullets connected.

He heard the Jeep's engine rumble to life and looked up, legs pumping beneath him. Molly was behind the wheel, and Bill was standing outside it. Both passenger side doors were open. Jack ran faster, Tackett rasping, trying to catch his breath as he did his best to keep up.

Bill had Molly's shotgun now, and he waited until Jack and Tackett were nearly to the Jeep before he pumped and fired twice in succession. Jack dove into the backseat. The sheriff climbed into the front, as Bill leaped in back.

The doors slammed.

Molly floored it in reverse and the tires squealed on the pavement. With a loud crumple of metal, she rammed one of the Prowlers. The others leaped on top of the Jeep as Molly shifted into Drive and accelerated again. Several of the beasts fell off.

One of them tried to hang on to the hood, but rolled off when Molly took a corner. But there was one on the roof, and another used the roof rack as a hand hold as he smashed the rear window with one huge, hairy fist.

"We've got to get them off!" Jack roared.

Jack slid down in the seat and shot two rounds through the roof of his Jeep. There was a wail of agony, and the beast up there tumbled off the side of the vehicle. Even as he sat up, he saw the sheriff take aim out the back window. He shot the Prowler back there twice, and would have done so a third time had the clip not run out of bullets.

They were free.

They had won.

Yet it did not feel as though it were a victory. Lemoine was still back at the police station. *We survived, that's all.* Jack tried to come to terms with that, for he knew that, for the moment, it would have to be enough.

Buckton was curiously silent as they rode toward the downtown area. Inside the Jeep, no one said a word.

Jack stared out the window at the street lamps casting their eerie glow upon the road, at the forest beyond, and the buildings that grew more numerous as they approached the Post Road. When he glanced up front again, he saw another car coming toward them. Its headlights reminded him of the sickly yellow illumination from the street lamps.

It passed them by going the other direction.

Phil Garraty's postal van.

Garraty's ghost glared sadly at him from behind the wheel as the spectral vehicle slid past in the night. One among many lost souls who were relying on him to destroy this Pack, not merely for vengeance, but to make sure they never killed again.

"Jesus," Jack whispered.

He closed his eyes, thinking about how many Prowlers were behind them—far more than he and Molly would have guessed. How many were still alive? They had killed maybe eight. Even if they could count on there being twelve or fifteen others back there, there was no way to know if they had even seen them all.

"Jack?" Molly asked, voice soft and anxious.

He opened his eyes.

"Are you all right?" she ventured.

They were passing through the main area of town now. The buildings looked almost abandoned. Dead. Ghosts themselves. There were a couple of people on the street, in front of the Empire Theatre. And along the sidewalks, he could see the ghost victims lining the road.

The ghosts stared at the Jeep as it rolled past, on its

way out of town. The spirits of the dead knew that he was going. Leaving them unavenged.

"Damn it," Jack snapped.

He felt Tackett staring at him. In the passenger seat up front, Bill turned around. He was human again, and Jack had not even noticed him changing.

"What is it?" Bill asked him.

Jack swallowed hard. "You got those grenades?"

Bill touched the small bag that was still strapped around his shoulder. In the rearview mirror, Jack could see the reflection of Molly's eyes studying him. Worry lines crinkled the skin around her eyes, and he thought how wrong it was that she should have lines at the age of eighteen.

Then he crawled over the backseat and pulled the top off the crate back there. He withdrew boxes of ammunition for the nine millimeters, and a carton of shells for the shotgun. He tossed them over onto his seat, then he pulled out the assault rifle.

When he slid back into his seat, the sheriff was staring at him wide-eyed.

"What the hell are you doing, Jack?" Tackett demanded.

Jack held up the assault rifle. "You ever fired one of these?"

"Maybe not that one exactly," the sheriff replied carefully. "But I was a marine."

"That'll do," Jack said. He handed the weapon to the sheriff, then started loading his own guns again. "Bill," he said, "hand back that shotgun."

Molly's eyes still watched him in the mirror. "Jack?"

"Turn it around, Molly. We have to go back."

"You're out of your mind!" the sheriff told him. "Now's not the time, kid—"

Jack rounded on him. "You can't see what I see, Tackett! You can't see the dead lining the streets. We can't just leave. How do we know what they'll do in the meantime? How do we know they'll even still be here? But right now they're all back there waiting, probably pissing all over your office, your duty to this town. We have to go back."

Tackett looked as though he'd been struck in the face. After a moment he blinked once, then popped the clip out of the assault rifle to make sure it was fully loaded.

Molly hit the brakes, and they turned around and headed back toward the police station.

"Make sure my shotgun is loaded," she said from the driver's seat.

It was quiet after that. Jack saw the ghostly postal truck in the road up ahead, but he did not mention it. Nor did he say any more about the phantoms that lingered on the sidewalks, moving swiftly along with them, keeping up with the Jeep as though it were no effort at all.

Yet though he did not mention the dead again, all three of his companions glanced furtively out into the dark from time to time, as if they might catch a quick glance of the lost souls who even now urged them on their way, crying silently for justice.

*   *   *

Molly's knuckles were white on the wheel. Her breathing was shallow and for a moment she felt as though she were underwater; there was pressure on her ears and everything sounded so far away.

Her foot was heavy on the pedal. The Jeep barreled up the road, covering the mile or two between downtown and the police station in what seemed like no time at all. The headlights seemed strangely dim. Beside her, Bill loaded her shotgun. Then he slid two grenades out of the bag and cradled them in his hand.

In the rearview mirror she saw Jack staring out the side windows, face slack and pale, ghostly. She knew what he was seeing. The lost souls, the victims of the Prowlers. He did not have to tell her. Molly wondered if the Meredith girl, the one they'd been unable to save, was out there, looking on.

It made her angry to think that. And the anger gave her strength.

The Jeep hit a pothole and the headlights seemed to blaze with renewed vigor. In the backseat, the sheriff checked the clip on the assault rifle again, and Molly tried not to think of the destructive capacity of that weapon. All guns scared her, but this one more so. It seemed so uncontrollable, even in the hands of a man with such confidence.

Of course, most of the sheriff's confidence was gone now. An expression of grim determination was etched on his face, but there was none of the air of authority around him anymore. He was just another soldier now.

"There," Bill rasped.

Ahead, the Town Hall was dark. As they cruised past it, the police station came into view, its shattered windows gleaming with light from deep within, a flickering jack-o'-lantern of a building. Dark shapes cavorted in the paved parking lot.

"They're still here," Molly whispered.

"It looks like they're . . . celebrating," the sheriff rumbled.

"They think they've won," Bill told them.

Jack grunted in the back. "Like hell."

"Molly, hit a few if you can, but get us right in front of the door." Bill rolled the grenades in his hand.

The faces of the Prowlers, their animal countenances, were almost absurdly comic when the Jeep turned toward them and the headlights picked them out, spotlighting them against the front of the station. Molly pumped the accelerator instead of the brake, and the Jeep surged across the parking lot. Several of the Prowlers were smart enough and quick enough to dive out of the way.

Two of them weren't.

The Jeep struck them an eyeblink apart, the impact of metal on shattering bone reminding Molly of big fireworks, and the way the explosion is heard first, and then the report right after. One of the Prowlers went under the tires and the Jeep bumped over him. The other flew up and struck the windshield, which splintered, and the thing slid off the spiderwebbed glass, limbs at odd angles, when she slammed on the brakes.

"Go!" Jack shouted.

Molly grabbed the shotgun from Bill, kicked open her door, and blew the arm off a Prowler that was coming for her.

They rushed the Jeep immediately, but only a few were still outside. As if enjoying the spoils of war, most of them were inside. Jack figured they were looking for Lemoine's journal. He could see several outlined in the open door, beginning to stream out, primal rage mixing with surprise as they prepared to finish what they had started.

Jack had the same idea.

He shot the first Prowler to rush him right through the window on his door. Then he kicked it open, dropped to the pavement, and shot again as the animal swiped a claw toward Molly's legs.

Gunfire split the night.

"Bill!" Jack shouted. "The door!"

Even before the words were out, he saw Bill pull the pins on a pair of grenades and lob them at the front door of the station.

"Cover!" Bill roared.

They all ducked their heads, shied away, but the blast was bigger than they expected, and when the grenades exploded, Jack and Molly were knocked off their feet. His head smacked the pavement hard, and he shook it as he got up.

Molly pumped the shotgun and decimated the chest of a Prowler that lunged at him. He fell beside him with a wet crunch and twitched only once.

"Stay down!" Sheriff Tackett snapped.

Jack glanced up at him from the pavement and watched in amazement as the aging man with the round belly and the thick, steel gray mustache opened fire with the assault rifle. There were four Prowlers remaining in the parking lot that were still on their feet when he started. Tackett swept the gun in a wide arc at gut level, and the Prowlers jittered like tacky plastic skeletons as the bullets thumped through their flesh.

They all went down.

"Let's move!" Bill snarled.

Jack was up in an instant. He grabbed Molly by the hand and pulled her up with him, and when they turned toward the station, he saw that the entire face of it, the front door and the wall around it, had been blown in. In the harsh light from inside, he could see several Prowlers getting to their feet. Others were scrambling over the rubble, howling with fury and bloodlust as they rushed to get out to the parking lot. Two kept going, along the side of the building, running for their lives.

Even as Bill reached into the bag at his side, his flesh rippled, the fur pushed through from below, and his bones stretched. It happened in three seconds.

In that time, he'd pulled the pins on two more grenades and tossed them into the open corridor of the police station.

"Ah, Jesus, the whole building—" Tackett began.

The explosion cut him off, a double-thump that shattered walls and cut the number of Prowlers down further.

"Now!" Jack shouted, throat dry, blood pumping hard. His whole body felt hot, as though the sun burned him.

But it was the darkest of nights.

Bill Cantwell let loose the animal in his soul. This was what he was. What he was always meant to be. Peace was what he wanted, but he would bathe in the blood of his enemies if they would not leave him to that peace.

With a howl that made him shiver with pleasure, Bill led the way into the ruined station house. He leaped over the rubble, with Tackett close behind him. The sheriff was shouting something, but Bill was not listening. He snarled a challenge in the oldest language on earth, a guttural, primeval voice that came up from deep within him.

The first of the Prowlers to attack him was a simple thing, already injured. Bill broke his neck with a quick twist. Others appeared in the hall. Tackett fired a burst from the assault rifle and three of them did a death dance and tumbled to the floor, bleeding out. Bill tried to figure how many were left.

Ten?

Fewer?

From a side corridor, one of them lunged at him, got a claw across his ribcage, and Bill hissed with the pain of it. He slammed the beast into the wall hard enough to shake plaster loose, but the Prowler came back at him immediately. He was strong.

Behind him, another went for Tackett. The sheriff

tried to shoot at him, but the clip jammed in the assault rifle. Tackett jammed the weapon into the beast's face and the thing lashed out at him. Claws raked the side of the sheriff's head, drawing blood, and Tackett staggered back against the wall.

Bill tore open the chest of his attacker, then went to Tackett's aid. He got there just in time, got his claws under the creature's jaw and tore his head right off his body with a grinding of bone and a thick, wet, tearing sound of tendons and muscles and skin being rent.

He glanced back at Tackett. The sheriff held a hand to one side of his skull, blood seeping between his fingers.

"Can you keep up?" Bill asked.

"I'll have to," Tackett replied.

"Stick with me then."

Jack ran up behind Bill and fired at several more approaching figures. He saw Tackett's bloody scalp and cursed loudly.

Molly pumped the shotgun and waited.

The figures disappeared back up the hall.

"Follow them. We're going to end this!" Jack roared.

Bill careened down the corridor ahead of them, toward the sheriff's office where it had all begun. Tackett followed, hand still clapped to his head. As he and Molly followed, weapons at the ready, Jack reminded himself that scalp wounds were supposed to bleed a lot, but he was concerned for Tackett regardless.

Bill was much faster than they were, and he reached

the office first. When he came even with the door and turned to go in, the Alpha was waiting for him. Henry Lemoine, lord of this Prowler pack, surged from the open doorway with his claws slashing down, and ripped bleeding furrows in Bill's chest.

Bill cried out in pain, voice sounding almost human. Tackett staggered back and away from them, swearing angrily at his own uselessness.

Tackett was out of the way, leaning on the wall, but the Alpha was too close to Bill for Jack to get a clear shot at him.

"Watch it!" Molly shouted.

Jack looked up even as she pulled the trigger. It stopped one Prowler cold but before she could even begin to pump the shotgun again, five of them were rushing from the room.

Bill and the Alpha continued to snarl and slash at each other, in a tussle on the floor. Molly tried to pump the shotgun and one of the Prowlers lunged at her.

Tackett grabbed her arm and hauled her out of the way. The monster slammed hard into the wall on the other side of the corridor. Then Jack was with them, propelling Tackett and Molly along, the soles of their shoes slapping loudly on the floor as they ran down the hall toward the rear of the station, where the cells were. Tackett's blood was dripping, leaving a trail behind them.

"We can't leave Bill behind!" Molly shrieked.

With a backward glance, Jack saw that all the others were following them. They had left Bill to the Alpha, confident in their leader's strength. He only prayed that they were wrong.

"No choice!" he told her. "Tackett, tell me you've got your keys!"

The sheriff glanced at him, one side of his head matted with blood. Understanding dawned on his face, and he reached into his pocket and pulled out his keys. Jack snatched them out of his hand.

"Molly, help him!"

Jack ran on, just ahead of them. At the end of the hall, he skidded on the linoleum as he raced around the corner, and saw the long line of jail cells. Even in those desperate seconds, his mind had been scrambling for a plan, a way to get out of this alive. The cells were their last chance.

He worked the keys in the lock of the first cell. When he hit the third key, Molly and Tackett stumbled up. The sheriff looked pale and shaky. The fourth key turned in the lock and Jack hauled the cell door open.

"In there!"

The Prowlers roared and loped along the hall toward them. Jack fired one shot over his shoulder, enough to make the Prowlers hesitate for the one second he needed to buy them. Enough. Just barely. When he slammed the metal-barred door behind them, one of the Prowlers hit the bars so hard, face-first, that it fell, dazed to the floor.

He barely moved.

A female paced tiger-like in front of their cell.

"Those bars won't save you!" she snarled.

Molly laughed, a mad, bitter sound. "What are you, stupid?" Then she pulled the trigger, and the female's head disappeared in a shower of bone and gray matter. Fur stuck to the wall in splatters of blood.

Jack opened fire, cutting down the other three that were still standing.

The one on the floor, nearly unconscious, was the last to die.

When all was quiet out in the hall, Jack turned to Molly, gasping for breath, and saw the tears streaming down her face. She dropped her shotgun and it clattered on the floor of the cell. He stared down at his guns in disgust, and let them fall as well. Behind them, Tackett had slumped to the floor. He sat leaning against the wall of the cell, face slack, eyes hollow. But he was alive.

They had won. Jack felt like throwing up.

But at least the monsters would take no more lives. Not in Buckton.

"Oh, God," Molly whispered.

She came to him then, and Jack took her in his arms and just held her, gently, rocking just a little. He did not try to wipe the tears from her eyes. After a moment he realized that he was crying as well.

"Bill?" Molly asked.

She lifted her gaze to him, and Jack stared at her. He bit his lip, almost afraid to wonder about the man, the monster that was their friend and ally.

Then they heard heavy footsteps out in the corridor.

The face that appeared in front of the cell was the face of the beast, but the eyes were so very human.

"Bill!" Molly cried in relief.

She snatched the keys from Jack's hands and pushed them through the bars to him. With a wince of pain from the wounds on his chest, Bill slid the key in and unlocked the cell.

The door swung open.

As Jack and Molly emerged amidst the carnage, the dead beasts all around them, Bill willed the change to come upon him again, building the false face that flowed to create skin and human features.

Then he stumbled and almost fell. Blood soaked through his torn clothing.

"Oh, my God," Molly said. She turned to Jack, eyes wide. "We've got to get them both to a hospital."

"No," Tackett groaned.

They turned to see him struggling to rise to his feet. He pushed away from the wall, expression grim but determined.

"Just go. Gather up the weapons you brought into town with you, get your things from the inn, and go. Don't talk to anyone, don't stop, and don't take Cantwell to a hospital within a hundred miles of Buckton."

"I don't understand," Molly said. "You need to have those wounds stitched before you bleed to death."

"I will," Tackett countered. "But the longer you stand here, the more blood I lose. Just get me to my office."

Jack glanced up at Bill. "Can you manage?"

"I'll heal," Bill grunted, though as he walked with them every step seemed painful.

Molly helped steady Tackett as they walked back to his office, weaving around Prowler corpses and splashes of blood as they went.

"What are you gonna do?" Jack asked the sheriff. "How are you gonna explain all this?"

"I don't have to explain. All anyone has to do is look around," Tackett replied. "I think they'll get it. I've lived in this town my whole life except during my time with the Marines. Even after all this, there are people I trust here. But there are also folks I don't know so well who'd be quick to call in the state police, and I don't want that.

"I don't want the media and state investigators and curious college kids driving up and down the streets here. There are people in this town I know will feel the way I do, once they've gotten over trying to convince themselves it isn't real. So I'll make a few phone calls, and I'll get stitched up, and by dawn, all these bodies will be burned or buried somewhere and the place'll be so clean it sparkles."

"What about all the damage? People are going to ask about that," Jack cautioned him.

"After the vandalism at the diner and the library, it'll be simple enough. The hard part's gonna be explaining where the Lemoines and Bernie Mackeson went, not to mention whoever else we killed tonight without knowing it."

Tackett shuddered at the thought and shook his head sorrowfully. "Damn, Tina. She was a nice girl."

No one had a reply for that.

"They'll just be disappearances," Bill said grimly.

"You'll get reporters, maybe even state police, but as long as no one says anything, eventually it'll just be a story people talk about."

Jack stopped them just outside Tackett's office. "Maybe not," he said. "People have seen us. Some of them have got to know you arrested us. There are going to be questions."

Tackett lowered his head and sighed. Then he pushed away from Molly and leaned against the door frame. "Henry Lemoine would have killed me if not for you. I'll cover for you as best I can, and no one I bring in to help me will talk about it.

"As far as I'm concerned, I picked you up because I don't like out-of-towners and had to let you go when Alan was killed. I let you out earlier this morning and you checked out of the Inn. You spent the day in town and then left Buckton after dinner. I saw you off myself, with my apologies for inconveniencing you. If you stick to that, and don't go back through town on your way out of here, this just might work."

The three of them stared at him. Jack wondered what rank Tackett had achieved in the Marine Corps, because he certainly had the makings of an officer.

"There might be a few who got away," Bill warned him.

"If they're smart, they'll keep running."

"Wow, I guess you've got it covered," Molly said softly.

Tackett pushed away from the wall. "I will if I can make the calls I need to make before I pass out."

She helped him into the office and over to his desk. The place was a shambles, dead Prowlers and shattered glass all over the floor, along with what appeared to be every book that had been on the sheriff's shelves. They were strewn about, some of them torn up.

Tackett picked up the phone and began to dial.

Which was when Jack noticed that Tina's corpse was not where he had left it. He had shot her between the desk and the door, but now her body lay on the other side of the room beneath a broken window. It had to be her, for she was the only female Prowler they had killed in the office.

Curious, Jack stepped over a dead beast and made his way through the books that had been tossed all over the place. A trail of blood led to where she lay, face to the wall. Her fur was matted with it and it pooled all around her head.

Jack stared. The bullet to the head had not killed her instantly. Somehow she had found the strength before she died to crawl all the way across the room. What he didn't understand was why.

Carefully, he reached down and turned her over.

Dead, jaws gaping open, eyes glossy, the thing they knew as Tina clutched a leather-bound book in her arms, held tight against her chest. He knew right away what it had to be. Jack crouched and slipped the book from her grasp. He stood and opened it, began to read from one of the handwritten pages.

"Is that . . . ?"

Jack glanced up to find Molly beside him, staring at

the book. He nodded. Bill came over to them then. He looked drawn, but the bleeding seemed to have stopped.

"You gonna be all right?" Jack asked.

"A little rest will do me a lot of good," Bill replied. "Maybe a few stitches. One of you is going to have to drive my car." His eyes went to the journal in Jack's hands. "Is that the book?"

"Yes."

"Bring it with you," Bill said. "It should make interesting reading."

After they were certain that Tackett had help on the way, they left the sheriff still on the phone and went back out to the Jeep. They drove back to the inn with the headlights off, and Molly slipped across the lot to get Bill's car. The two vehicles moved quietly through the dark until they were well outside of town.

They were exhausted, and Bill was wounded, and they were a long way from home. But Jack knew it would be all right now.

For as they drove out of Buckton, he did not see a single ghost on the sides of the road. The victims of the prowlers, the souls who had wandered lost among these mountains, had finally left Buckton behind.

E P I L O G U E

On Monday Courtney let them sleep all day as business went on as usual in the pub. She counted the hours until the kitchen would close and not once did she let slip that three of Bridget's best employees were lazing around like slugs upstairs. After Jack, Molly, and Bill had rolled in that morning, just after six A.M., they had given her the wee-hours-of-the-morning version and all fallen into bed, exhausted.

At last, going on eleven-thirty that night, the restaurant area was cleared. Courtney had Matt make last call at quarter to midnight. By ten past twelve, the place was empty of patrons and staff, and Courtney locked up after Matt with a gentle smile of thanks and a hasty wave. Tired, but thrilled to finally be able to ascend once more to her apartment, Courtney limped across the pub, her cane thumping on the hard wood, and climbed the stairs.

When she opened the door, she heard tinny television voices from the living room. She locked up behind her and went in to find them lolling on chairs and sofas with some ancient black and white rerun on Nick at Nite unfolding to canned laughter on the tube.

Jack spotted her first. Courtney's heart had been so heavily burdened by fear for him in his absence, and now she felt so much lighter, in head and heart.

"Hey," Jack said.

Molly and Bill both glanced up at the sound of his voice, then smiled when they saw Courtney enter.

Her brother rose from his chair and walked over to her. He wore sweatpants and a T-shirt, and it was clear they had been his uniform all day. It had been that kind of day.

Jack took her face in his hands and kissed her forehead. Then he hugged her close and Courtney let herself lean on him.

"Gotta tell you, little brother," she said in a half-whisper, "for a minute there I—"

"Don't say it," Jack interrupted.

"I know, I know. It's over now."

A frown creased his forehead. "Over? I wish it was. Just getting started, I think."

Courtney wanted to argue, to trot out all her fears for their safety, all the reasons why it was not their problem that there were other Prowler Packs all over the country, probably all over the world. But she could not, because she agreed with him. It had been she, after all, who had set them on the path to Buckton in the first place.

It wasn't over. It would never be over.

Gently, she hugged him, kissed his cheek, then limped over to Molly. The girl gazed up at her, a wan smile on her face, seeming happy and content, and yet there was a shadow over her eyes. Once they had sparkled brightly. That sparkle was still there, but Courtney thought it might have been dimmed somewhat. She hoped it was only an illusion.

"You all right?" she asked.

Molly took the question seriously, seemed to turn it around for a moment. Then she nodded with grave sincerity. "I'm all right."

Courtney turned toward Bill. "And you," she said. "Mister ignore-those-blood-stains-I-heal-pretty-fast. You come with me."

Without another word, she turned and moved away from them, into the hall. Bill got up and followed, padding silently after her.

Jack watched, a bit taken aback, as Bill followed his sister into the hall. A moment later he heard Courtney's bedroom door open and close, and then the sound of soft music began to drift out to where he and Molly stood in the living room, gaping stupidly at nothing in the hall.

"Wow," Molly said at length.

"Yeah," Jack agreed. "I'd say we missed something."

Their eyes met then, and Jack felt his chest tighten. His breath caught in his throat, and it was as though something was tickling his stomach from the inside— only he wasn't ticklish there.

"I don't think we missed anything, necessarily," Molly told him, a bit of a rasp to her voice. She swallowed visibly and her smile seemed uncertain. "I'd say it was there all along, like a puzzle somebody only built halfway. We just weren't paying attention when the rest of the pieces got put together."

With a tentative chuckle, Jack shrugged. "I guess. All the same to you, though, I'm going to try to block it out. She's my sister, y'know?"

Molly smiled sweetly. "Yeah. I know." With a tiny shiver, she stretched, and tried to stifle a small yawn. "I'm glad we're all back in one piece, Jack. And I'm . . . I'm glad we went. It was the right thing to do."

I'm glad we went. Jack's mind swirled with images of horrible violence and bloodshed, and he shook his head in amazement.

"Yeah. Me, too."

For a moment, Molly searched his eyes. Her smiled faltered. "Well, good night."

"Night," Jack replied.

Molly paused, then started for the hallway. Just short of the open door, she stopped. As he watched her hesitate there, Jack held his breath. Molly half-turned toward him, eyes downcast, lips pouting slightly. Her mane of red hair fell across her face, partially obscuring her expression.

Then she lifted her head, chin raised, and strode toward him. Her step was determined, but her eyes were wide with fear. Molly reached up with both hands, grabbed Jack by the back of the head, and pulled him down to kiss her. Their lips met, and Jack felt as though they burned a little. It was a deep kiss; his heart thundered in his chest, and it seemed he had never felt so invigorated and yet so weak at the same time.

The kiss slowed, became softer, more gentle, as if they were merely tasting each other's lips.

Molly lay her head on his chest a moment. Jack caressed her upturned cheek. A sweet smile blossomed again at the edges of her lips. She stood back, shook her head as if in disbelief, and then turned to walk toward the hall again.

"Good night," he called weakly after her.

"Sleep tight," Molly replied almost in a whisper.

She hurried from the room and he stood and stared after her until he heard her door close softly down the hall.

"Oh, my God," Jack gasped. "What the hell do I do now?"

"What you have to do."

Jack spun, startled, and yet he was not truly surprised to see Artie shimmering there in the middle of the room. Through the spectral form, Jack could still see the television screen, and the canned laughter that filled the room made the scene even more surreal.

"You were watching?" Jack asked quietly.

"Just the last few seconds. I just got here," Artie explained. "Sorry. I wasn't peeping, though. Seriously."

As if slowly deflating, Jack sank onto the sofa. "What do I do now, Artie? This whole thing . . . you . . . Molly . . . it's too complicated. Before it was hard enough, but now I feel like you're this big secret I'm keeping from her. It feels wrong."

Artie nodded solemnly. "I know, Jack. But you know it's for the best. As for what you're gonna do now, you're gonna just keep doing what you've been doing. Taking care of business, and taking care of Molly."

His black eyes flickered, and the ghost glanced away. "You should be with her, Jack. It's . . . it's harder for me to take than I thought it would be. I mean, I know it's the right thing, but . . ." Artie's entire form seemed to ripple, as though the air itself was folding in around him. Then he solidified again, and he stared at Jack.

"This is the way it should be. Let it play out."

Jack exhaled slowly, with a shake of his head. "I just . . . maybe, Artie. But can we change the subject? Not talk about this for a while?"

For the first time, Artie had turned to look at the television set. Onscreen, Dick Van Dyke was having a bad dream, restless in bed.

"Oh, I love this one," the ghost said excitedly.

As though he could still feel it beneath him, the spirit of Artie Carroll settled down on the sofa next to Jack. They watched television in silence for a few minutes. In some ways it was wonderful for Jack, filled him with a nostalgia for simpler times with Artie. For those same reasons, it was also painful.

"What you did up in Buckton was really something," Artie said at the commercial break. "Lot of lost souls not so lost anymore, thanks to you."

Jack frowned. "They really have moved on, then?"

Artie nodded. "But why the long face? You should be happy for them?"

"Well," Jack said slowly, "no offense, but, we took care of what was keeping you here a long time ago, but you're still around. I just . . . I mean, why?"

The ghost smiled.

"Somebody's got to watch out for you, bro."

The wind whistled through the trees on Pine Hill, but aside from that, the mountain was dead silent. It was as though even the wildlife was afraid to move, afraid to cry out. Below, in the town of Buckton, people tried to make sense of the disappearance of more than two dozen of the small town's citizens.

In the clearing upon Pine Hill where the Bartleby place had once stood, the two survivors argued about what to do next. One was determined to have vengeance upon Sheriff John Tackett. The other wanted simply to flee. And so they argued, and they hunted for meager sustenance, and they lingered there together, wondering how long it would be before Tackett came to the clearing.

They were still there when *she* arrived, tall and thin, with eyes so cruel they both lay quickly before her, offering their throats. They had not the heart to fight. The face she wore, the façade, was dark and exotic by human standards, but they could sense the power of the beast underneath. She demanded to know what had happened, and they told her all of it.

"This cannot be," she whispered. "This was supposed to be the sanctuary, the place to rest and to start again."

"The sheriff killed them all. A boy and a girl, outsiders, they helped him," one of the survivors replied, "and one of us. He killed his own."

The female sniffed the air. "I can smell them. They have been here, fouled this sanctuary with their presence. Their scents are familiar."

Fury raged in her, but she forced herself to be calm. "Come then. We'll begin again together, we'll gather others around us. A great Pack, just as Tanzer dreamed of. And when the moment is right, we shall all have our vengeance upon these murderers."

The survivors bowed their heads to their new mistress. She laid a hand upon each of them, reassuring, and yet also establishing her place as their pack leader, their Alpha.

"Just as you say, mistress," said one of the survivors.

"Jasmine," she corrected. "Call me Jasmine."

ABOUT THE AUTHOR

CHRISTOPHER GOLDEN is the award-winning, *L.A. Times* bestselling author of such novels as *Straight on 'til Morning, Strangewood, Prowlers,* and the *Body of Evidence* series of teen thrillers.

Golden has also written a great many books and comic books related to the TV series *Buffy the Vampire Slayer* and *Angel.* His other comic book work includes stories featuring such characters as Batman, Wolverine, Spider-Man, The Crow, and Hellboy, among many others.

As a pop-culture journalist, he was the editor of the Bram Stoker Award-winning book of criticism, *CUT!: Horror Writers on Horror Film,* and co-author of both *Buffy the Vampire Slayer: The Monster Book* and *The Stephen King Universe.*

Golden was born and raised in Massachusetts, where he still lives with his family. He graduated from Tufts University. He is currently at work on the third book in the *Prowlers* series, *Predator and Prey,* and a new novel for Signet called *The Ferryman.* There are more than four million copies of his books in print. Please visit him at www.christophergolden.com

Everyone's got his demons....

ANGEL™

If it takes an eternity, he will make amends.

Original stories based
on the TV show
Created by Joss Whedon
& David Greenwalt

Available from Pocket Pulse
Published by Pocket Books

BASED ON THE HIT TV SERIES

Prue, Piper, and Phoebe Halliwell
didn't think the magical incantation
would really work. But it did.
Now Prue can move things with her
mind, Piper can freeze time, and
Phoebe can see the future. They are
the most powerful of witches—
the Charmed Ones.

**Available from Pocket Pulse
Published by Pocket Books**